S[illegible] COLD

An absolutely gripping crime thriller full of twists

EMMY ELLIS

Detective Carol Wren Mysteries Book 4

Originally published as *Time Stands Still*

JOFFE BOOKS

Revised edition 2023
Joffe Books, London
www.joffebooks.com

First published in Great Britain in 2022
as *Time Stands Still*

This paperback edition was first published
in Great Britain in 2023

Cover art by Nebojša Zorić

ISBN: 978-1-80405-895-4

PROLOGUE

21 Larch Lane — Scudderton

Little Carol Wren woke to the sound of the key turning in the lock. She scrambled upright on the sofa, her heart thudding, her mind still twisted with sleep. Rubbing her eyes to clear them, she held her breath, wondering what to do. If she ran upstairs, Dad would see her, chase her, and give her a good wallop, but if she stayed here . . . he'd do the same.

She couldn't win either way.

Young as she was, she'd learned the art of looking after herself. She could make sandwiches, use the hob, the toaster and even the kettle. Dad loved nothing more than going to the Lion of a night, blocking out his "troubles" as he called them. Carol fended for herself, lonely but at the same time pleased he wasn't there. Since Mam had gone, Carol hadn't formed any lasting bond with anyone. She didn't trust that they'd stay, that they wouldn't leave her, too. She had no affinity with Dad, the drunken bully, and had few friends at school.

The handle of the living room door bent downwards, and Carol almost let out a shriek. But Dad didn't come in, someone else did. Frank, the man who worked at the cinema.

Carol wished she could go there, but Dad wouldn't let her. She missed out on so much because of him.

"All right, nipper?" Frank asked, coming to sit beside her.

Carol smiled, but it faded as Dad stormed in.

"What the fuck are you still doing up? Bedtime is at seven."

He lunged forward, fist raised, and punched Carol in the stomach. She cried out, clutching her belly, then Frank shot up and stood between her and Dad.

"You should keep your hands off her," Frank said, "or you'll have me to deal with. Cut her some slack, okay? You can see she's been asleep."

"Yeah, with the fucking light on and the curtains open," Dad snarled. "Anyone going past would know I left her on her own. They'll say I'm a shit father."

"You *are* a shit father." Frank pushed Dad towards an armchair and forced him onto it. "And people know she's on her tod anyroad, because you don't see a babysitter knocking at the door every night, do you?"

"Aww, fuck off, will you?" Dad got up and stormed out, likely going into the kitchen.

Frank turned to Carol and smiled. "Do you want me to take you up to bed, lass?"

Carol nodded, and Frank took her hand, guiding her upstairs. He tucked her into bed, reading her one of the stories Mam used to.

She wished she lived with him instead.

The story ended, and Carol wanted more, but Frank stood.

"Any trouble, you remind him about me," he said. "He'll stop then."

Carol drifted off to sleep, wanting to believe him, but Dad was a law unto himself, and nothing would stop him from doing what he wanted, she knew that all too well.

CHAPTER ONE

Undisclosed Location

Sofia sat at the back bedroom window and stared out at the big Tesco, its lights bright in the darkness. Her home stood on the top edge of Coldwater. Years ago, before the estate had expanded, the two-storey used to stand alone, her neighbour half a mile away. She'd watched the landscape change, the buildings appearing, more and more of them creeping ever closer until the new one in front was all but sitting on her doorstep, the ones to the sides huddling nearby, forming a street. There was still the expanse behind, the supermarket to the left across a country road hugged by hedges, and in the far-far distance, the intermittent square glows of the windows in cottages on the moors. One set of squares had been dark since that surgeon's arrest. She only wished she'd sat here when he'd been driving home from murdering people. She could have phoned the police with a sighting of his SUV or that daft little sports car he used to drive.

She'd have had someone eager to hear what she had to say, maybe that Carol Wren woman who'd been on the news, a detective who'd have been so grateful for what Sofia told her.

She turned over the hourglass on the sill, watching the blue sand filtering into the bulbous bottom, creating a pyramid. When the top part was empty, she'd go out.

She opened the window to let in the autumn air, and convinced herself she picked up the sounds of the fairground on the pier — music, shrieks from holidaymakers — but it was all in her head. Sitting there for the time it took for the hourglass to filter through wasn't a hardship. She enjoyed these moments where she pretended she was the only person on the planet. It gave her time to think, to go over her plans.

At last, Sofia closed the window and went downstairs. Everything was neat as a pin, clean, scrubbed daily. Austere, the dictionary would call it, or maybe sombre, all dark colours with no life to them, bland and boring to the eye. The same as it had been for years. Her room was pink, though, but she hated everything inside it, even the colour. One day, she'd have a blue house, the same as the sand in her hourglass.

She checked the time. Ah, only eight o'clock. She could go out for quite a while. Join in the fun on the pier, if only as an outsider. It was better than being lonely.

CHAPTER TWO

The Pier

"You ready for this?" Nathan whispered to his best mate, anxious for some reason. Maybe it was because he'd seen so many people he knew on the pier this evening. He'd be right in the shit if he got caught, especially because there was CCTV now Chippy June had pushed the council for it. What a do-gooder old cow.

"Yeah," Bestie said.

"Then let's get a shift on."

They split up, doing what they did best, mingling, collecting, then acting normal, like they hadn't just robbed some holidaymakers. The pier during tourist season was the best place to be — rich pickings from people too intent on having fun to notice their missing purses and wallets until the time came to pay for a ride or buy a hot dog. Twats.

He swallowed down a glut of excitement at the thought of what they did. Not just pickpocketing but the other thing. Nathan couldn't stop doing *that* if he tried. It was their secret. Soon, they'd find a plaything and hurt it, kill it, then go home and pretend they were good people. Playing a role Nathan didn't want to play.

He hated following rules.

CHAPTER THREE

The Pier

Old Clem, the Ferris wheel man, got on Madeline Cotter's nerves. He was old, grumpy and brusque nowadays, always acting as though he didn't like his job. She reckoned if he didn't enjoy his life he should change it, the same as she had recently. Like one of the memes she saw the other day: *If you're unhappy with where you are, you're not a tree — move!*

Madeline was moving. Not in the sense that she'd pack up her belongings and relocate, but *moving*, doing something different from her usual day-to-day activities. Stagnation was never a good thing, yet once upon a time she'd loved stagnating.

Funny how things changed.

She walked past Clem, who stood inside his little booth, and gave him a filthy look because, God, he really did annoy her and had since she'd been a teenager. Since his stupid controls had developed a fault and she'd got stuck at the top of his precious wheel for an hour, frightened out of her mind. Since he'd encouraged her to go on a date with Kevin. She held grudges like a bottle holds water, churning around inside with her agitation, reminding her they were always there.

She had several of the buggers and planned to do something about them.

No, she most certainly wasn't a tree, not anymore, nor was she a doormat.

Madeline smiled and left the pier, heading for the Little Devil. She'd sit in there with a vodka until the pier closed, get seen, get an alibi — the latter was always a bonus when you had it in mind to commit murder.

She'd taken to leaving the house each night, a daring thing, smothered by the once-comforting four walls, desperate for something different, exciting, less mundane. She wasn't getting any younger, and life had a habit of passing you by. Before, she'd been happy with that, especially after the debacle with her ex-husband. All she'd needed when Kevin had first left her was peace, for every day to be the same, some stability, a big contrast to how it was when they'd lived together. Pins and needles, she'd been on them daily, wondering which woman he'd fuck next behind her back. He'd thought she wasn't aware.

Until she'd let him know she knew.

Boredom had set in six months later, and in a warped, not-a-good-parent way, she was glad when her daughter showed symptoms. It meant Madeline had something to do, to focus on, other than Kevin and his antics.

Pushing *those* thoughts out of her head, she entered the pub, scanning the crowd. Monday, bingo night, the various events at the Devil giving people something to do every evening of the week if you needed company and mild stimulation. Madeline needed that these days, to let her hair down, to be herself instead of a carer. Her sick daughter took a lot out of her. Madeline felt it was okay to leave her in the evenings, to have a life of her own for a few short hours. She was always back by half eleven to see if Poppy needed anything, but that time might change over the course of this week. Poppy was always asleep when Madeline returned anyway, so there was no rush, was there? Her child slept like the dead.

She paid Reg, the landlord, for a bingo card and her fortifying drink of vodka, lots of tonic, planning to play the next four or five games after this one had finished. Hopefully she'd win and could shout "House!" loudly, gaining attention. In the meantime, she'd chat to other customers, several of them, and hope, if it came to the police questioning anyone, they'd remember she was there.

It was important they did.

* * *

Sofia wandered the pier, a baseball cap pulled low, her straight hair hanging in her face. Well, it wasn't *her* hair but some clip-in extensions she'd added, ones she'd found in Claire's Accessories. She'd dressed in old clothes, nondescript, nothing people would take any notice of. While she didn't want to be lonely, she didn't want to speak to anyone either. Being in their company was enough, on the peripheral of their lives, listening to them, watching them having a good time, and the best bit, a ride on the Ferris wheel. She had coins in her pocket from the jar in the kitchen cupboard, five quid, to pay Old Clem and get a cup of hot chocolate from the food cabin. Burger Shack had changed hands, the son, Gordon, running it now his father had died. Sofia had gone to nursery school with Gordon, but he wouldn't know her these days. She'd found people forgot faces quickly.

She waited in the queue for the ride, anticipation and excitement flowing through her. A few people got on, then Old Clem took her money, no smile, only a grunt and a gesture for her to climb aboard. She was relieved he didn't insist she share her cabin with someone else. He closed the door and secured it with a bolt on a chain, then ambled into his booth to move the contraption so others could take their seats.

Her carriage rose to eight o'clock then stopped, and she stared out at the sea. A flash of moonlight on the water reminded her of an elongated triangle, and the moon itself smiled, welcoming her into the hustle and bustle of pier life. She looked to her left and down. People milled around, and the lights of the fairground, so pretty, lifted her mood. Music played, some modern tune or other, one she hadn't heard on the radio yet, but it had a bouncy beat, something to encourage her limbs to move.

She loved dancing.

Sofia remained still, though. Old Clem might get funny if she jiggled the cabin. Tell her to get off.

It rose again, halted, swinging enough to churn her stomach, and she sat at eleven o'clock, her breath taken away by the view. Ahead and to her right, the vastness of the sea, and to the left, the strip of road, the woodland behind the pub, then the Coldwater estate beyond, the Tesco sign a gleaming red, tiny but still recognisable. She felt on top of the world, free from burdens, and was glad she'd come here again.

At last, the wheel went on its journey, round and round, Sofia's tummy plummeting with every downwards pull then rising with every lift. She was four again, that little girl who'd enjoyed everything life had to offer, someone who was free and without the worries of the world on her shoulders.

She studied the crowd and spotted a few people she knew, glad she was up here and out of their way. Questions weren't welcome: *How have you been? Is everything okay now?* No, she didn't have the energy for those, especially: *What are* you *doing here?*

Why *shouldn't* she come to the pier? Why *shouldn't* she have a good time?

Oh God. Sofia caught sight of a woman strutting along the road towards the pub. She'd recognise that walk anywhere. Thank heavens for small mercies that she wasn't coming to the pier — but why was she going to the Little Devil? Sofia didn't have her down as a public drinker. She didn't want to see her, to speak to her. She needed time to enjoy herself, and being waylaid and dragged into a conversation was low on her list.

She just wanted to *be*.

* * *

Clem was getting too old for this shit. He used to smile at the holidaymakers, enjoy watching them having a good time, but these days, all he wanted to do was sit around and revel in well-earned retirement. His neighbour, June, ran the chippy at the end of the pier, and while she still had energy in her bones, she said, she was going to keep running her business. Clem would love for the pair of them to pack it all in and spend what was left of their lives together, but June was a strange one. He couldn't work out if she wanted his company or something more. To be together as a couple. A prim and proper sort, was June. He still had it going on down there in the trouser department, he was lucky his equipment worked at his age, and he could do with reliving his youth, sowing his oats again. He missed his wife in that regard. She'd always been there with open arms, God rest her soul.

Mainly, he wanted a cuddle. To feel loved again.

He switched the lights off on his Ferris wheel, sending the fairground into darkness. Everyone else had shut down already and gone home. He stared out of the window in his booth at the black sea painted with a strip of moonlight, sighing at its magnificence, wondering how many others had bothered to view it tonight instead of ignoring it. Too many people were fixated on getting a thrill that they failed to notice the natural beauty of the planet.

He turned to face the fair. The waltzers stood immobile on their wavy wooden platform, hulks in the black now the flashing lights had gone off, the dodgems unmoving ghosts, their poles stretching to the canopy. All the stalls' shutters were down, hiding what lay within — the shooting range, hook a duck and Burger Shack, among others.

This place had been his life, his reason for existing, but now he wanted peace. No shrieking tourists, no littluns' mouths dripping with ice cream or sticky with candy floss, no standing in his booth when the weather turned nasty, rain battering the panes, the sea as choppy as anything.

He stepped outside his booth and locked it, and with his takings bag in hand, heavy with coins, he wandered up the far end towards June's Chippy, dodging happy people on their way to bed. As usual these days, he'd help her clean up, take the rubbish out for her and walk her home, which he'd done for a while but especially since Ortun's murder — he didn't want her finding another body in the water or even on the decking behind the chippy. It had rattled her more than she'd let on to the police, especially once she'd found out her husband, who'd been washed ashore many years ago, dead, had been connected to the case. In the private times Clem shared with her, she'd confessed to thinking her old boy had been playing away with holidaymakers and someone had taken umbrage. Murdered him. Ortun *had* murdered him, but not for shagging around.

Clem reached the chippy and used the key June had given him. She stood behind the counter in her royal-blue tabard, spraying cleaning solution and wiping up the oil splashes from the steel edging of the lidded fryers.

"That was a busy night," she said.

He didn't disagree. It was like all the caravan dwellers had converged on the pier, eager to squeeze every last drop of happiness from their holiday, likely the last before winter set in. "The bloody teenagers are getting worse."

"Rude, the lot of them." June came round the front and doused the glass food cases, pulling the trigger of the bottle as though shooting the teens. "D'you know, I wonder if anyone teaches their kids manners anymore."

Clem smiled. She was bordering on "In my day . . ." territory, where the elderly complained about the youth of today. He did it himself on occasion, but he felt so *old* when he started spouting the differences between generations, so he reined himself in, buttoned his lips so he didn't sound like his grandad, God rest *his* soul, too.

It didn't work this time. "One of them tried to sneak on my wheel for free, and when I pulled him up on it, he told me to fuck off. He can't have been more than thirteen, and his mam, she was *laughing*, egging him on."

"Disgusting." June swiped a cloth over the glass. "Slung up, not brought up, and they have too much leeway. All this cosseting going on, parents afraid to put their foot down. Thank God the council finally agreed to CCTV. If you report the lad, they might find him on camera and give him what for."

"Hmm." So she didn't bang on, he said, "I'll pop my takings in your safe, like usual, and get on with sorting the rubbish." He had an ominous feeling, one of dread like he'd had just before his wife had died. "If owt ever happens to me and my takings are still in your safe, keep them. Buy yourself something nice."

"Morbid sod."

Clem went into her office, stashed the money, and walked into the rear preparation room. June had already put the tray of batter in the fridge and washed the worktops, which still gleamed with wetness. He collected the black bags she'd removed from the bins. As always, a flutter of nerves skittered through him upon opening the back door. He half expected to find a body, or a killer committing murder, but deep down, he knew it was the lingering horror of what had happened out there before. He tromped onto the decking, looked left and right, then deposited the bags in the wheelie bin. A quick check that the new struts in the railings were still there, intact, and he returned inside, gladly locking up. He helped June finish cleaning by lifting the chairs upside down onto the tables then mopping the floor. The next half an hour crawled by, and finally, it was time to go home.

June had some paper packages in hand. "Thought we could have a fish supper."

Clem smiled. She said the same thing every night, claiming it was food left over, but he reckoned she cooked it special, right at the last knockings, just for them. "Lovely. You're a good woman."

"Shame my husband didn't think so."

He winced at the hurt still jabbing at her after all these years. "He didn't know what he had. Didn't appreciate you. You're a diamond."

She blushed, and hope flared inside him. Maybe he should compliment her more often. He might just get that cuddle off her yet.

* * *

Walkabout Avenue

Nathan wanted to laugh so hard but couldn't. If he did, someone might come out and catch them. He was fucked if he'd admit any blame. He'd used his BB gun to shoot a tabby cat four times, and the stupid thing had squealed and run into some bushes. Nathan was trying to pull it out, but it was a feisty animal and kept clawing at the sleeve of his jacket.

"Bloody fucker's pissing me off." He rammed his foot under the hedge, wanting to crush the moggy's head, and the cat hissed in protest.

"Leave it."

Nathan stared at Bestie in the darkness. "You what?"

"You're going to get hurt if you keep on. It'll go mental at you. Think about the time when that black cat nearly took your eye out."

"Fuck's sake." Nathan didn't like being thwarted, but time was ticking on, and they had to get going.

There would be other nights. Other cats.

* * *

Hiddleston Croft

Madeline stood beside Old Clem's place, anxiety building. He'd gone into June's ages ago. What if he stayed the night? As far as she'd seen over the past month, he hadn't done it before, but there was always a first time. She was going to be late getting home; half eleven had already come and gone.

"Fucking hell," she whispered.

Another ten minutes passed, and she was about to sack this off and go home, but a spill of light came from June's front doorway, and Clem stepped out. Madeline clutched the weapon down by her side, a wrench that had belonged to Kevin, a tool that was heavy and long enough to cave in Clem's stupid fat head. It was Ferris Fucker's fault, what she was doing. He'd helped set off a chain of events in her life that had brought her to this. If he hadn't, well, who knew where she'd have ended up. She wouldn't have to live off Kevin's divorce payout and the generous amounts he sent her each month. She wouldn't have a sick daughter at home to care for all day.

Clem wandered along June's path then onto the pavement, turning to enter his garden. Madeline moved back, down the side of his place so she stood in complete darkness, and scraped the wrench along the bricks to gain his attention.

"Who's there?" Clem called out, his voice rumbly and low.

Madeline scraped the bricks again.

"Bloody kids," he said. "I'm telling you, if I catch you, you'll be down the nick faster than you can blink."

Footsteps. Coming closer. Madeline's excitement grew — she was righting a serious wrong — and she lifted the wrench. Clem, orange-tinted from the streetlamp, stood ahead, peering into the darkness. Could he see her? Not that it would matter. He wouldn't be alive to tell anyone she'd paid him a visit.

He grew bigger as he approached. Two feet away from her. She swung the wrench, and it connected with his temple. He let out an "Oof!" and staggered sideways, his shoulder banging into the wall.

"What the hell?" he muttered, sounding angry, surprised and disorientated all at once. He clutched his head, groaning.

She struck him again, swore there was a crack of bone, and he sank to his knees. Everything reared up inside Madeline, all the hate, the pain, the desperation, the degradation, and she attacked him over and over, splashes of blood slapping onto her face. Laughter burbled in her throat. She held it in, giving Clem another wallop for good measure, then gripped the wrench with both hands, raised it above her head, and brought it down fast on the back of his head.

Panting from adrenaline and exertion, she paused to regulate her breathing. She knelt on the side path, uneven bobbles of concrete digging into her knees where the screeding hadn't been done properly. She pressed two fingers to his neck, her nurse-type gloves tight, and waited for a pulse. A faint throb, so she hit him again until something gave, his skull, the wrench embedding in a hole. Another pulse check, and she was satisfied.

She stuffed the wrench under Clem; that would serve Kevin right, his fingerprints would be all over it. Framing him had been the best idea she'd had in years. Forensics took a while to get results back, so she had enough time to finish off the others on her list. Then the man she'd married, the man she'd loved, given every part of herself to, would be pulled into the station.

She stood and walked along the quiet street away from June's so the old bitch didn't spot her going past. Madeline cried happy tears on her journey home, a release of sorts gushing free from inside her, replaced with euphoria. Life had been difficult, and now, someone was going to pay for it. She continued on, heading into Scudderton proper, along the verge on the left-hand edge of Coldwater. No cars came past, and even if they did, she presented as a dark figure, hood up, head bent, and the drivers would be unable to identify her.

She'd thought about this for a long time. Planned it to the last detail.

There was no way she'd get caught.

The best bit of the night prior to murdering Clem?

She'd won fifty quid on the bingo.

CHAPTER FOUR

Undisclosed Location

Desmond had a job to do, and as he prided himself on getting things done to the letter, he'd come up trumps for his boss if it was the last thing he did. Boss might well think it'd be the last thing Desmond did because Boss had implied in the past that people he used to do his dirty work had a habit of disappearing. The thing was, Desmond might look big and dumb, but he was far from thick. He'd arranged things nicely so when he'd completed his task he could disappear, far away from Boss's reach. He'd already been paid a fortune to do this, and that money was tucked up tight in an offshore account. And there was more to come. Boss wasn't the only one who knew how to do dodgy things. Desmond was a pro at it.

He straightened his jacket and admired the shiny buttons. The outfit suited him, although the job it represented wasn't his usual gig. He preferred dressing as part of the crowd, watching and waiting, and if anyone stepped out of line, he decked them. The element of surprise was on his side because he'd hidden in plain sight, and no one expected him to step up and clock them one.

For this job, he'd had to change his appearance, which wasn't so bad, except the glue from the fake beard itched like a motherfucker and wreaked havoc with his skin. A rash had formed already, and he'd had to resort to using poncy moisturiser to stop it going flaky. God, the things he did.

This was his last venture. Soon, he'd be on a beach somewhere, catching a tan. His mother had told him his big-headed attitude wouldn't get him far, but what did she know? It'd got him to where he was today, hadn't it?

He smiled at his reflection in the mirror. Even she wouldn't recognise him like this, and that was exactly what he wanted.

His real self disguised.

CHAPTER FIVE

Hiddleston Croft

In the morning sunshine, Chippy June waited for Old Clem to knock. They walked to and from the pier together every day, and she was glad. Since she'd found Ortun's body in the sea, tied to the struts of the pier railing behind her chip shop, she'd been a jittery mess, although she'd never admitted that to anyone other than Clem. She'd grown so fond of him lately, enjoying the evenings they spent together, eating their fish suppers and reminiscing. What he'd said to her last night about the teenager trying to get a free ride had been playing on her mind. She'd suffered a fair few young people getting arsey in the chippy, moaning about the price of a portion of chips and trying to get her to sell them cheaper. Cheeky buggers. It didn't help that Sammy, her assistant manager, had gone off to Spain for a fortnight with his wife and child. June had a woman standing in for him, and Verity was as sour as unripened grapes, so the kids liked to wind her up.

Maybe it was time to jack it all in and retire like Clem had suggested.

But what would I do? I'd be bored.

Impatient, June left her house and walked up Clem's path. She knocked on his door and rang the bell, too, in case he'd overslept. The curtains were still open, which wasn't surprising. He'd gone home later than usual last night and probably went straight to bed. Another round of knocking and bell jabbing, and she bent to peer through the letterbox.

"Clem? Wake up, you old fart!" she shouted and glanced up and down the street. There weren't many homes along here, all of them occupied by the elderly, although June didn't class herself as such. Yes, she was old in years, but inside, she was still young, just more seasoned.

She sighed.

"I'll have to go around the bloody back," she muttered. "The silly fool likely hasn't locked the kitchen door even though I told him to start doing it."

June walked past the window of his little toilet and turned the corner. She stopped, blinking, trying to make sense of what she saw. A heap, just clothing she'd like to think, but those clothes were on a person, and that person was Clem. Shock rendering her feet immobile, she slapped a hand to her mouth. Blood, so much of it, soaked his white hair, a burgundy patch on the back of his head. Was that a *hole*? His face was flat on the path, and she imagined, if he'd fallen, that his nose was broken.

"Oh God . . ."

At last, trembling, she got herself going and stepped forward a few paces, lowering to her knees beside him. "Clem? Are you okay?" She shook his shoulder and, with no response, checked for a pulse, sickened by the blood that had dripped down his neck. She had to *touch* it. A shudder ripped through her even though the blood was dry, and guilt formed a well inside her — she shouldn't be repulsed, this was her *friend*, for Pete's sake, but she was.

Cold and frightened, she stood and stepped backwards, staring at Clem all the while as if he'd rise as a ghost and chase her away. There had been no steady throb beneath her fingertips, and he'd felt stiff, cold. She shifted her gaze to his surroundings. Blood spattered the pale bricks in arcs and splashes, some coating a line of weeds that had grown beside the concrete path near the grass, the leaves speckled with it. The path itself had a small dried puddle of dark red where blood must have seeped down from that horrible hole in his skull, gathering, congealing, forming a skin.

Like custard.

She turned and ran home, inserting the key, her hand shaking, and she heaved at the scent of blood she swore came from her fingertips. Inside, she left the door open and fished about in the drawer of her telephone table for the business card Carol Wren had given her a while ago. Stabbing at her phone screen, she dialled the number and held her mobile to her ear.

"DI Carol Wren."

"It's me. June. Chippy June. Clem's . . . Clem's dead."

"Oh no, I'm so sorry to hear that. Did you find him in bed, then?"

June shook her head — stupid, because Carol couldn't see her. "No, he's . . . he's down the side of his place. There's blood, and he's got a hole . . ."

"A hole?"

"He must have tripped over." But she was lying to herself. "Or someone's killed him. I can't see where he'd have fallen and smacked his head on owt but the path, but that wouldn't make a hole, would it?"

"Are you still there, at his?"

"No, I'm at home. I had to get your card."

"Can you bring yourself to go back to Clem's and stay there until we arrive?"

Could she? She didn't want to see his broken skull again, all that blood. "Do I have to?"

"No, but can you go outside and make sure no one else goes near him? We can't have anyone messing up the scene."

"Okay." June took a deep breath. "All right, I'll do it."

"We'll be there as soon as we can."

"Hurry up. I . . . It's so awful."

June ended the call, wishing she'd asked Carol if she could stay on the line, but that was daft, the woman couldn't mollycoddle her. Gathering her mettle, June went back outside, took her keys out of the lock and pocketed them in her tabard. She closed her door, wanting to go back in and hide from this, but she owed it to her friend to remain strong.

She stood on the pavement between both houses, anxious because Betty would be coming out soon, off to Buns 'n' Bread to pick up her usual loaf and a cake of some sort for lunch. Betty liked to get there before the doors opened so she always got the freshest things. June didn't need the hassle of explaining to Betty what had happened, but she had no choice, did she?

Unless I skate over the fact he's dead.

Ten minutes crawled past, and June calculated how long it would take for Carol to drive from the village of Mollengate, where she lived, to Scudderton. It wouldn't be long, but what if she had to call in at the station first?

June glanced at her watch again, but only one minute had gone by since she'd last checked it.

A door farther up opened, and a white-haired Betty appeared, tugging out her tartan shopping trolley on wheels. She must be going to the market as well, then, to the veg stall, which, she'd proclaimed, was the only way to get produce that lasted more than two days anymore. She effed and blinded at a wheel getting stuck on the threshold, her ample cheeks jiggling with the force of her wrenching.

She locked up and stomped along the pavement, big boobs bouncing, taking no notice of Clem's place and stopping close to June. "Clem's having a lie-in? Unusual for him."

June swallowed down her anxiety. "Did you see anyone last night? Along here, I mean."

Betty frowned. "Now you come to mention it, I did."

June's stomach rolled over. "A man or a woman?"

"I couldn't tell, I was half asleep. Got up for a wee, didn't I? Why?"

"Clem's . . . Clem's been attacked." That was a better way to put it.

"Attacked?" Betty shrieked. "What's this town coming to? We've only just come out the other side of that mad surgeon killing people, and now this? Where is he? Inside? And why are you out here?"

"I'm waiting for the police. They'll likely want to speak to you if you saw someone."

"Deary me. I haven't got time to hang about. You know I like a fresh loaf."

"Then expect them to knock at yours when you come back." June folded her arms. "I'd have liked nowt more than to go to my chippy and take in the fish delivery, but some of us have kind hearts and opt to stick around when there's trouble." She sniffed in disdain.

"There's nowt I can do anyroad." Betty sniffed back at her. "Except maybe go and sit with him. Shall I do that?"

"No," June said, too quickly, remembering what Carol had said. The last thing the copper wanted was Betty lumbering all over the garden. "No, he's better off being left alone."

Betty shrugged. "You know him best." She smirked, probably thinking June and Clem were an item doing rude things of a night. "I'll be seeing you."

June watched her walk down the street, suddenly wishing her neighbour would come back, then alarm grew at a van coming up the road. It parked, and a man got out, the same man who'd been at the pier on the morning she'd found Ortun. Todd Butcher.

He approached and gave June a cuddle. "I'm sorry you had to find him, love."

So was she. Oh God, so was she.

CHAPTER SIX

Hiddleston Croft

Carol couldn't believe their luck. They'd not long solved a murder case, so to have another so soon was a shock. Plus she'd had to deal with her mother's body being exhumed from beneath the patio of her childhood home. The poor people who'd bought it had moved out and still hadn't sold it. Seemed no one wanted to live in a crime scene.

Carol had blocked a lot of her upbringing out, but during the previous case, memories had been unlocked, and she'd recalled her father laying slabs on the night Mam had supposedly walked out on them after a row.

She hadn't walked out. How could she when Carol had seen Mam fall and smack her head on the hearth? She wouldn't have had her wits about her enough. The post-mortem revealed she had a broken hyoid bone. Dad had strangled her, buried her, then lied to Carol about it for the rest of his life. Carol had felt abandoned, left with an alcoholic monster who'd hit her, treated her badly. It was a wonder she'd grown up as good and caring as she had, but that was down to her not wanting to continue the cycle of abuse, needing to be the opposite of her father. And why she hadn't had children. She couldn't put a kid through what she'd endured, couldn't risk turning into *him* when times got rough.

Dave sat in the passenger seat. She'd just parked outside June's place, needing a small breather before she jumped into the fray. SOCO in their all-in-one suits milled around in Clem's front garden, one of them dusting for fingerprints at the front door. June was nowhere in sight. PC Alan Pitson, her favourite copper after Dave, was today's log officer, and he stood at Clem's gate talking to Richard Prince, the scene sergeant. Rib's van was already here, so the pathologist was likely in the tent with Todd, the lead SOCO. Carol had needed a shower before coming out, and she'd actioned for Alan to get here as soon as possible, plus Todd and Rib. With that covered, she'd had time to get ready, stick some toast in and make a coffee.

She and Dave had eaten on the way here. They were bumbling along lovely in the cottage they shared, getting on as easily at home as they did at work. If she'd still lived in her flat, she'd have asked him to stay over most nights since her mother had been dug up. Nightmares had come, fuelled by guilt and grief — hideous faces that had no nose, no eyes, no mouths, pointing at her, accusing her. *You should have told someone about your father laying that patio, you should have known your mam had been dumped in a hole in the garden.* She was getting better at not taking the blame, though. How could she have been aware of what had gone on after Mam's fall? Carol had been sent to bed. As an adult, she cursed her younger self for being upstairs when Dad had his hands around Mam's throat, but as the child, she'd had no control over the situation. Even if she'd stood there while he'd committed murder, she'd have been too scared of him to run and get help. With Mam now cremated, her ashes sprinkled in the sea at Scarborough, her favourite place, Carol had been able to finally lay her to rest. Carol hadn't been abandoned by her, and that was the saving grace of it all.

"We'd better get on, then," she said.

Dave nodded. "Clem, though. Who'd want to kill him?"

"God knows. I thought everyone liked him, but what do I know?"

Carol got out and went to the boot, sorting their protective clothing and putting it on. A stickler for not contaminating any scenes, she took out three pairs of booties and tucked them beneath her arm. Dave took his and did the same.

She approached Alan at the gate. "Morning."

"Not a good one." Alan had been a bobby for years, content to remain in that role.

"No. It's a sad state of affairs when someone like Clem gets it." She signed the log. "And it doesn't help that we're still in season. There are tourists everywhere."

"Could have been one of them." Dave signed in, too. "Maybe he pissed one of them off and they followed him home."

She hoped not. Sifting through all the people staying in caravans, hotels and B&Bs wasn't something she or uniform would enjoy doing. It stalled the process, and with the golden hour possibly already long gone, she was behind time as it was.

"Where's June?" she asked Alan.

"At her place. Whitney's with her. I thought it best I phoned her to come out."

Whitney Faulds was their main family liaison officer. She'd announced the date of her wedding last week. She was marrying Alton Sinclair, the night-time station sergeant. They'd opted for a beach ceremony next summer, which would be lovely — if the great British weather behaved itself.

"Good call." Carol smiled. "June must be in bits."

"She was in a hell of a state by the time I got here." Alan scrubbed at his chin. "Todd and his lot were already here, and she'd held it together until she saw me. I suppose I'm a familiar face, what with me being involved when her husband was found on the beach."

"Bless her. We'll go and see her in a few."

Alan opened the gate. "She mentioned Betty Saunders had seen someone last night. Betty's gone into town, to the bakery and the market, so hopefully she'll be back by the time you need to speak to her."

Carol nodded. "We may as well do it while we're here. Saves a uniform doing it or Michael and Katherine leaving the incident room. Katherine will want to dig into Clem's past and see whether he's on social media."

Carol and Dave slipped booties on.

"But it's a possibility, a pissed-off holidaymaker," she said, her mind wandering back to that part of the conversation. "We can't rule it out at the minute."

She picked her way along using the evidence steps, up a path, then moved to the side of the house. A tent stood ahead, about halfway down, and she took note of its surroundings. A large tree to the left, leaning drunkenly, its naked boughs lending a protective arm over the tent. A slice of grass beside this path, a small wooden fence blocking off the front area, about ten inches high. Leaves in golden colours had sailed down and settled, and forensics had one hell of a job on their hands sifting through that lot.

Dave came up behind her. "In you go."

She grimaced, switched her booties for another pair so she didn't transfer anything from the path, dropped them in a designated bag beside the tent flap, then raised her mask. She stepped in. Rib stood on a low step among several evidence markers on the grass and path, Todd doing the same. A photographer worked around them, snapping pictures.

"I'd stay where you are, Bird," Rib said to her. "Saves owt getting mucked up." He gestured to the markers. "A lot of blood spatter. By the way, did you enjoy your dinner in the Lord last night? I had the same as you, and to be honest, the chicken was like cardboard."

She smiled. "Glad you had a dodgy meal. Mine was lovely."

Rib's eyes crinkled over his mask. "You never pass up a chance to be mean."

She laughed. "Just giving you back what you used to dish out to me. It's not nice when the shoe is on the other foot, is it?"

"That's where you're wrong. You know I wind people up to prove they've got a bit of life in them. I've just been telling Todd he needs a haircut. It's like a fucking bush under that hood."

"At least I've *got* hair, baldy," Todd said.

"I happen to have hair, I just shave it off." Rib must have poked his tongue out because his mask extended in the middle.

"Morning, Todd," Carol said.

"Morning. Not a good call first thing, is it?" He flung out a gloved hand at Clem.

"Nope. Okay, give me a second to see what we have here," she said and geared herself up to look.

Clem lay face down, his right arm squashed between his side and the wall of the house, his left resting across the path as if he'd reached for something. Right leg straight, the left bent at the knee. If it wasn't for the blood, it would appear as if he'd fallen asleep. But there *was* blood, a lot of it, *and* the hole in the head June had mentioned.

"That wound." She pointed to it as the photographer's flash went off. "A fall, like the edge of the path dug in, or . . . ?"

Rib shook his head. "There isn't any evidence of that, nor any debris from the ground. This is more like a weapon. I know you won't want to look closely, but think of something with a rounded end."

"That could be one of many things," she grumbled.

"Okay, this might help. A Babybel. The hole is deeper in the centre, so if you imagine pushing a Babybel into soft butter, that's the shape we're talking about here. A smooth implement, nowt ragged that would splinter the skull into tiny, grit-like pieces, although there *are* larger fragments where I believe he was struck more than once and some chipped off."

Carol shuddered. "Your descriptions are foul. You've put me off that cheese for ever."

Rib laughed. "Serves you right for being cruel to me just now."

Todd chuckled. "You two . . ."

Carol supposed, to the onlooker, that them having a laugh when someone was lying dead at their feet was disrespectful, but it was a way of coping. No one wanted to take in the full enormity of a scene without some form of light relief. It could send you mad.

The photographer lowered his camera. "I'll go out in the garden, so call me when you turn him over."

"Will do," Rib said.

The officer left.

"So we're talking murder," Dave said, the tent flap slapping into place.

"We are." Rib took a tool like a chopstick out of his bag and leaned down to lift some of Clem's hair back. "See that temple? I'd say it was the first strike. The core of the bruising is the same shape as that on the back of the head, and the bruising surrounding it is a result of blood rushing to protect the site. No signs of an egg bump, so that strike wasn't as hard as the others."

"Done to subdue?" Carol asked.

"I'd say so, although we could be talking about a hesitant killer here, someone who didn't hit him hard enough at first because they didn't know *how* hard to do it." Todd folded his arms. "He took a battering, as there are contusions in various places all over the head, but that hole was the killer blow."

Rib nodded. "I'm betting it was. I suspect his face will be a mess because it hit the concrete. A broken nose at the very least."

"Ouch," Dave said. "Poor bastard."

Carol couldn't imagine the pain of faceplanting on concrete let alone wallops to the head. "Let's hope he was out of it before he hit the ground. Alan said Betty Saunders saw someone round and about last night. Does that fit with an estimated time of death?"

Rib cleared his throat. "Excuse me. Got a frog in there. Err, yes, full rigor, so we're talking six hours ago at least. I'm guessing more. He's stiff as a board."

"When will you do the PM?"

"Today. I've nowt else on. I finished with my current lab resident last night. The death at home you rang me about. Nowt suspicious. Heart attack."

"That's good, then. I was beginning to wonder if Clem was a second victim, what with them being similar ages." Carol scratched her head with the back of her wrist. "No idea why someone would kill Clem. You?"

Rib shrugged, and Todd frowned.

"Okay." Carol sighed. "We're going in blind once again." She looked at Dave. "June's it is, then."

* * *

In a plaid dressing gown, June sat on her chair by the fireplace, flames crackling, throwing out more warmth than was necessary as the early autumn weather was milder than usual. Mind you, she was probably in a state of shock, going by the way she shivered. Whitney sat in the chair on the other side. Clem had used it last time Carol and Dave had been here to inform June that Ortun had killed her husband.

That felt like a lifetime ago.

Carol and Dave perched on the sofa opposite, Carol glad to be out of the protective clothing and getting on with the nitty-gritty. A tray of tea paraphernalia, provided by Whitney, sat on the coffee table between them, and the FLO poured while June cried in silence, staring at the floor, a crumpled tissue held in her gnarled hand.

"I'm so sorry," Carol said. "I know you two were close."

June sniffed. "I was only just thinking of more, too."

"More?"

"Yes, me and Clem. Friends who could maybe live together. It would have saved on the outgoings, and he's here every evening after we close anyroad. It'd make sense. And now . . . I didn't get the chance to tell him."

Carol felt sorry for her. "Life, as you know, can be cruel."

"Can't it just." June wiped her nose and tucked the tissue beneath the wristband of her gown. "Clem didn't deserve this. Is . . . *is* it murder?"

"Yes." Carol didn't think June would appreciate any beating around the bush. "Are you ready to tell me about your movements last night?"

June bobbed her head. "He shut the wheel down at ten, as usual, and came to help me in the chippy. Took the rubbish out, mopped the floor. We walked back — no one followed us or owt — and this street was empty when we got here. We came into mine for our supper — I'd done us some fish and chips — then we sat and watched a film. *Grease*, it was, because I love a bit of John Travolta. Mind, we didn't watch all of it. Clem had nodded off, so I woke him and said it was time to go home. I wish . . . I wish I hadn't. I was going to leave him there with a blanket then go to bed, but I wasn't sure how he'd take to waking up in my living room. He saw himself out, I locked up, then went for a wee, a shower, and got into bed."

Carol thought about that. If the bathroom window was shut, the sound of the shower might well have dampened any noises from outside. "What time was that?"

"Five to twelve."

Dave wrote in his notebook then gave Carol a quick glance: *Bet he was killed just after he left here*. Did that mean someone had been waiting for him, that this was premeditated rather than a random, chance attack?

Whitney sat and observed, as she always did, and Carol looked her way. Whitney shook her head as if to confirm she didn't believe June had done this. Whitney would have casually nosed around to detect any signs of blood or a struggle, and monitored June's behaviour.

Carol picked up her tea and sipped. She cradled the cup. "So you didn't hear anyone around after Clem left?"

"No. I got up as usual this morning." She went on to relate her movements. "And here we are. I washed my hands, is that okay? I touched . . . touched his blood. It was dry but . . ."

Carol would have preferred her not to have done that, but as she was only checking for a pulse and certainly not a suspect in her eyes, she'd let it slide. "Don't worry about that. I'm more concerned over how you're feeling. Do you need Whitney to stay with you for today?"

June shook her head. "I'm going to the chippy."

"Do you have to?" Whitney asked.

"It'll keep my mind busy, and there's Verity, standing in for Sammy while he's away, she'll be waiting for me soon. Then there's the fish delivery. Callum will be wondering where I am. He's already phoned, and I said I'd be there within the hour."

"So Callum took over Skipper Kinnock's boat, then?" Carol asked.

"Yes, he runs the *Poisson Mort* for Violet."

Skipper had been killed by Mason Ingram, and Violet was a lovely Irish woman who hadn't deserved to lose her husband in such a terrible way.

"Okay, well, if you're sure you want to go in. Whitney can give you a lift," Carol said.

"Someone's been in to swab me and take my clothes," June said. "I knelt by Clem, see, so can I get this dressing gown off and have a shower now?"

Carol nodded. "You do that."

"Finish your tea." June rose. "Oh, I nearly forgot. There was a teenager last night. Clem said he'd tried to get on the Ferris without paying. There's CCTV now, so maybe you'll spot him on it. For all we know, what with the way the kids are these days, he decided to attack Clem."

Carol perked up at that. "Did Clem give a description?"

"Only that he was about thirteen and his mother was with him. She was laughing at her son wanting a freebie."

"Did he say what time that was?"

"No, sorry." June left the room, closing the door behind her.

Dave wrote in his book then took his phone out. "I'll message Michael, get the ball rolling on CCTV."

Carol thanked him and raised her eyebrows at Whitney. "Thoughts?"

"She's shaken up, but you know her, she's no-nonsense and wants to get on, although she did admit that this on top of finding Ortun has made her reassess life. She said something about moving up the coast to a retirement cottage, reckons Scudderton is turning into murder central."

"Can't say I blame her," Dave said. "She's had a fair bit of tragedy, and we've had a few murders lately. I don't believe she'll leave Scudderton, though. She's part of the furniture." He lifted a cup off the tray and drank half in one go.

"Have you got steel guts or what?" Whitney said.

"Can't stand it lukewarm or cold." Dave downed the rest.

Carol took another sip of hers and placed the cup on the table. "We should go and see if Betty's in yet." She stood, thinking of June sitting in her chair night after night, no Clem for company. Tears pricked the backs of her eyes.

"You all right?" Whitney asked.

"Yep, just contemplating the vagaries, that's all. One minute she's thinking of asking Clem to move in, and the next he's gone. Anyroad, enough of that. We'll see you when we see you."

She opened the door and left the room, the tinkle and slosh of the shower reaching her, and it struck her how different that shower would be. In last night's, June had been looking forward to bed, not a care in the world, and in this one, she was probably crying, her tears meshing with the water.

I know that feeling, love. I've cried in the shower more times than I can count lately.

* * *

Betty Saunders, a blowsy woman with the energy of a wasp trapped in a jar, flumped down on a chair at her kitchen table and pursed her lips. "Murder? Bloody hell. June only said he'd been attacked."

"He was," Carol said from her standing position by the sink. "Can you tell us what, or who, you saw last night?"

Betty glanced at Dave, who sat at the table with her. "What I saw is easy, but as to the who, your guess is as good as mine." She got up again and poked around in a tartan shopping trolley, producing a large, mud-smeared cauli and a brown paper bag with rabbit ear twists keeping it closed. She thumped over to a veg rack in the corner of the dining area and placed the cauli on top, then emptied the bag in the tray beneath. Potatoes. "It could have been a man or a woman, young or old. All I saw was someone in dark clothing. I couldn't even tell you if they had a hood up or owt, it was literally a whole black figure."

Dave scribbled that down. "What about the height and size?"

Betty rammed her hands inside her trolley again, bringing out another paper bag. "A bit taller than me, so five nine, something like that, although I've shrunk over the years. I used to be six foot, you know." She tipped onions onto the rack and scrunched the bags up. "Size, let me think. Average."

Carol held back a sigh. "Average to one person isn't the same as it is to another. Any reference to clothing sizes? Maybe that will help you think."

"I don't know what bloody waist they take!"

Carol let out the sigh then. "I meant a twelve, fourteen or whatever."

"Oh." Betty trundled to the bin and threw the bags away. "Maybe a sixteen?"

"Thank you," Dave said. "So you didn't get even the slightest idea of the sex?"

Betty harrumphed. "I said not, didn't I? One of them androgynous people where you can't tell." She walked towards Carol and leaned across the worktop to stroke a loaf of bread.

Alarming.

"Prices have gone up," Betty mumbled. "This cost me twenty pence more than two days ago. Disgusting. I'm on a pension."

"It's getting bad, yes." Carol was lucky in that her father had left her his worldly goods when he'd died, including the house she'd sold, and she'd finally spent some of the money by buying the cottage and a static caravan. She had income from work, plus the van, and Dave paid his way in the cottage, so she didn't have to worry about twenty pence here and there. She felt bad for anyone who suffered from the pinch these days. "Which direction did they go in?"

Betty stopped petting the bread and stuffed her hands beneath her armpits. "Up there." She jerked her head. "So, away from Clem's, not going past June's."

"Can you recall what time that was?"

"Well, I woke up at five past twelve for a wee. I heard footsteps. I went in the spare bedroom and had a look out, and there they were, turning right into the woods."

A ten-minute murder window. He left June's around five to twelve.

Carol thought about where those woods ended. It was the long road that led to big Tesco, she was sure of it. So did the killer live on Coldwater? Or had they gone the other way to one of the caravan parks? Residents of Scudderton also lived up there permanently, so it wasn't just tourists.

"Is there owt else you can remember?"

Betty shook her head. "No."

Sadly, this meant they didn't have much to go on, although a figure standing at five nine and the direction they'd gone in was better than a poke in the eye with a sharp stick.

She and Dave said their goodbyes, let Betty know a uniform would be along to take an official statement later, and left the house.

Richard Price stood in the middle of the road with PC Mulholland, their notebooks out as though they were comparing. Carol went and joined them, Dave going over to speak to Alan at Clem's gate.

"Owt from the other neighbours?" Carol asked.

Richard pushed a hand through his greying hair. "Sod all. Same for Mulholland. Everyone was in bed."

Carol bit her lip. "Okay, me and Dave will head down to the station. You never know, Katherine and Michael might have unearthed something."

Hope still resided in Carol, although at times it had deserted her. She thought of Mam, alone in that damp hole under the patio, and the times Carol had played hopscotch on the slabs, no idea her mother was beneath her. And the hope she'd allowed to bloom that Mam would come home and rescue her soon. The hope she'd held on to that the body wouldn't be hers. Then the crashing emotions when DNA had proved it was.

Life. It really was a shitbag.

CHAPTER SEVEN

Undisclosed Location

Sofia turned the hourglass over and daydreamed at the window. In her mind, she sat on a sun-drenched beach and stared out to sea. It wasn't the one in Scudderton but a turquoise expanse that sparkled as if diamonds perched on the surface. The sun was different, too, and there was none of the humid air you got back home. She was on the Costa del Sol, a multicoloured sarong over her bikini, her body tanned, the scent of various sunscreen lotions all around her. And voices, happy people, as glad to be there as she was. Some rested on loungers and read books or sunbathed. Others listened to the radio and shared out cheese butties speckled with sand, sipping cocktails through straws from the Beach Hut bar.

She loved imagining different scenarios. It gave her hope for the future. A dream she could cling to. One day, she'd go abroad if her finances allowed it. If she got rid of the roadblocks in her way. She wasn't sure she had the courage yet, although she'd thought about it often enough and she was certainly angry.

Those thoughts brought her hurtling back to reality.

Last night, she'd put the loose change in the jar in the cupboard. She hadn't bothered with a hot chocolate from Burger Shack, as tempting as it had been. After seeing that woman going into the Little Devil, she'd just wanted to get home. She'd put the clothing back in the wardrobe and got into bed, falling into her usual pattern of inciting a dream, one she could coast into naturally and that would carry on after she'd drifted off.

She'd put herself on a cruise ship, the *Merry Belle*, walking the many floors, taking a tour, a ghost-like participant. The dance hall, the two restaurants, the theatre where resident actors performed their version of *Cabaret* to much clapping and cheers at the end. She'd watched *Titanic* and based the interior of her ship on that one, and she was Rose, looking for her Jack. She floated around, smiling at everyone she passed, then went up on deck and gripped the railings, lifting her face to the sun. The sea breeze whisked past her cheeks, sifting through her hair, transforming it into rippling ribbons behind her, and the sound of people in the pool had her smiling.

She'd opened her eyes, and the moon had taken the place of the sun, a gale snatching the breeze, and the shrieks from the pool turned into screams of terror. Like the *Titanic*, her ship was going down, and people rushed around, desperate to line up for the lifeboats. Sofia couldn't move — dreams were nasty like that — and as the *Merry Belle* listed, she had listed with it, toppling over the railing and into the violent waves.

She'd woken up drenched in sweat, convinced for a moment it was the sea dripping down her body and soaking her nightdress. The fog of the dream dispersed, shunting her back into her bedroom, and she'd cried, wishing she was in the sea again, drowning despite the fear she'd experienced, swallowed by the water and dragged down to the bottom.

Stop doing that. Be happy. It's almost at an end.

She pushed herself back to the Spanish beach and forced an ice cream to appear in her hand. It reminded her of childhood, on the occasions when she'd sat on the sand at Scudderton Cove, a bucket and spade nearby, her mother and father laughing, talking about God knew what — she'd been too young to remember or even understand. She cried again, for what once was, and told herself to get a grip and stop mourning the person she missed so much, the man who'd left her for another woman. He wasn't coming back, and the sooner she came to terms with that, the less she'd hurt.

She licked the ice cream and wiped her tears away.

That's better.

CHAPTER EIGHT

Undisclosed Location

Desmond was bored. Boss had told him to remain impassive, to blend into the woodwork. That was all well and good, but the position he held for this malarky wasn't one where he could act the shrinking violet. Sometimes, Boss got right on his nerves with the way he dished out orders, but it was to be expected. After all, he ran a tight ship, and there were many secrets Desmond had picked up on by standing in the background. They'd be the reason Boss would want to make him disappear when this was over. Scandals, stuff the public shouldn't know, like what really went on behind the scenes. Plus what Desmond was doing now. Boss was taking a huge risk — not that Desmond couldn't deliver the goods, but if it ever got out, well, a hit on someone never went down a storm and tended to get you put away.

Boss wouldn't like it in prison. He'd got too used to the high life.

There was no question Desmond wouldn't do the deed. He'd been paid and always stuck to his word. He'd kill the target but take no pleasure in it. Since Desmond had got to know them, he'd found Boss's nemesis to be pleasant, a person who gave their time freely, no matter how stressed they were. You didn't get many of them to the pound.

It was time to make the second move. The first had been infiltrating the target's world, and as Desmond had detected no signs of suspicion directed his way, he reckoned it was safe to proceed.

He wrote what had to be written, then left where he was staying, on his way to work, smiling, because this shit was far too easy.

CHAPTER NINE

Ridgebrook Close

Madeline had arrived home in a jubilant mood last night, popping her bingo winnings away. Maybe she'd treat Poppy to a new book. *Cinderella* would be nice, or maybe *Snow White and the Seven Dwarfs*. A weight had been lifted by killing Clem, and she could only imagine how she'd feel once everyone else was dispatched and Kevin was rotting away in prison. He'd soon regret leaving some of his belongings here, but mainly his toolbox. It would be his beautiful downfall.

She hated him for buggering off once he'd made his fortune. He'd created a social media platform, much like Facebook, but it had taken years to catch on. ChatSesh was his baby, one he'd nurtured for a long time, and she'd helped him to create it, offering advice, making him cups of tea late into the night, and looking after Poppy by herself. Poppy hadn't been poorly when Kevin had lived with them, that had come afterwards, yet he still hadn't given the child the attention she deserved. It seemed even a sick kid hadn't tugged at his heartstrings.

In a way, Madeline was glad he'd walked out. His many affairs had worn her down, and after she'd told him she knew what he was up to, he'd taken it with a pinch of salt. He'd promised to stop it, which was something, then he'd come in a month later with a big bunch of flowers, apologising for "falling off the monogamy wagon". Time and again she'd taken those flowers, her heart aching, her eyes stinging, and told him she forgave him.

Until the day she hadn't.

She'd given him an ultimatum: *It's me and Poppy or you're out.*

He'd hired a small van and packed up the majority of his things, only coming back to see Poppy once a month, then he'd changed it to taking their daughter out instead so he spent as little time with Madeline as possible — his words, not hers. Then he'd stopped seeing Poppy altogether.

To this day, she couldn't stand the scent of flowers. It reminded her of how pathetic she'd been. A doormat. God, she'd been such a fool, but not so much that she hadn't taken him to the cleaners. She'd been awarded half of his fortune that had accrued up until the end of their marriage, plus he'd paid two hundred thousand for Poppy, placed in a trust fund so Madeline couldn't get her "filthy mitts" on it. She wouldn't have touched what wasn't hers anyway, and she gladly paid for her upbringing with the settlement, but Kevin's sour words and treatment throughout the divorce, and him ghosting them a few months afterwards, had shown her who he really was.

As had him shacking up in one of the big houses on the cliff recently, sold to him by Gary Cuttersby, who'd decided to move on with his sons, settling in Runswick Bay so he was closer to his illegitimate daughter and her mother, Charlotte. Madeline had heard he'd started seeing Charlotte again, although this time it wasn't an affair but a proper relationship. His dead wife would be turning in her grave.

Kevin's new pad had a glass ceiling above the living room — Madeline should know, she'd been up there to have a look, knowing he'd be in his posh new office building, working on ChatSesh with his minions. Christ, he behaved like he'd invented Google, kitting the premises out inside like their corporate headquarters. He had a dubious logo, too, and many a time she'd thought of alerting Google to the similarities. She'd bet they'd take him to court.

She'd spoken to Kevin's neighbours, Willy and Lise, who'd informed her he'd moved in with a redhead. Madeline wasn't surprised, but she was sickened all the same. *She* should have been living in that house, her and Poppy, and Kevin should have cherished them, not cast them aside.

Bastard.

She got on with loading the food tray for Poppy and taking it upstairs, bypassing the stairlift her daughter had to use. It was such a shame the way Poppy couldn't live a normal life, how Madeline had to cater to her every whim, but she'd do it without complaint. At least Poppy had *one* parent she could rely on, who wouldn't let her down.

She swivelled on the landing to open Poppy's door using her bum, then entered and cocked a leg out to stop it from slamming. Tray placed on the over-bed table, she walked to open the curtains and the window. Fresh air always did a body good, didn't it, and she wanted Poppy to get as much as she could before winter crept around in its frosty boots.

"Morning!" she said brightly and returned to the bed to pour orange juice from the glass jug into a plastic sippy cup.

Poppy stirred, opened her eyes and winced. "Is it morning already?"

Madeline gave her an indulgent smile. "It is, and the sun's out. Shall we go for a walk later? I was thinking of buying you a motorised wheelchair instead of the one you've got. It's getting tiring pushing it around. No idea why I didn't think of that before."

"Okay." Poppy eased herself up, but her elbow bent, and she flopped back down.

"Let me help you."

Madeline pulled Poppy into a sitting position, packed pillows behind her and wheeled the bed table closer. "Porridge today with golden syrup. Your favourite."

Poppy smiled and, dear as she was, picked up her spoon and ate. Madeline was glad she didn't need feeding, at least not yet, but she'd be there to play aeroplanes with her food if she couldn't manage it, zooming the spoon towards her open, bird-like mouth.

"Nice?" Madeline asked.

"Yes."

"Well, I'll leave you to it, then I'll be back to help you in the shower."

Madeline gave her precious child one last loving glance then left the room. She had cleaning to do — without little eyes watching — which involved scrubbing the clothes she'd had on last night. Because Poppy didn't get much stimulation other than books or what was on the telly, she tended to pose a million and one questions if things weren't the norm. Madeline couldn't be doing with her asking why she was attacking her boiler suit with a scrubbing brush — "And why are the bubbles pink, Mammy?"

God, no, that would never do.

In the kitchen, she poked at the clothing which had been soaking overnight in cold salty water, then rummaged inside a carrier bag to pull out the gloves. She smiled at how bloodied they were, although it had dried, turning burgundy rather than bright red. She went out the back and put them in the fire pit, getting the blaze going good and proper, then returned to the kitchen to scrub, scrub, scrub.

Suit clean, Madeline made tea and drank it outside, dropping the carrier bag in the fire pit and watching the flames, thinking about the person she'd be visiting later. This one wouldn't be killed at night. She'd arranged for a carer to come and sit with Poppy, claiming she needed some respite, so a bit of shopping would do wonders. She needed to be seen in town afterwards, minding her own business, not a murderer at all.

Today was going to be such a good one.

She did what she'd promised and helped Poppy have a shower, then she dressed her and carried her over to the armchair by the window while she changed the sheets.

"Where did you go last night, Mammy?"

The question had Madeline pausing mid tug, the end of a pillow in one hand, the case in the other. "I didn't go anywhere, darling."

"I heard the front door shut. And footsteps."

Bloody hell. "Oh, *that*! I went into the front garden to water the plants."

"Oh."

Crisis averted, Madeline finished her job, listening to Poppy humming a tune. She put new bedding on, pleased with the smell of freshness from where she'd hung them on the line to dry. With Poppy in bed a lot of the time, it tended to get musty.

"Shall we go for that walk, then?" she asked brightly, closing the window then scooping Poppy up to place her in the stairlift. "Maybe we could go to the pier and have an ice cream."

Poppy clapped.

She was so easily pleased.

* * *

Cove Pier

A sudden gust of wind pushed Poppy's ponytail to one side, a hairy streamer. Madeline tucked it into her daughter's collar and pulled up her hood, continuing to push her up the pier towards the fairground. Oh, this was intriguing. A few of those special police officers prowled, and Madeline received a jolt of excitement. Were they here because of what she'd done, talking to people to see if anyone had seen anything going on last night? She wanted in on that action so headed straight for an officer standing by the Ferris wheel, which was moving, someone else in Clem's booth, a lad of about twenty.

"What's going on?" Madeline asked the female plod.

"We're asking after Clem Talbot. The Ferris wheel man. Do you know him?"

"I'm a resident, not a tourist, so yes, I know him, but not that well. He's a fixture around here, like the pier — you notice it all the time but don't necessarily visit."

The copper frowned. "Right . . ."

Madeline knew what that kind of "right" meant. The PCSO thought she was a willy weirdo, someone not to be taken seriously. Well, they'd better take her seriously, because she meant business. This woman here would soon find out Madeline was a force to be reckoned with come this afternoon.

"Where do you live?" the officer asked.

Madeline wasn't about to give her the actual address, she didn't feel it was necessary. "On Coldwater."

"Were you here last night?"

"On the pier? No, I went to the Little Devil, though. Won fifty pounds on the bingo. What's happened?"

"Did you see owt when you walked past?"

Hmm, so she was avoiding answering Madeline's question. Maybe the police were taught to evade, to keep information to themselves. She supposed it saved people going into a panic. She hoped Clem hadn't come back to life. That would be annoying. "Nowt out of the ordinary. It was the same as always, people having a good time."

"Thanks." The PCSO moved away.

Madeline was tempted to put a hand out to stop her — she needed more details, fuck it — but the wise side of her warned she shouldn't push it. Instead, she went to the candy floss stall and bought a pink cloud on a stick for Poppy, biting the inside of her cheek and letting her mind wander. What if Clem *hadn't* died? He wouldn't have known who she was, it had been too dark, but he could give details of the attack.

No, she hadn't felt a pulse. She was being silly.

Madeline walked them to the end of the pier and glanced inside June's Chippy. The CLOSED sign was on the door, but June was in there with that annoying Verity woman who stood in for pier business owners when they needed a day off or a holiday. She'd have been manning the Ferris if Sammy wasn't in Spain. Maybe Verity's son had taken over the wheel for the time being, although Madeline hadn't seen him for years so wouldn't recognise him.

Madeline tapped on the chippy door and waved to June, who looked over. She had a pink tabard on today, which was odd, because she usually preferred the blue one. She came to open up and cocked her head in question.

"Everything okay?" Madeline asked. "Only, some copper asked me about Clem . . ."

June's eyes watered. "Haven't you heard? He's been murdered." Her bottom lip quivered.

"Oh my God!" Madeline slapped a hand to her mouth to hide her smile. She lowered it and whispered, "That's awful. I'm so sorry. You were good friends, weren't you?"

June nodded. "He was attacked. Blood everywhere. I'll never get over it."

Madeline pulled a suitably empathetic expression. Was that the reason for the tabard switch? Ooh, had the police taken the other one? Talk about exciting. "You *saw* the blood?"

"Yes, I was the one who found him this morning."

"Oh no, love, that's terrible, that is. I can see you're upset, so I'll let you get on."

June smiled sadly and closed the door, drawing the blind down over the glass, either instantly dismissing Madeline or making it clear to other people that they shouldn't knock. The chippy didn't open until eleven lately, but that wouldn't stop hungry holidaymakers from demanding food.

Madeline pushed Poppy back down the pier, stopping every so often so her daughter could watch her try to catch a duck or shoot tin cans for a teddy. For once, Madeline won — she must have luck on her side, what with the bingo last night. Poppy chose a fluffy penguin, likely because she loved the film *Happy Feet.*

"I'll put it in my bag for the minute so you don't get it sticky," Madeline said and stuck the toy inside. She took out a packet of wet wipes and got on with cleaning the candy floss off Poppy's hands. "Right, *now* you can hold it." She gave her the penguin. "What are you going to call it?"

Poppy clutched it in her small hands and sighed. "Karlos."

"Lovely. Shall I try to win you something else?"

Poppy sighed again. "All right."

Madeline bristled slightly. "You don't sound very enthusiastic. Do you want to go home?"

"No." Poppy gazed at the sea. "Can we see if the dolphins are out?"

That meant a visit to the Beach Hut Café where they could sit by the window. Poppy knew exactly what she was doing, the crafty sod. She'd get a Coke, a slice of lemon meringue pie and attention from the locals, especially the new owner who'd taken over from Yolanda — she'd been killed by that dreadful Mason fella. Bernard had stepped in to run the café, and he loved Poppy.

"Okay." Madeline never could stand firm when it came to her child. "We'll stay until twelve, then I have to get back. Yasmeen's coming to look after you this afternoon while I nip to town, don't forget."

She wheeled her to the café and turned her back to push the door, but someone rushed over to hold it for her, a welcome do-gooder. She thanked them and went inside, glad Poppy's favourite table was unoccupied. Bernard came and took their order, and for the next wee while, mother and daughter stared at the sea, seeing which one would spot a dolphin first.

CHAPTER TEN

Tour Bus

Sofia remembered the time she'd sat on the top deck of a tour bus in York. She'd gone there to get some peace. The tour taught her many things, but Dick Turpin stood out the most. He'd been hanged in a big field, all the townspeople coming to watch him die, and instead of waiting for the hangman to do his thing, Dick had jumped, thus killing himself. He'd been in control, something Sofia wanted in life, to be the conductor, the one who held the baton.

Soon.

She ducked, low-hanging branches from the trees trying to swipe at her hair. The tour guide spoke into his microphone, but she tuned him out, imagining herself on the castle walls, actually walking along the top, daring fate to send her sprawling. She shouldn't do that, tempt fate, but lately she'd become the sort of person who had to think of all the pitfalls.

There was a lot at stake. A bit like it had been for Turpin, who'd holed up in York prior to his death, probably hoping he wouldn't get caught. Would she get caught? Maybe she ought to switch to plan B. It would mean she'd have to have her wits about her more, to watch what she was saying and doing to a greater degree. She didn't want to end up with a metaphorical noose around her neck.

The tour came to an end, and she contemplated going around again, but no, she'd seen enough. Instead, she stepped off the bus and walked to the nearby art museum, although it didn't hold her interest, and she ended up leaving to buy an ice cream, sitting on a bench and watching the tourists walk by. Maybe she should go inside York Minister, have a gander in there. Would she be touched by God when she walked through those doors? Would she see the light and not go through with her plan?

She doubted it.

CHAPTER ELEVEN

Ridgebrook Close

Madeline couldn't stand this, Kevin leaving. How could she get him to care? He didn't seem bothered at all, more relieved that he was walking out on her and Poppy, his chance to get away and live the life of a single man, spending his fortune.

I should never have married him.

Poppy, understandably upset and confused, chased after him down the garden path, calling his name and asking what she'd done wrong, and she'd be good if he stayed, she promised. He ignored her and dumped a suitcase in the back of the van he'd hired, slammed the door and got in the driver's seat.

On the pavement, running along to get to him, Poppy tripped, her little body going sprawling, and she landed on the gritty tarmac on her hands and knees, a wail coming out of her gaping mouth. Kevin drove off, the utter bastard, and Madeline raced to her daughter, crouching to help her up. Poppy cried, tears streaking her sweaty red face, and Madeline inspected her scrapes. The palms weren't too bad, so she swiped the dirt away, but one of Poppy's knees had a gash from a jagged stone, and blood dripped down her shin, heading towards her white, lace-edged ankle socks.

"It's all right, Mammy's here," Madeline soothed. "I'll always be here."

Poppy hiccupped and pushed Madeline away. "But I want Daddy!"

She dashed back up the garden path, tripping once again, flying through the air onto the grass. At least it was a soft landing this time, but her poorly knee sank onto a pile of dog mess. Poppy screeched and gave Madeline a filthy glare as if it had been her *fault.*

Madeline went to pick her up, careful not to get any poo on herself, and she heaved at the scent. Next door's chocolate Lab had a habit of jumping over the low hedge and leaving his deposits, and now look what had happened. She took a snivelling Poppy upstairs and plonked her in the empty bath, undressing her and switching the shower on. She pulled her cleaning gloves on and washed the shit off, the heat of the water exacerbating the smell, clinging to the rising steam. Madeline was close to being sick, but she had no choice, she was a single mother now, and everything was left down to her.

With Poppy clean and wrapped in a towel, her clothes disposed of in a bin liner, Madeline led her to her bedroom and dressed her. She applied a large plaster to the worst knee and held her close until she stopped crying.

"Is Daddy coming back?" Poppy asked.

"No, but he'll visit you, so don't you worry about a thing."

* * *

The next morning, Madeline found Poppy in bed, breathing erratically, her skin pale. It seemed she had symptoms of a fever, yet she wasn't burning up, nor was she shivering. Madeline cared for her as a mother should, taking a day off work, but by the end of the afternoon when Poppy was talking gibberish, she phoned the doctor.

The visit hadn't gone as expected. In everyone's life there's a moment when time stands still, and this was it for Madeline. The world stopped spinning, her vision narrowed to a blue pin on a corkboard above the doctor's desk, and her body turned cold. Poppy was rushed to hospital. The words "possible sepsis" and "maintain systolic pressure" and "bacteraemia" were bandied about, the latter an infection of the bloodstream, bacteria present. Madeline knew only too well what could happen. She was a nurse here. She'd seen people die of sepsis, comforted the grieving families. This couldn't happen to Poppy, it couldn't!

She remembered the dog poo then and, with something to go on, a source of the issue, the doctors worked diligently. Poppy made a full recovery. The attention Madeline had received as a parent of a sick child had been exceptional, and when they'd gone home a few days later, she'd felt so lonely, the house too quiet, nobody giving a monkey's about them anymore. Kevin hadn't answered any of her calls, and to go from such a caring environment to this was a shock.

At the end of the following week, Kevin finally showed up, and Madeline told him about the fright she'd had and how Poppy had been a trooper.

"No harm done, she's fine now," he said. "So put it behind you."

"Like our marriage?" she asked spitefully. "There are some things you can't put behind you, and Poppy being ill is one of them. You weren't there, you didn't see her, so you'll never know how frightening it was."

"Give over, woman, she's right as rain."

He'd spent an hour with Poppy, pretending to be interested in colouring in with her, but the crayon he held didn't even meet the page. Madeline hated him then, the kind of hate that sent you batty and you wanted to pick up a knife and stab someone.

She endured six months of quietude, needing time to heal from their breakup, but with Kevin's visits waning, his days out with Poppy turning to pipe dreams, Madeline yearned for something more.

That was when she put some of her own faecal matter on a cut Poppy had got from a piece of paper, leaving it there for an hour while her little girl slept.

Someone would care for them now.

CHAPTER TWELVE

The Oak Tree

Nathan kicked at a stone. It skittered off and landed in a clump of scraggy grass. "I'm so bored of this place. Can't wait to leave."

Bestie shoved his hands in his pockets and leaned back on the tree trunk. "People have noticed the cat thing, did you see?"

Nathan nodded. "Yeah, I'm on social media. What was it they called me? The Cat Killer?"

"Bloody stupid name."

Nathan dreamed of bigger, better targets. He'd even thought about the top of the food chain — people — but he only had his BB gun. He'd read the books about killing, knew he had to learn, to pace himself. "I should switch to dogs or something."

Bestie laughed nervously. "And how the fuck are you going to do that? Dogs don't wander around outside like cats do."

"Yeah, but they're let out in the back garden for a piss before bed."

"I don't think I can stomach watching you doing a dog."

"What are you, a fucking baby?"

"No, I just . . . No dogs, Nath."

Maybe it's not on your list, pal, but there's nowt stopping me doing it by myself . . .

CHAPTER THIRTEEN

Incident Room

Carol had made coffees and handed them out. Katherine was digging into Clem's past, and Michael helped PC Lloyd, going through CCTV from the pier. As the nights were drawing in earlier, it was difficult to make out faces on the footage unless fairground lights flashed and lit them up. Hopefully, the teenage lad they were searching for would be by those lights and they'd get a good look at his face.

Dave sat at his desk helping Katherine out on social media, but so far, Clem's name hadn't popped up on Facebook.

"I'm still going through Twitter, so try ChatSesh," Katherine said. "It's big now, and you never know, he might be on it."

Carol got on with adding to the whiteboard. Michael had already written Clem's name, address, age and profession, so Carol stuck a recent picture of him up there, taken from an online news article about the benefits of visiting Scudderton, and she listed the details she'd received from Rib. The DCI had once again told her to "get on with it" and "don't bug me until you have to", something that suited her, the team, and the DCI himself. No, it wasn't the usual protocol, but it worked, and so long as cases got solved, who cared how it had been achieved?

"Let's take a break and have a natter." She placed the marker pen on the lip of the board. "Okay, Rib estimates the time of death as possibly more than six hours before he got to the scene. I believe it's around midnight, going by when Clem left June's and Betty Saunders saw someone walking up the street. Blunt force trauma, several hits to the head, using a curve-ended weapon, the top something like a Babybel in diameter."

"Sounds like a wrench to me," Michael said.

"Hmm, I agree," Carol said. "We'll keep an eye out for that. So, the teenager. He tried to get on the Ferris for free, so did he get arsey for being caught? Did he follow Clem home, then wait around two hours for him to appear? Really? The fairground and chippy shut down at ten, and Clem helped June tidy up, so let's say they got to hers at quarter to eleven. That's still an hour and ten minutes of waiting. Do we buy that?"

"If he's in a rage, yes," Michael said. "Maybe the anger grew worse so the kid stayed until Clem came out of June's."

Carol glanced at Lloyd, who was glued to a monitor, searching for said kid. "If we knew what time the lad boarded the wheel it would help, but we bloody don't. Lloyd, don't forget we have a mother in the mix, one who found it amusing what her son was attempting to do. It might be easier to find a laughing woman."

"Yep."

Carol smiled at Katherine. "What do we know about Clem?"

Katherine swung her chair round to face her. "Wife, deceased. Seems he's the last of the family line. Todd said some of his team gained access to the house so will look for funeral arrangement papers. I'll get on to any directors here to check with them, too, plus I'll query solicitors to find out if he had one so they can get the ball rolling on his estate.

There's his house, although he doesn't have a car registered in his name anymore. He must have given up driving."

Carol sighed. "No past arrests?"

Katherine shook her head. "Nowt, although he is mentioned in our files. He was spoken to by uniforms about the Mason Ingram case, what with the bodies being on the pier, plus there was a fight years ago that he broke up between arguing holidaymakers, so he gave a statement. Other than that, he was clean."

Carol took her phone out. "Give me a second, I need to phone the Oracle."

"Who the chuff's that?" Dave asked.

Carol had forgotten she'd kept that name to herself. "Richard. He knows a lot about the people around here, so I'll pick his brains." She walked into her office and closed the door, dialling Richard then plonking her backside on her comfy chair behind her desk. "Got owt to report yet?"

"We've moved to the nearby streets and the woods to see if we can pick owt up there. I've put someone on walking the route through the trees and timing it so we know when they'd have come out on the main road. PCs Fisher and Howard are on the pier with PCSOs, although I think the specials can deal with it on their own now, it'd be good for them. Grebe is with a couple of other specials, talking to people on Coldwater. Other than that, fuck all. You?"

"We're in the same boat. I'm ringing because as far as we can tell, Clem didn't get into any trouble. I was wondering if you knew of something that might point to him being killed. I'm thinking a grudge, but of course, it could be a random attack, an opportunist after his wallet and whatnot."

"He wasn't robbed, I checked in with Rib on that. He even had his pipe in his coat pocket. SOCO are still in his house, and there are no signs of forced entry, nor does it appear owt's been stolen. As for a grudge, no, Clem was surly in his old age, but he used to be one of the happiest men I knew. I think losing his wife sent him into a spiral of depression, but June helped him with that. She certainly stopped him from raising a whiskey or ten in the Devil."

"So he drank there after his missus died?"

"For about three months, then June swept in and saved the day."

"Poor man."

"I know."

"Okay, I think we'll go and speak to Reg. If Clem got into any altercations, he would know. Thanks for your help."

"No problem."

Carol slid her phone away and went back into the incident room. She told them what Richard had said. "So unless Reg can fill us in on any arguments, we're stuck for a motive apart from revenge by the teenager. I could send uniforms to the pub, but it seems like they're all busy around Clem's area or on the pier, and I don't want to overburden them."

"It's sounding more and more like a random attack to me," Michael said, "although if they weren't after his wallet, what was the point? For kicks?"

Dave stood. "Or it could be someone practising on him."

That idea was ominous, disturbing, and Carol shivered. "Before they go after their real target?"

Dave shrugged. "Who the hell knows? Let's go and see Reg."

"Err, hang on." Lloyd pointed to his screen. "I've found the kid and his mother. Clem looks angry, waving his arms about, and in the end, the mam hands over the fare."

"Do you recognise them," Carol asked, "or do you think they're tourists?"

Lloyd pointed to the teen. "That's Asher Welding. We had him down here on suspicion of shoplifting about two weeks ago. He's a scally, and his mam's not much better. She's called Heidi. They live on Coldwater. Fifteen Ridgebrook Close."

Coldwater. Hmm. "Let's watch it, then."

Lloyd rewound to where Asher waited in line with other boys, then pressed PLAY.

"Seems to me Clem had every right to pull him up, and as for the mother . . . She's laughing, then gets lairy. Could *she* have killed him?" Carol looked at Dave. "We'll go to see her first, then Reg."

"Suits me." Dave shrugged on his lightweight jacket. "I'm feeling generous today, so I'll pick brunch up for everyone on the way back. Buns 'n' Bread sausage butties?"

Everyone but Lloyd agreed.

"I'll need to get back on duty now I've found the lad," he said.

Carol raised her eyebrows. "Not if I find you something else to do, you won't."

Lloyd laughed. "All right."

"Help Michael with sourcing images of weapons so it frees him up to do something else."

She walked out, thinking about Lloyd and how much he was always up for helping them out. If ever there was a miracle where the budget went up and Richard could spare him, she'd nab him as a permanent player in her team.

People like him were hard to come by.

* * *

Ridgebrook Close

Heidi Welding was indeed a scally, one with a big mouth and plenty of opinions. Red-faced, blonde hair in a loose bun, she'd shouted all the odds on the doorstep, claiming her son was an angel, despite the allegation of shoplifting, which, according to her, just so happened to be a case of mistaken identity. Whatever. She was obviously a woman whose mantra was "Not my boy!" and she didn't believe he could be anything but perfect. She'd given in and let them inside, so that was progress, although she'd said her husband, Mark, would have something to say about it. Carol didn't care if he did, he could say what he bloody well liked. This was a murder inquiry, and whether Heidi and her husband thought the police coming round was "harassment" or "invading their privacy", it was tough shit.

In a living room in sore need of a feather duster, Heidi sprawled out on her grey crushed-velvet sofa and lit a cigarette. The so-called scary husband was at work and the son at school. Carol and Dave remained standing, him by the door, Carol by the window.

"So you're here about that bloody Clem, are you? Why, did he report what went on last night? Figures, the moody bastard." Heidi blew out a stream of smoke. "What, do detectives do house calls now about a kid forgetting to pay him?"

"Forgetting isn't quite what it looked like to us on CCTV." Carol folded her arms. "He clearly got on the ride with the idea of not handing any money over. While his mates paid, he hid himself among them as they boarded."

"*Duh*, he thought they were paying for him."

"Did he? We'll have to go and ask them about that." Carol had no intention of doing so, but an officer might need to speak to them, depending on what Heidi said. If all the lads went home together, they might also have been at Clem's last night. Who knew, it may not be one killer but several.

"Do what you like." Heidi sucked on her cigarette.

"You were seen laughing at your son being caught by Clem, but then it appears you were angry. Shouting, it looks like. What went on there?"

Heidi snorted, and smoke sailed out of her nostrils. "Clem was giving it some, having a right go, and it got my back up, didn't it. Only me and my old man can shout at Asher, not that we have to do that often because he's a good boy. I told Clem to fuck right off and get a life. It was only a quid, for fuck's sake, nowt to get up in arms about."

"Not to you maybe, but it was Clem's livelihood. Where did you go after you left the pier?"

"Home, where d'you think?"

"Was Asher with you?"

"Nah, I left him there for a bit with his mates."

Carol's spine stiffened. "What time did he get in?"

"Eleven, something like that."

"And you know that for sure, do you? You saw him come in?"

"Yeah, I was watching the telly with Mark. What are you asking me this for anyroad?"

"Where are the clothes Asher was wearing last night?"

"Drying on the line."

Fuck it, Carol hadn't expected them to have been washed yet. She could still take them, but honestly, with no proof she needed them bagged, she'd likely face resistance. Still, she'd give it a go to see Heidi's reaction. "Can I take them?"

Heidi frowned. "What the chuff do you want *them* for?"

"To rule Asher out."

"For what?"

"Murder."

Heidi's face drained of colour, and she reached over to stub her cigarette out in a crystal ashtray. "Hold the fuck on. Are you saying my boy was involved in something he shouldn't be? You're barking up the wrong oak, woman. He wouldn't hurt a fly."

Carol didn't have enough fingers to count how many times she'd heard that line. "So are you refusing to hand the clothes over?"

"Nope, I'll go and get them now. Asher's got nowt to hide. Who's he meant to have killed, then?"

"Clem."

Heidi's anger dispersed, and she roared with laughter. She got up and approached the door, Dave moving out of her way. "Well, if you find owt, it'll be a miracle. Blood, I assume. He didn't have any on him when he got home, and if you'd viewed the CCTV properly, you'll have seen he was wearing all white, so I'd have *seen* blood, no problem. Some detective you are."

She stomped out, Dave following, and they came back a minute or so later, the clothes in a carrier bag and Dave's face bright red.

Heidi thrust the bag at Carol. "Here you go, and while you're at it, stick them up your arse. At least those lab people will be able to find something on them that way. Now then, I've got my shows to watch, so piss off and don't come back until you've had the test results and there's an apology on your smug little mouth. You think you're great, don't you, because you've been on the telly, but let me tell you something for nowt, I'm not a fan."

Carol smiled. "No, I'm not a fan either." *Of you.* "Thanks for not obstructing the investigation. Yes, the test will likely show nowt, but we have to be sure."

"I should have made you get a warrant." Heidi sat and lit another ciggie.

"But you didn't, you were a responsible parent, and I respect you for that." Carol almost choked on the words, but she'd kill this woman with kindness if it was the last thing she did. She wrote out a receipt and handed it to the woman. "Thank you for your time. We'll be in touch."

"Aren't you going to go to the school to arrest Asher, then?"

"No, we don't need to do that at present, but an officer will be round later to ask him where he was."

"I'll get his passport ready so he can do a runner as soon as he gets home." Heidi rolled her eyes.

"What are his friends called?" Dave asked.

Heidi winked at him and reeled them off as well as their addresses. Dave wrote them down, blushing, and Carol frowned. What was going on here?

"Right, now bog off." Heidi switched the TV on, whacking the volume up to painful levels.

Carol walked out and, at the car, placed the carrier in an evidence bag. Yes, she'd probably have egg on her face over this, the clothes might yield nothing, but better she got it done now than later down the line if it looked like Asher was who they were after. She filled out the relevant information on the bag and got in the driver's seat, sending a message to Richard to ask him to get someone to pay a visit to all the lads later and that Dave would send the details.

Dave flumped in and rested his head back. "Bloody hell . . ."

"I know. She's a rare one. I need you to message Richard with the lads' details. We'll drop that bag off then go to the Devil. I wouldn't say no to a large glass of wine after that visit, but we're on duty."

Dave laughed and put his seat belt on. "She came on to me in the garden."

Carol stared at him, eyes wide. "Oh my God! What did she say?"

He cleared his throat. "I quote: 'If you ever feel like whipping out your truncheon, you know where I am.'"

Carol ugly laughed, tears streaming. "You poor bastard."

"I know."

She wiped her eyes and clipped on her belt, then drove away. "The people we see in our jobs, eh?"

"Hmm." Dave got his phone out to contact Richard. "If those tests are negative, a uniform can take the clothes back, because I'm not doing it."

Carol laughed again and ribbed him about his new potential girlfriend all the way to the lab.

* * *

The Little Devil

In a quiet area of the pub, Reg scratched his head. "Clem, dead? Blimey. It's a wonder any of us are safe anymore. What the hell is this place coming to?"

"It's a crime hub, apparently," Dave muttered.

"You're telling me," Reg said. "There must be something in the ruddy water, turning people into killers."

Carol leaned an elbow on the bar. "I'm glad I buy bottled, then. When Clem used to come here after his wife died, did he get into any rows with anyone?"

Reg frowned. "Nah, he was content to sit on his own. Didn't want company, and who could blame him? He was married for over fifty years. Must have been a shock finding himself on his own. You wouldn't know what to do with yourself, would you?"

Carol knew all too well; she'd never really had a relationship where she'd been heartbroken. She'd walked away from her last lover, Noel Bartlett, and thank God she had, because he'd turned out to be a nutter, the killer surgeon they'd caught recently. Dave, on the other hand, knew what it was like to love and lose. His wife had been having it away behind his back, kicked Dave out, and now played happy families with some fella and their baby.

"Can't say I do," she said, "but I can imagine it must have been awful. So there's nowt we can look into, then? I mean, no one held a grudge as far as you know?"

"Nope."

That was that, then. With nothing more to be gleaned, Carol led the way out of the pub and waited for Dave on the path. "Shall we nip to the pier, see the uniforms there?"

Dave nodded, and they walked in silence, past the marina then on towards the pier, which appeared to be bustling. Visitors had once again parked in the Backstreet over the road, which wasn't allowed, and the vigilant warden had slapped tickets beneath their windscreen wipers. The wind had picked up since this morning, tossing her hair about, and she moved a strand that had made itself at home across her eye. She contemplated what to have for dinner, and the whiff of fish and chips solved that for her. They could eat in June's Chippy, then go to the Lord, crime permitting.

* * *

Cove Pier

Carol approached one of the specials who'd been left to question people. "How's it going?"

"It isn't." PCSO Donna Wilbor shrugged. "No one seems to have seen owt, and the problem we've got is not everyone here today was on the pier last night."

"News will spread that you're asking about Clem, so someone might come forward by tonight. If not, we'll have to hold a press conference tomorrow." Carol hated doing those, but as the DCI shirked his responsibility there, she wouldn't have much choice if something didn't give soon.

They chatted for a while, coming up with blank after blank, so there was nothing for it but to nip to Buns 'n' Bread to collect brunch.

Donna wandered off to talk to more people, and a woman pushing a wheelchair came rushing over, her face showing concern.

"Carol Wren, yes? I've seen you on the telly."

Carol smiled to hide a cringe. Her celebrity status wasn't something she liked to dwell on. "Can we help you?"

"I heard about Clem. I'm Madeline Cotter. I was in the pub last night and didn't see owt. I just wanted to say that."

"Okay . . ." Carol glanced at the occupant of the wheelchair, who held a stuffed penguin close to her chest, her hood pulled low, obscuring the top half of her face, then Carol smiled again at Ms Cotter. "If there's nowt else . . ."

"No, nowt else at all. Me and my daughter here were in the café spotting dolphins just now, and I dashed out to speak to you."

It seemed Ms Cotter had a case of being starstruck. She gazed at Carol with something close to adoration. It was weird and uncomfortable.

"Don't let us keep you, then." Carol watched her blush and walk away.

The daughter leaned out and peered back, staring Carol right in the eye.

Carol sighed. "Well, that was awkward."

"Must be a day of meeting oddballs." Dave pointed across the road. "Food."

She dismissed the encounter as one of those things and followed Dave down the pier. A doorstep sandwich was calling her name. After they'd eaten back at the station, she'd think about the next steps. At the moment, she had no idea which direction to go in, and that never boded well.

CHAPTER FOURTEEN

Undisclosed Location

Desmond had watched the fallout from what he'd written, his face impassive, showing no signs of either knowing about it beforehand or how he felt about it now. He supposed he was meant to display some kind of disgust, to let the target know he wasn't on board with what the words said, but Boss had told him to play it calm at all times, and if he was asked, he was to say he'd been employed for a specific reason, and giving his opinion on matters like this wasn't included in the job description.

The target wasn't happy, but their partner didn't seem afraid. Said partner brushed it off, acting as though it was nothing, par for the course, the words not creating the desired effect at all.

Desmond would have to change that.

CHAPTER FIFTEEN

Train Carriage

Sofia sat on a crowded train on her way to London. It was nice to be among people, to breathe the same air, to see the same sights through the window. She'd thought about the man when she'd sat in her reserved seat, how she missed him, wanted him back in her life. The heart never forgot someone you loved, and she'd expected him to be with her for ever. There might be someone else in the future, another who could give her what she needed, but to be honest, she didn't think so. He'd been perfect for her, yet he'd ended their relationship.

Could you love more than one man in your lifetime? Would it be the same with someone else? She'd have to get used to all of the new one's habits, and she'd compare, make mental notes, and the dissimilarities would stand out a mile. But in order to move on, she'd perhaps give it a go, find another perfect person to dish out the love she craved.

A woman across the aisle struggled with her two kids, a boy and a girl close in age, maybe three and four. Sofia would love to have children, but first she needed to get her house in order. There was so much to do, and she had no idea how to get her name changed so she could start again elsewhere. Depending on which route she took, she might not need to do that. Scudderton was a stale place, and while it breathed life in the tourist season, and there was the sea, the pier, she had to make a clean break. After completing everything, and if she stayed, she risked bumping into the man who'd left her for another woman. She couldn't handle him ignoring her as if she'd never existed and they'd never known one another. She'd read that some relationships went that way, a complete break.

Sofia was in first class, so a train worker came by with a trolley. Today's perk was a bacon roll and a can of wine. She ate and sipped, watching people working on laptops. Everyone was so *busy* all the time, yet here she was, sitting back and relaxing. People took different paths, didn't they, their worlds going in distinct directions.

It was time for Sofia to finish plotting *her* new course. If everything turned out as she predicted, she'd be happier by putting the shit behind her.

Nothing good ever came of living in the past.

CHAPTER SIXTEEN

The Odeon

Poppy had spotted the dolphins first, or so she'd thought. Madeline had spied a pod, waited for her daughter to clock it, then claimed Poppy the winner. She'd left her asleep in Yasmeen's care, so the support worker didn't have to do anything but be there. Madeline doubted Poppy would wake. She loved her afternoon naps.

In her hooded boiler suit, gloves and a clown mask taken from Poppy's toybox, she crouched behind the back of the Odeon beside the industrial-sized wheelie bins. The prick who'd made comments to her and Kevin when they'd gone on their first date still worked there. Frank was around seventy now, and she'd never forgotten what he'd said.

"You two make a lovely couple."

That had convinced her they did, and she'd gone in harder to make Kevin like her. To be funnier, more attractive, someone he'd grow to love. If Frank had kept his big mouth shut, Madeline wouldn't have got any grand ideas. Before Frank had said it, she hadn't expected Kevin would be that interested in her. Yes, he'd asked her on a date and Clem had encouraged her, but to be honest, she'd thought it was one of those nasty jokes where boys asked girls out for a bet.

She should never have listened to Frank.

He'd be out in a minute to put the rubbish in the bin from the previous showing, all those disgusting people leaving their mess. Sweet wrappers, drink cartons and popcorn scattered on the floor. She'd watched him a few times from across the yard where she'd hidden behind a pile of old chairs that used to be in the cinema. They'd replaced them with those comfy ones that had cup holders in the armrests, so it'd said in the local rag. A waste of money in Madeline's book, but there you go.

The fire door opened, and out came Frank, the doddery wanker, clutching two black bags. She gripped the hammer tight in her gloved hand, excitement ramping up, the knowledge that justice would be served. People couldn't get away with ruining someone's life, and she'd show them all how their words and actions had affected her, what they'd turned her into.

Frank didn't pick the bin she was next to, so she crept closer to the edge and poked her eyes round. He wheezed — must be all that smoking — and took a moment to cough up phlegm. She shuddered at the sight of him. Wispy hair, a bald spot on top, his skin ruddy, a strawberry nose. He spat on the ground, hawked again, then slung the bags inside, slamming the lid and walking towards the door. The sunlight glanced off his hearing aid, and she checked the yard, standing upright.

Madeline raced out, the hammer raised, and smacked him on the back of the head with it, the flat end used to wallop nails. It dented his bald spot, and he let out a weird, deep shriek, more of a groan, sinking to his knees the same as Clem. Blood seeped into his hair, and he put a hand to the wound at the same time as flopping forward onto the concrete, banging his temple on the hard surface. She straddled him and did a two-handed lift, learning from her time with Clem, bringing it down so hard the crack of his skull rang out along with a dull thud. She gripped a clean section of his hair and wrenched his head back, swinging the hammer at his face. The blow landed on his nose, skewing it sideways, blood spurting from his nostrils and the gash she'd made.

She'd always hated his nose. Too big.

She struck his face several times, the last connection on his forehead, another dent, and more blood that seeped over his eyelids, streaking down his cheeks in rivulets. She breathed heavily, her skin hot beneath the mask, and turned the hammer around so the curved, two-pronged side pointed towards him. She stood, kicked him over onto his back, and brought the tool down, the end digging into the ravaged dent on his brow. It sank deep, and she imagined it had gone into his brain. Conscious someone could come out and see where Frank had got to, she quickly checked his pulse.

Nothing.

The hammer stuck fast, so she had a hell of a job to get it out. She stashed it under him and, on her way back through the yard, laughed quietly, a pleasurable stream of happiness wending through her. She opened the gate and closed it behind her, walking halfway down the alley that would take her behind some side-street shops in town. She washed the blood from her face with wet wipes and stripped off her boiler suit, gloves and mask, stuffing it all in a large handbag she'd left there. The mask would burn well in the fire pit later. Then, having stuffed her bloody hair up into a sunhat, she casually strolled into the winding cobbled street full of souvenir shoppers, her pretty skirt swishing with every step. There was quite a crowd, and she acted like them, nosing in windows at the displays, a hand to her mouth as if she contemplated whether she *really* needed to buy a box of fudge.

Satisfied she'd remained innocuous, she dipped between shops and came out the other side, Superdrug to her left, the post office on the right. Once again, she merged with the thickening crowd, slipping into Yours to buy herself a present, a dress she'd seen last week.

Madeline browsed for fifteen minutes, smiling at the sound of sirens — someone had found the old duffer, then.

Good. She paid for the dress and went into several more shops, spending two hours in town, all told.

She got on the bus and went home. It wouldn't do for her child to wake and talk to Yasmeen. Kids came out with silly stories, didn't they, like their mother making them ill and injecting them so they fell asleep for hours.

Such nonsense.

* * *

Ridgebrook Close

Yasmeen smiled from her seat on the sofa. "She's slept all this time."

"I thought she would. I took her to the pier this morning. It's all that sea air."

Madeline saw her out, then checked the video baby monitor on the sideboard in the living room. Poppy was still in the land of nod, and Madeline estimated she had another half an hour or so before she roused. It was so easy, using the drugs to knock her out.

The fire pit scoffed her gloves, the mask, the sunhat and the handbag. She put the boiler suit in the washing-up bowl to soak and made herself a cuppa, sitting in a deckchair to imagine the kerfuffle going on in the cinema yard, her smile wide, her heart on its way to healing.

CHAPTER SEVENTEEN

Incident Room

News had come in from Todd that Clem's body had been moved and a wrench found, confirming the theory. Lloyd had been going through Instagram looking for an account Clem might have used. This job was much harder, what with people using names different to their real ones. Clem could be "Ferris_Wheel_Lover" for all they knew. They'd all taken half an hour to eat their sausage sandwiches and drink tea, then the team had got stuck in, searching for leads online. Carol had liaised with Richard again — still nothing to report — and she'd got in contact with PCSO Donna Wilbor to check what was happening at the pier.

No one had seen or heard a thing that could be classed as ominous, although a few had noticed Clem and June leaving the pier. Lloyd had found the couple on CCTV, walking down the pier and off it, but with no cameras along the stretch of road where the marina and the Little Devil stood, nor the route they'd have taken to their homes, *who* had been hanging around them at that time was anyone's guess. Those Lloyd had recognised as locals were being spoken to, but as for the visitors, that meant two officers had the long job ahead of them of speaking to everyone in caravans, hotels and B&Bs to see if any of them matched the still shots taken from the footage and whether they'd seen anything going on.

Beyond frustrated, Carol consoled herself that at least forensics would be back in a few days regarding any DNA or fingerprints on the wrench, or indeed, on Clem's body once the PM had been completed. She hoped the tests would get done sooner but wouldn't hold her breath. In the meantime, it meant officers canvassed all over Coldwater, especially the houses closest to the edge of the estate nearest to Tesco, asking if anyone had been seen walking through or on the outskirts of the estate.

"ANPR checks haven't thrown owt up." Michael sat back and massaged his temples. He must be tired after cross-referencing for the past three hours. "Everyone spotted in vehicles in that area last night appear to have legitimate alibis — I've phoned all fifty-two of them. I double-checked their journeys to see if they were caught on camera going in the direction they said, and they were telling the truth — unless one of them cruised while waiting for the murder to take place, an accomplice sort of thing. All those who'd been to Tesco will be matched with the CCTV we have coming from the store, the car park cameras in particular. It should be with us by the end of the day, so I'll get cracking on that first thing tomorrow if it comes in too close to the end of our shift."

"Thanks," Carol said. "And yes, it looks like we'll be going home on time because we're hitting roadblocks left and right. Unless the uniforms have any luck with the fairground lads, we're stalled." Her work mobile rang, and she looked at the screen. Joy Parsons, the station sergeant during the day shift. "Hi, Joy, what can I do for you?"

"There's been another one. Frank West from the Odeon."

"Aww, bloody hell." The news hit Carol hard. Frank had played a significant part in her childhood, and she'd never forget his kindness that night, nor how, when Dad had died, Frank had come to her and told her grieving was optional when it came to Harry Wren and no one would blame her if she didn't shed a tear. She'd wondered why he'd even been friends with him if he'd felt that way. Or had he remained friends after he'd witnessed Dad hitting her so he could keep an eye out?

Joy tapped something, the sound tinny. "Have we got a case of serial elderly bashing here?"

"I was just wondering the same thing." Carol hadn't been doing anything of the sort, but she wasn't about to share a poignant memory with Joy, no matter how nice she was. Reminisces like that were precious gems she wanted to keep in an imaginary jewellery box, safe. "Are SOCO and Rib en route, because Todd said Clem had been taken in about an hour ago."

"Rib's at the cinema now, but Todd's sending Ben Asher to head a team there because there's still work being done at Clem's. And it's not the cinema itself. It happened out the back in the yard. There's a cordon set up at an alley behind, and all officers have been told to go that way. Robin Hood Street. Saves the emergency vehicles parking out the front so everyone can gawp."

"Good idea. Okay, me and Dave will go there now. What about uniforms, are there enough? I've had to ask Richard to get some to question people caught on CCTV last night at the pier."

"I've been speaking to him. We're working it all out. Alan will do the log at the alley. I've sent PC Howard to take over from him at Clem's. Good job it's an otherwise quiet day. Let's hope it stays that way."

"You could have jinxed it by saying that, you know."

Joy laughed. "Don't, two murders are enough to be getting on with, thanks. Tarra for now."

"Tarra." Carol put her phone in her pocket. "Um . . ." The words got stuck in her throat, so she chose the route she'd normally take, brisk and to the point, her detective head on. "Frank West's copped it."

"Ah, fuck it, he was one of my favourite people." Michael appeared truly saddened. "He always used to slip me a bag of sweets when I went to see a film."

"Same," Katherine said. "He had a satchel, if you remember, and he handed them out in the queue. Mam said it's because he didn't have any kids of his own. His wife had trouble getting pregnant."

"Yeah, they were little white bags, weren't they?" Michael chuckled. "Like he bought in bulk and portioned them out."

"I didn't know that." Carol would have done if she'd been allowed to go to the cinema. Even as a teen she'd had to make excuses as to why she couldn't join her friends, not that she'd had many, and they didn't ask her after the first few times — what was the point when she always said no? Her eyes stung, and she swallowed a lump in her throat. God, who would want to kill someone as kind as Frank? "Dave, we need to go." Shit, that had come out broken, raspy. "Lloyd, I need you to stay on Clem. Michael and Katherine, switch to Frank."

Carol left the incident room, wiping her eyes and trying to get a hold of herself. She remembered wishing she'd lived with Frank, that *he* was her father and he'd read her a story every night. She'd never have got smacked, punched or punished in the most hideous ways if he'd been in charge of her.

She'd have been loved.

"Fuck it," she muttered, annoyed at her emotions getting the better of her.

She walked out of the station, vision blurred, and sat in the car. Dave joined her, and he didn't say a word. She'd told him the Frank story once — she didn't mind sharing her jewels with him — so he'd know she needed a few minutes to process things. Frank may not have known it, but he'd done her a favour that night. Dad had still hit her, just not as hard, especially when she'd cried, saying she wanted Frank.

A reminder to her father that despite what he'd thought, she *did* have a lifeline available to her . . . if only she had been brave enough to reach out and take it.

She hadn't, and she'd regret that for the rest of her life.

CHAPTER EIGHTEEN

21 Larch Lane

It was so weird being back here, the childhood home Carol had sold after Harry Wren, the liar who'd made up some crap story about his wife walking out on him, had passed away. He'd drowned in his bath, and Carol had found him, shocked by the sight of his body but relieved it was over, he'd gone. Forever. That was sometimes what happened when an abused person was freed from their tormentor. She was glad she wasn't the other kind who mourned the one who'd screwed up their life, desperate to see them again even though some part of them detested the deceased for what they'd done. The abused experienced a complex set of emotions, and, grateful she'd joined the police and had been trained in what to spot, what to do, how someone may feel, she'd fully applied it to her day-to-day living after Dad had died. Shame she hadn't done it while he'd still been alive. As an adult, she'd managed to stand up for herself more when he'd got in her face, so that was something, but he'd still had a hold on her, that all-too-familiar fear of him keeping her from saying what she really felt.

The fact she'd been a police officer hadn't bothered him at all. He'd said what he had to say, regardless of whether it would hurt her, or if it would be classed as illegal. Bullying. Coercive manipulation. Mental cruelty.

Normally, a family member might not choose to be present at an exhumation, but Carol had insisted, wanted to be here, to glimpse the first sight of what might be her mother in years. Prior to the slabs being pulled up, dogs had been brought in to sniff the scent of death, of a skeleton beneath the patio. Their barks had chilled her earlier this morning, ringing out so loudly, a portent of what was to come. And also a relief. She hadn't imagined those memories.

"Got something," someone said, a man — Ben Garrett — in coveralls, on his knees at the edge of the exposed area, clutching a tiny trowel.

Carol glanced into the hole from her spot on the astroturf the owners had laid — they'd said the patio was about to be replaced and were relieved this hadn't happened after they'd done it, then the wife had slapped a hand over her mouth, realising what had been said. Carol had assured her it was fine, a natural thing to think — "think" being the operative word, because saying it was highly insensitive, but Carol hadn't said that bit.

What appeared to be a finger bone poked out of the earth — earth heavily mixed with sand which had obviously been placed prior to Dad laying the slabs. And that sand had helped to preserve the bones for decades. Now another memory arrived, of the empty sand bags, discarded on the grass, one of them floating along on the breeze until Dad had put a large stone on top of them all.

Was this that first glimpse, a small bone? She'd expected a face — like in her nightmares.

Rib stood beside her for moral support, plus he'd take the remains back to his lab and work on them with some man who'd been called in to help, one who was more au fait with this kind of thing. She'd asked Dave to stay away. She'd be too emotional with him here, more likely to cry, and she didn't want to do that. Yet.

"Deep breath, Bird."

Carol did as he'd told her, reaching out to grasp his hand tight. Funny how she'd never have done this before their truce, how the thought of even touching him had repulsed her. Now they were friends, and he was proving it by stroking the back of her gloved hand with his thumb, wanting to soothe, to comfort.

"Will there be any flesh left?" she asked. Her face, I want to see her face one last time. *"Mam's features must have rotted by now, surely."*

"Not necessarily. We'll maybe get some hair if we're lucky, or body matter that hasn't disintegrated, preserved by the sand. It's thick in places."

"What does sand do?"

"It absorbs moisture, so bacteria doesn't stand a chance in destroying the flesh. Although, with those slabs on top, and if there was rain back then, it would have got to her. Until we see all of her, we won't know."

That bone tip, it stood out in the dark mud, and Carol shivered.

Ben carefully moved surrounding earth and sand, digging deeper, and the bone tip, the distal phalange (she remembered that from Rib telling her when she'd viewed a PM ages ago), fell away.

Rib gave her another lesson. "Next will come the middle phalange beneath. Your poor mam, reduced to being bone names. Next comes the proximal, the metacarpal, and all the other small bones that make up the base of the hand, then the radius of the wrist."

And on and on it would go, all the puzzle pieces that made up Mam's skeleton, except her flesh wouldn't be on it in places, sections of her recognisable façade eaten by bugs. She was like any other dead person who'd been gone for a while, the basics, but at least they had those basics.

"In fertile soil alone," Rib said, "this could have been an entirely different situation. After twenty years, the bones dissolve, but the soil would have given up the secret anyroad, that she'd been there. Proof of the burial."

With Carol's naïve dream gone — of staring at Mam's face one more time to see if it matched her memories, which had frustratingly faded after so long with no photos to keep it alive — she turned away, tugging Rib to the bottom of the garden with her. If some of the preserved flesh remained, Carol didn't want to remember her that way. She looked to the bright-blue sky, the sun warm, and closed her eyes, hot tears wetting her cheeks, cold by the time they snaked over her jaw and down her neck. Dad had ruined it again, keeping something from her, dictating her life even now from beyond the grave.

It's over, my sweet lass. Let me go.

Mam's voice, loud in her head, like it had been when Carol had sat on the wall at Scudderton Cove with Dave to eat fish and chips straight out of the packet, and she'd told him what she'd remembered of that terrible night and the day after. Dad digging that hole, putting those slabs down, slabs that might well be traced back to wherever he'd bought them from, and that sand — something for the cold case team to get their teeth into. Of course, Carol had agreed — not that she'd had any choice — to allow the cold case lot to do their jobs. She didn't have it in her to poke about into her parents' past, to keep a level head when things cropped up that she might not like.

Soon, she could find out how Mam had died if the bones revealed the truth. From that knock to the head on the hearth during her argument with Dad? Or had she been strangled? Suffocated by one of the sofa cushions? Where had Dad kept her body while he'd been busy preparing to get rid of it? On the floor where she'd fallen? Questions, questions, too many she hadn't been able to answer, and maybe, if she were brutally honest, she didn't want to know.

"Fancy going to Scarborough?" she asked Rib. "It'll be ages before you need to transport her."

He glanced at his watch. "Unlike you, I haven't got the day off. I'd rather stay. Make sure she's . . . you know."

He didn't have to say it: Make sure she's looked after right. She would be, this team were the best around, but she appreciated his care. If she couldn't handle staying, he would.

She nodded, rested a hand on his shoulder, and stared him in the eye. "I'll never forget this. You. Staying."

For once, he didn't come out with some snarky comment to rile her, to get a reaction to prove she was alive. "We'll get to the bottom of this, then you can try to move on. I'll be here for that as well."

Carol glanced away, forcing her gaze to the fake grass so she didn't see the sincerity in his eyes. A wren dared to land, unfazed by the amount of people in the garden, and it stared at her, its beady eyes flicking. "She didn't deserve this, any of it. She'd finally stood up for herself, confronting Dad about the other woman, and he . . . he did that to her. To me." She left her tears unchecked. "I wish he was alive so he'd go to prison, pay for it."

"But he isn't, Bird, and that'll be one of the hardest parts going forward. That there's no justice."

The wren came closer, brazen, clearly used to humans, and it cocked its head.

"I can't get over her being down there all this time."

"Don't carry any guilt over that. You were a kid. Look at it this way. In the end, you remembered what happened, we've found her, and at least, once everything's been done, she'll get a proper send-off."

"That's why I want to go to Scarborough. To see where I'll scatter her ashes. She loved it there."

"Then maybe it's best you go alone. A pilgrimage."

Carol nodded.

The wren chittered, and she wondered what it had to say.

It observed her one more time then flew away in the direction of Scarborough.

* * *

Scarborough

In North Bay, Carol stood on a path in front of different-coloured beach huts — yellow, blue, red — and stared out to sea, the remains of Scarborough Castle to her right. It sat on a rocky promontory, and Carol remembered Mam telling her about the master gunner's house and how, as a little girl, Mam had wanted to live there inside the beige-and-grey stone walls and the faded rust-red roof. Mam hadn't got her wish, of course she hadn't, but the memory served as a reminder that Mam hadn't just been Mam. She'd been a child with fanciful dreams, a young woman with aspirations, then she'd married Dad — God only knew why — and life had been so far from castles and royalty it wasn't funny.

I should go there. Stand where we stood that time she took me to see it.

It had been a visit Dad hadn't wanted to partake in — of course he bloody hadn't, he'd preferred propping up the bar in the Lion — and Carol had loved it. She'd *wanted to live in the master gunner's house, too, but only with Mam. Dad could stay in Larch Lane all by himself. Carol must have known even then that he was a baddun if she thought of a life without him.*

The wrong parent had been taken from her.

She returned to the car park and moved her vehicle to the pay and display at Marine Drive. On foot, she followed the signs around the headland to the South Bay side and found a set of steps she knew she'd struggle with. They led up the hill the castle stood on, although they changed to a steep path that killed her calves and shins. What a hike it was; she had to sit on every bench along the way and was out of breath once she reached the top, cursing herself for being so unfit. She passed through a stone archway then found the entrance, another archway. In the gift shop, she paid to enter the grounds. She declined the offer of a tour from one of the English Heritage staff members — after all, she wasn't interested in the castle. All she wanted to do was stand in front of that house and imagine her mam doing the same: dreaming, wishing, hoping.

She picked the exact spot where she'd stood with Mam all those years ago, between two stone walls to her right and two small black cannons on her left. She faced the building. Five windows on the top floor, four on the lower with white shutters, two either side of the door. Yes, it was impressive, and she brought to mind what the view would be like from the rear windows, all that sea and land.

She wandered along a pathway to her left surrounded by long grass that she assumed had been left to encourage insect wildlife. All around the promontory edge was a black wire mesh fence and warning signs stating a sheer drop. She stopped and took in the vastness of the sea on the North Bay side, then turned to look at South Bay. She'd thought this would be the perfect place to release Mam's ashes, a clump of land that seemed on top of the world, but there was too much scrubby foliage on the other side of the fence. It didn't seem a fitting end. There were no laws regarding scattering ashes on the Scarborough coastline, so yes, she'd do that, but farther along maybe.

Carol walked quite a way towards some large slabs of stone on the ground, going up a few steps to stand on a landing of sorts. Here, she was higher, and there was no scrubland beyond the fence, just a rocky ledge. She bent over to stare down at the sea, the white-capped waves swooshing up to the base of the cliff. She'd be better off releasing Mam here. The ashes would sail on the wind, some of her hopefully landing in the sea.

While Mam wouldn't end up living in that house, she'd be close to it.

Carol sat on the landing and hugged her knees.

And cried.

CHAPTER NINETEEN

The Odeon Yard

Suited and booted, Carol observed her surroundings from her spot at the top of the alley leading to the yard behind the cinema. SOCO, some on hands and knees, inspected the ground and placed evidence markers. Ahead, about twenty metres to her left, a row of large green wheelie bins. To her immediate left, stacks of old cinema seats. Some had been attacked by rodents, stuffing poking from splits in the red fabric, droppings left as evidence the pests had been there. On her right, empty space, and directly ahead, a tent covering the body.

Dave came through from the alley and stood beside her. "Are you going to be okay?"

"I have to be. It's daft, because it's not like I really had much to do with Frank. He was just significant at one point in my life, and I held on to that as one of the rare good memories. Let's face it, I don't have many of those, not from childhood anyroad. It got easier as I grew older, but to a degree, Dad still ruled my life right up until he died. I was always afraid of him no matter what age. It's only now he's gone that I can see him for the pathetic man he was. If he woke from the dead, I'd have no trouble telling him what I think of him now."

"It took him dying for you to get stronger, though, to be yourself without recrimination and ridicule."

"You're not wrong there." She clapped her gloved hands. "Right! Let's get this bit over and done with, then we'll have to go and see his wife. No one's been sent out to her yet. Joy knows I prefer giving the bad news over a uniform doing it, when it's murder anyroad."

At the tent door, she switched her booties, gave the old ones to a SOCO nearby and went inside. Ben Asher and Rib, one either side of the body, stood on evidence steps. The photographer from earlier stooped by Frank's feet, snapping away. Three steps had been placed inside the tent flap, so she opted for the one on the left. Dave came in and took the right.

"Afternoon, Bird." Rib pointed at the body. "He's got more wounds on his head at the back. This one's a hammer, by the way. Whoever this is likes hiding the weapons under the body. I don't see the point."

"Is someone going through their sodding toolbox or what?" Dave said. "What's next, a chisel?"

Carol thought about his suggestion. At least with using tools from their own box, it meant they weren't caught on camera buying any — so someone had planned this, had known the risk of purchasing them. On the other hand, if they'd been used around the house, they'd have not only DNA on them but also possible paint flecks that could be matched, and wood, dust, any number of things.

But they'll probably point to your average household, so that's no good to us.

"What state are the wrench and hammer in?" she asked.

Ben rocked on his heels. "The wrench is silver, has faint scratches on it, so while it isn't old, it's been used. The hammer's the same. Maybe they're from a toolbox someone doesn't access very often, only for odd jobs and the like."

"So long as there's DNA on them from the killer, I don't care." Carol turned her attention to the body, something she'd been putting off.

Frank lay on his back, elbows bent, hands up beside his head. His face . . . Jesus Christ, did he even *have* a forehead anymore? It was difficult to tell with all the blood, but June's description came into her mind. A hole. Was that significant?

Silly cow, being fanciful.

His cheeks had been pounded, livid bruising already black and purple. Blood where the skin had split. His nose had taken a battering, leaning to one side, the skin broken, and if she wasn't mistaken, there was a round shape on it, different to the gash on the forehead. The killer must have used both sides of a claw hammer.

He didn't look like Frank anymore but some misshapen, bloodied mess, streaks of scarlet over his closed eyes — and that was something at least. Had he fallen unconscious quickly? He must have had them shut when the blood had oozed from his forehead.

"He was upright when the forehead was struck?" she asked. "I'm thinking of the blood flow down his face. It'd go to the sides if he was on his back."

"Yes," Rib said. "I'm guessing he was hit from behind to incapacitate him, then he fell to his knees — see the grit on his trousers there? He went forward, and somehow he must have got up again, his attacker going for it. I'll know when I do the PM whether the nose and cheek injuries were from the front or behind, I need to inspect them properly, but the forehead . . . It was a side-on strike, so the prongs of the hammer entered, the tips pointing towards his left temple. I noted a curved entry."

Ben chipped in. "So the killer is either left-handed or they chose to use that hand to throw us off."

"Must be a strong killer to pull the hammer back out," Dave said.

The photographer walked out, distracting Carol. She couldn't look at Frank anymore anyway, so she was grateful to have her sight directed elsewhere. Images paraded through her mind in grief-laden boots, children, their faces lighting up when they saw Frank with his satchel at the head of the cinema queue. How was it she could be more upset about his passing than her father? It just went to show that blood wasn't thicker than water at all, it was kindness you remembered about the dead, how you'd been treated. There would be hundreds of people mourning his death when the news spread.

"Is there owt else that might tell us what the hell's going on here?" she asked.

"We'll be able to determine the approximate height of the assailant soon," Ben said. "Going by the depth of the wounds, we could also guesstimate their weight by how much force was needed to hit Clem and Frank. By the way, the wrench is a large one, pretty heavy, so maybe the killer is used to lifting?"

Dave nudged Carol. "This could be any number of people. Gym users, carers, nurses, bricklayers."

"Or it could just be an angry person," Rib said. "Being riled up changes people, they get energy, become stronger from adrenaline."

Carol got her head back in the game, thankful the kids' faces had slipped from her mind. "Was owt stolen?"

"No, his wallet was in his pocket." Rib crouched. "Another cinema employee found him. A young girl, about eighteen. She went inside with an officer who's taking her statement."

"I'll have to have a quick word, see if she saw owt, but I won't bother her for long. So, there's nowt much for us to stick around for?"

"No, Bird. I'll get hold of you about the results of the PMs. I'll do Clem's by the end of the day, but Frank's will be in the morning."

"Okay. Are you in the Lord tonight?"

Rib shook his head. "Nope, it's gaming at my place. Got a mate coming round. We're getting a Chinese."

"Okay, then, I'll see you when I see you."

She didn't relish speaking to the poor cow who'd found Frank, but it meant Carol could stall going to see Frank's wife, and she felt wicked for feeling relieved about it.

* * *

Clementine Way

Carol sat beside Dave in the car outside Mrs Irene West's bungalow.

"Do you ever think about how people are only one breath away from disaster?" she asked.

He let out one of his nervous laughs. "Bloody hell, that's a bit deep."

It was, but she'd had a lot of time to contemplate it since Mam had been exhumed. "Like, Frank went to work today, kissing his wife goodbye, and neither of them had any idea he wouldn't be going home. They didn't have a chance to say all that needed to be said, his life was snatched away, same with me and Mam, and now his wife will be left wishing she'd told him she loved him as he walked up that path, that she looked forward to him coming back."

"She might well have done that every day for all you know."

"I get that, but do you see what I mean? Shouldn't we all be saying things *now* instead of keeping them hidden for the 'right time'?"

"I suppose so . . ."

"There's no 'suppose so' about it. I love you, Dave. You're my best mate, and I don't think I could do this life bollocks without you. I appreciate you more than you realise, and I wanted you to know that before . . . well, before it's too late."

"Same." He coughed.

They stared through the windscreen, then Dave leaned over, grabbed her tight and knuckled her head.

"You made me cry, you daft mare." He drew back, his eyelashes wet. "We hold each other up, don't we? Always have. Through thick and thin, that's us. If I didn't have you when the ex fucked off . . ."

"I know." She swiped her eyes dry and took a deep breath, flattening her hair where he'd messed it up. "It's the same for that poor sod who found Frank, but in a different way. She's going to be changed for ever."

"Shame she didn't spot owt, though, someone leaving the yard or whatever."

"We can't win them all." She checked her face in the rear-view mirror. "Bloody state of that. Come on."

She forced herself out of the car and waited for Dave on the pavement. ID in hand, she walked up the path to number five. A net curtain twitched, and she felt bad because Mrs West was oblivious, her only concern who was coming to her door, and soon she'd be devastated.

Carol didn't have to ring the bell. The door opened, and a diminutive woman, her hair dyed dark brown — or was that a wig? — smiled wide.

"Oh, it's little Carol Wren! How are you, dear?"

Carol put her ID away and didn't bother introducing them. "Hello. I'm okay, thank you. Can we come in?"

"Of course! Is it Clem? I heard about that when I went into town this morning. A nice lady called Donna asked me some questions on my way to the Beach Hut."

Carol felt the murders were linked but wasn't about to come out with that straight off the bat. She had to deliver the bad news first, and anyway, she might not mention the suspected connection at all. It depended how Irene coped. "No, it's Frank."

"Gawd, has he had trouble at the Odeon again? He should be retired by now, but he won't have it. Loves going there, he does. Come through. I'll make us a drink. The kettle's just boiled."

Trouble at the Odeon? Carol glanced at Dave, who shrugged. She followed Irene into a galley kitchen that was separated from a dining area by a breakfast bar. Everything was modern, as though the kitchen had recently been installed.

Irene filled cups from the kettle. "Have a sit down, I'll be with you any minute."

Carol thought it best to let the woman play host for a while longer. She sat at a high-gloss white table, Dave opposite, a vase of pink roses in the centre, a pile of cork coasters beside it. Irene chittered on about the nice summer they'd had and how autumn was taking its time showing a full face — "Even the leaves aren't dropping as much as usual, are they?" Tea brought over on a tray with a picture of kittens on it, Irene sat with her back to the wall and waved for them to take a cup.

"You said about trouble at the Odeon." Carol lifted a mug and placed it on a coaster. "What's been going on there, then?"

"Oh, there are some scallies who go there, mainly that naughty Welding boy, Heidi and Mark's son. You must know him, he's always up to something. Frank's had no end of bother with that lad, mouthing off, you know the sort of thing I mean, stealing sweets even though Frank hands his out for free. A boy playing at being a man, that's what Asher is. Frank's had to escort him out twice now, and Asher's on his final warning. He'll be banned before long, you see if he isn't. Is that why you're here?"

At the mention of Asher Welding, Carol's hackles had risen, and Dave had jotted something in his notebook.

"No, love, that's not it." Carol swallowed. "I'm so sorry, but someone attacked Frank in the cinema yard, and I'm afraid he lost his life."

A woman screaming in grief was never a good thing to watch or hear, and Carol's heart bled for her. Dave went to the rescue, jumping up and hugging Irene to his side — he was good at being a shoulder to cry on, Carol knew that only too well. Irene clutched at the front hem of his suit, her arthritic fingers knobbly, the knuckles red, her eyes scrunched shut as a god-awful wail took the place of the scream. The noise was pure despair, as if it had boiled deep inside her then flashed up and out of her body. Carol had to look away, couldn't stand the sight of the tears glossing over the parchment skin of Irene's cheeks, over the wrinkles, every one of them deeper now mourning had entered her soul.

Carol might appear not to care, but she took her cup regardless and stood at the back door, staring out into the garden to stop herself from breaking down. A vegetable patch. A brick shed with a wonky blue door and a rusted padlock. A rotary washing line with some of Frank's clothes flapping in the breeze, clothes he'd never wear again.

Yes, we were all a breath away from disaster, and the fall-out from one such event played out in a kitchen, in a seaside town, in a world that was cruel and unjust.

Carol let her tears fall.

CHAPTER TWENTY

The Oak Tree

Nathan was hacked off. This wasn't how he'd planned to spend the next two hours, by himself, but he supposed he could use the time to think about the dogs. Mrs Larkin at number six had one, a scrappy thing called Herbie with grey fur that always looked like it needed brushing. Mrs Larkin was old and had scabby hands, like the branches of the oak tree Nathan sat beneath, so maybe it was too hard for her to keep the animal tidy.

He imagined going to her house and asking if he could help her out there. Brush the ugly fucker and take it for a long walk. That way, he could practise hurting dogs, getting to know when it was likely to bite if he pinched it or poked a finger in its side. Or if he tugged on its tongue until it yelped.

Pleased with his idea, he decided to do it alone. He didn't want Bestie putting a downer on it, which he would. Bestie wasn't quite on the same level as Nathan. He was too worried about getting caught, plus he was daft about dogs. Nathan hated all animals. They were pointless pests, smelly, and didn't deserve to live.

He wouldn't kill Herbie — lucky pup — just use him as an experiment.

He might up his game and kill Mrs Larkin, though. She got on his tits.

* * *

Mrs Larkin's House

"What a lovely boy you are, Nathan. Nowt like my son, who doesn't care whether I'm alive or dead."

Handy to know.

The old bag handed him a glass of cloudy lemonade. "Herbie doesn't get out much anymore. It's my legs, see, so the walks will be welcome." She turned to the mutt. "Won't it, darling?"

Nathan rolled his eyes. His elder sister, Chantal, called her dog a "fur baby", and Mam said it was her "granddog", like it was a fucking person. That was just stupid if you asked him, and he wanted to stab Chantal and Mam in the eyes every time they said shit like that.

"It's no problem," Nathan said. "I love dogs." He cringed at saying it.

"Would you like to take Herbie out today?"

"Yeah, but I thought I could brush him for you first."

"Oh, would you? How sweet. It's best to do it in the garden, because that fur will get everywhere."

Nathan had already seen that for himself. The living room carpet had never seen a hoover by the looks of it, and the place was filled with old-fashioned furniture and loads of knick-knacks.

She ferreted in a sideboard and found a steel brush with a rectangular end. He almost laughed at the thought of dragging it through the knots, the dog yelping.

"Won't that hurt him?" he asked.

"Oh, he'll complain, whine a bit, but if you're careful, it won't be too bad."

"Maybe he needs a shave at one of them groomer places, then you wouldn't need to worry about brushing him."

"Not with winter coming up. Herbie will get cold."

Nathan liked the idea of that. A bald dog left outside in the snow, shivering and whimpering, getting frostbite on its paw pads.

He stifled another laugh.

Herbie looked up at him, matted tail wagging.

The stupid bastard didn't know what was coming.

CHAPTER TWENTY-ONE

Undisclosed Location

Desmond reckoned he was making an impact now. He'd written some more things, so horrible even *he'd* winced at them, and the result was that Target had finally got worried. The message had hit its mark, and a few more like that might mean Desmond was elevated in his position here.

He needed that to happen. Boss was getting antsy.

Desmond had explained to Boss why he was taking so long. If he did what he'd been told too early, fingers would point his way. Wasn't it better that he went down the softly-softly route so no one thought it was him?

"This is so disgusting!" Target's faced paled, and they wrung their hands, pacing up and down, most likely trying to think who could be doing this.

Desmond chuckled inwardly. They'd never find out, even if they called in the police. He'd ensured he was safe, and if some piggy or other poked into it, they'd come to a dead end. Boss had set it up, and *he* should know how to do such things like hiding email servers. Desmond had to hand it to him, Boss was a clever bastard.

"This is unacceptable. I won't let this sort of crap happen." Target stopped pacing and gripped the edge of the desk, their knuckles going a weird colour. "What do you think about it?"

Desmond hadn't expected to have to give an opinion, and Boss had said he shouldn't give one. *Fuck Boss.* "It's rude. Seems someone's got a gripe and won't come right out and say it. They're hiding behind a keyboard."

"Exactly what I thought. I'll get someone onto this."

It wouldn't do any good. Like the police, whoever Target employed would be stumped. Boss was good at what he did; it was fascinating how he could work shit out.

Target flopped onto a chair and massaged their temples. Their face had taken on a red hue, anger building, which was understandable, considering what Desmond had written. He'd dug deep and come up with the most hurtful things he could say.

"Sorry if I'm speaking out of turn," Desmond said, "but I've got a pal who can sort things if you ever catch who did this."

The frown said it all. "Sort things?"

"Yeah, you know, get rid of them."

Target gaped at him. "We don't do things that way here, I thought you knew that."

"My apologies. I was just thinking of how I'd feel in your shoes, that's all. Fit to be tied."

"Don't get me wrong, I am, but I can't go down that route."

Desmond shrugged. "The offer's there if you change your mind. I'd even do it for you if it made you feel better."

"I appreciate your offer, but no."

Target opened their laptop and fired off an email, likely to whoever they thought would solve this problem. Desmond zoned out, thinking of how he could get closer to Target in order to do what had to be done. The things he wrote were designed to get Target to take Desmond into their confidence, for them to become closer.

The next step was to get Target to invite him to their house so he could memorise the layout, and although Boss had procured the blueprints, Desmond preferred seeing things for himself. The distances between rooms. How far the exit was from where he'd do the deed. How quickly he could get away.

The devil was in the details.

CHAPTER TWENTY-TWO

Ridgebrook Close

Poppy had been in hospital a few times now, and the doctors were at a loss as to why she kept getting faecal matter in her bloodstream. At first, Madeline had blamed next door's Labrador, but the test results indicated it had been human faeces. So she'd suggested, in a quiet area where Poppy couldn't hear, that her daughter wasn't wiping herself properly while going to the toilet, had perhaps got some on her hands and picked at her innocent scrapes or cuts afterwards.

"Please don't say owt to her about it," she'd pleaded to an old colleague, Laura, who happened to be looking after Poppy that day. "She'd be so embarrassed. I'll have a word about hygiene and how important it is. God only knows she must see that when she's in hospital every few months."

"I'm more worried it's psychological," Laura had said.

Madeline would usually have been affronted by that, but it only fuelled her ideas. If she could get Poppy seen by a psychiatrist, there'd be more reasons to receive attention. It would work well, too, because if Madeline told her daughter to speak freely there about this particular issue, Poppy would deny ever putting poo on herself, and that would lend credence to a mental disorder.

"I thought about that," Madeline had said. "All this illness started when Kevin left. Do you think Poppy's trying to get him to notice her?

Doing this to herself? I mean, he's barely been to see her or take her out, so maybe she feels abandoned."

"Poor kid. That's a bit extreme, though, isn't it? What child her age would know to do that to make herself ill?"

Madeline had bitten her lip. This was getting awkward. "Maybe she saw something on the telly?"

"Hmm, I'd have thought she'd be more into cartoons. Dr Johann might see her."

Oh. Was he working here? Madeline hadn't known that. She'd never forgotten about him. How could she? Ian had been a big part of her life, consuming her thoughts during a certain phase she'd been going through. They'd gone to university together to study medicine, had a few drinks in a crowd as friends. Then there was that big party. "Do you think he'll slot her in somewhere as a favour? See whether he thinks she needs more sessions?"

"I should think so. He's nice like that."

Madeline had nodded, her plan taking shape. She'd have to think about this properly, envisage any pitfalls so she had her answers straight. The conversation with Laura had bordered on scary, Madeline out of her depth because she didn't have all her ducks in a row. Then there was Ian . . . It could become a complication.

She skated a thin line, and it was obvious she'd have to stop using the faecal method of making her daughter ill. The attention was addictive, though, so she couldn't give it up, and seeing Dr Johann was the perfect next step. It had become her drug, doing this, one she desperately needed when the last high had worn off — one she couldn't bear to let go, even though it was wrong. She consoled herself with how she wasn't a monster — she waited until just the right moment to take Poppy into A&E, the child was never in any real danger, although Madeline worried it would go too far one day and there'd be no happy ending. Kevin still didn't seem bothered by Poppy's hospitalisations, so it was about time Madeline did something more about it. Maybe a crazy child would get him to sit up and take notice.

She'd learned many things as a nurse, and if this were the only viable option, she'd have gone for it: anthrax poisoning from coming into contact with infected animals or contaminated products. It wasn't likely, though. Yes, there was a farm nearby where sheep were present and could be petted, but an anthrax outbreak was rare in this country, and she didn't have access to it. It wasn't like she could just steal a petri dish from somewhere. Still, if she could have poisoned Poppy with the inhalation of spores, there would have been a nice set of symptoms. A cough. Fever and chills. Tiredness, aches, nausea and vomiting, but no, it wouldn't happen, so it was pointless thinking about it.

Pesticides was another angle, but how would she get Poppy to swallow it so the explanation to the hospital looked legitimate? Having it poured into a drink would mean either Poppy or Madeline had knowingly done it, and while Poppy did as she was told and didn't speak to the nurses and doctors much about subjects on Madeline's "no" list, Madeline couldn't take the risk.

It could be another pointer to the mental health angle, though . . .

"I didn't do it!" Poppy would say.

"But you must have been having an episode and don't remember," Madeline would respond.

She could make out her daughter did things without knowing it, like her mind blanked and she came out of it with no recollection. Or what about sleepwalking?

For now, while she waited for an appointment with Dr Johann, which could take ages to come through, she'd settle on food poisoning. Raw chicken mixed with the cooked inside a premade sandwich from a supermarket. The bonus here: a payout. More attention by going to the newspapers. Madeline imagined all the neighbours coming to her doorstep once Poppy had been discharged, grapes on hand for the poorly child, words of comfort, just like they'd done all the other times.

She cut the raw chicken breast into small pieces and placed it in one half, mixing it with the mayonnaise already there. Then she doctored the other half and put it back in the packaging as evidence when she contacted the shop. They couldn't deny it if raw chicken was in play, there for all to see. It could be put down to employee sabotage at the factory. That would make a big splash in the nationals. She imagined the woman at the Customer Services desk would try to fob her off with a refund and an apology, but that wasn't going to be the end of it.

Not by a long chalk.

CHAPTER TWENTY-THREE

Ridgebrook Close

Richard Prince had taken it upon himself to speak to all the lads who'd been with Asher Welding on the pier and afterwards, since Carol had mentioned Asher playing Frank up at the cinema. It wasn't that he didn't trust other uniforms, they were brilliant, but he felt his rank might go some way to lending a more serious air to things. Asher sounded as if he was on the verge of becoming out of control, and if he was a teenager who thought he ruled the world, a constable might not be seen as anyone to be wary of. A sergeant, on the other hand . . .

As with the others, Richard wanted to watch Asher's expressions, how he held himself, whether he looked guilty. His friends had already been questioned, and each of them said the same thing — they'd hung around on the pier, mucked about down by the marina, and got home around eleven, one of them admitting he'd been grounded because he was supposed to be in by ten. His mother, smug as anything, had added that she'd confiscated his phone for the duration of his punishment.

A quick check with Lloyd, who was helping Carol's team out, proved they were telling the truth about what time they'd left the pier; the CCTV had confirmed it. Their parents, who'd been present at Richard's visits, had agreed with what their boys had said, and to be honest, he was inclined to believe them.

Then came the sad business with Frank, but they couldn't have killed him as each of them had been in school, Richard had already checked, but Asher . . . he was a different story.

Richard sighed and knocked on the door of the Welding household, aware he'd face resistance, especially if Mark was around, but Heidi opened it, an ice cream scoop in one hand with what appeared to be clumps of mashed potato on it.

"Come on, then," she said, "let's get this malarky over with. It's all a waste of time, but I suppose you've got to earn your wages somehow, and us minions just have to put up with it."

Richard had phoned ahead to ensure Asher would be home. He stepped inside, the scent of sausages hitting him. He could do with some grub himself, *and* being at home with his feet up, but he had this to get through first, then he could hand the reins over to another sergeant, Oliver Havers.

In the kitchen, Asher sat at the table with Mark — *oh, great, I've got him to contend with* — and Richard stood by the huge, American-style fridge-freezer. Heidi waved the scoop at him, indicating he take a seat, and he chose one opposite the lad and his father.

"We'll be eating while you interrogate our son." Heidi used the scoop to create perfect domes of mash on the plates. "Do you want some?"

Richard did, it looked delicious, but he had to decline. "No, thank you."

"Fair enough." Heidi handed the plates out. "If you can't bring yourself to eat commoner food, then you're a bit of a wanker, to be fair."

"That isn't the case at all, Mrs Welding." Richard couldn't be doing with this at the end of his busy day. Arguing. Placating. "I'm not allowed." That excuse would fly. Heidi wouldn't know whether he could eat with people or not while on duty.

"You're a rule-follower, then." She sniffed.

"It makes life easier."

Richard got his notebook ready, sensing Mark's heavy stare on him. There had been plenty of times Richard had dealt with a drunk Mark, who always got far too lairy in the Devil and threatened to punch people's lights out. As he didn't fancy a black eye, Richard would take the same approach as he had with the other boys — to act as if he was on their side. Policing wasn't just about upholding the law but learning how to handle people to get the best results.

Heidi sat and tucked in.

Richard took a deep breath. "Okay, this is just to clear Asher of any involvement. Of course, we don't think for one moment he had owt to do with Clem's death, but it's normal for us to question those who've had any recent interaction with the deceased, especially the negative variety. I'm not inclined to believe Asher got the hump after being told off by Clem and decided to kill him, because that would be ridiculous, wouldn't it?"

"Too fucking right." Mark stabbed the air with his fork. "He was home, so that's that. You can bog off now."

Richard was concerned about the time Frank had been killed. "I'll be going shortly, but . . . Asher, I've contacted the school, and you signed in at registration today, this morning's and after lunch, but one teacher can't recall you being in his class. Where were you during double maths?"

Heidi jumped in. "Oh, so he's skiving now, is he? Jesus Christ. What else are you going to pin on him?"

"But perhaps he was, Mrs Welding, and that's something we've all done, haven't we, and providing Asher wasn't doing owt he shouldn't be while not in school, that's a problem for you and the school to deal with. So, Asher, where were you?"

"In maths." He speared a slice of sausage and stuffed it in his mouth. "Mr Bains is a blind old bat, so he probably didn't see me. He's too busy reading his book anyroad, hardly looks up at us lot."

Richard smiled, the kindly uncle, but inside, he was annoyed that this family always put up roadblocks. Nothing was ever simple with them. "Right, in order to strike you off our list regarding the skiving, you need to let me know where you really were."

"Why?" Mark asked. "What's he done, killed someone else?" He laughed, revealing chewed-up sausage in his wide-open mouth.

Richard didn't enjoy the sight. He'd been nice, but now he'd get to the point. "Unfortunately, Asher not being in school was around the time another murder was committed."

"Oh, fuck me!" Mark leaned back, shaking his head. "Are you *serious*? I mean, he's a kid. Thirteen years old. What's he done, got a gun and gone on a rampage?"

Richard shrugged. "As I said, I don't think Asher is involved, but I have to ask these questions. And a gun isn't even in the equation."

Mark cuffed his son around the back of his head. "Where were you?"

"Down the wreck with someone." Asher blushed.

"Who?" Heidi asked.

"I don't wanna to say. You'll rib me."

Mark nodded. "A girl, then. So what? If it gets you off the hook, tell the copper, for fuck's sake."

Asher scooped up some mash, pouting. "Fine, I was with Jessie Smith, *okay*?"

"And where does she live?" Richard wrote the name down.

"Next door at seventeen," Heidi said, "and she'll get a right bloody bollocking off her mam for skiving, which is why our Asher probably didn't want to say it was her. He's caring like that."

Richard didn't think Asher cared much about anything except himself, but he wasn't about to say so.

"Who's snuffed it now, then?" Mark bit into a sausage. A spurt of fat shot out and landed on the table.

"Frank West from the Odeon." Richard watched them for their reactions.

Heidi's eyes filled with tears, something he hadn't expected from her, and Mark appeared shocked and saddened. Asher widened his eyes and looked uncomfortable.

"Aww, no." Heidi put her cutlery down. "He was a good bloke."

Richard nodded. "We're aware Asher was a little . . . annoying at the cinema on two occasions and is on his final warning. Any more mucking about, and he won't be allowed in."

"What sort of mucking about? I didn't hear jack shit about this." Heidi folded her arms. "Asher's a good boy, so it must have been someone else."

"Just tomfoolery." Richard wasn't aware of the facts. "Let's get back to last night. You're sure Asher came in by eleven?"

Mark shoved his chair back, the damn thing barking loudly on the laminate, and he got up, letting out a weird growl, one Richard had heard on the night Mark had been arrested for affray. It didn't bode well, the man was volatile, so Richard braced himself for a verbal attack.

Surprisingly, it didn't come.

Mark fetched his phone off the worktop beside the bread bin and poked at the screen. "Here's the proof." He came over and thrust the phone in Richard's face.

Video footage, presumably from a doorbell camera, showed Asher using his key to get in. Digital numbers in the bottom-right corner revealed the time and the seconds counting up. As Richard had suspected, a gang of children hadn't decided to commit murder, but getting to the bottom of things was his job, and it unfortunately involved pissing off people like this.

"I'll need a copy of this."

"Fine." Mark retook his seat.

"Thanks. Well, I'll leave you to your meal." He stood and slipped his notebook and pen away.

Asher stared up at him. "Are you going to ask Jessie about the skiving?"

"I'm afraid I have to. If you want my advice, keep yourself out of trouble, all right?"

Asher nodded.

"I'll see myself out."

Richard popped next door and remained on the garden path while a screeching mother shouted at her daughter, sending her to her room once she'd confirmed she'd played truant today. Satisfied Asher wasn't their killer, he went back to the car and phoned Carol to let her know.

Back to square one with no suspects.

Bugger.

CHAPTER TWENTY-FOUR

The Oak Tree

Nathan had come out for a breather. He waited for Bestie. On the nights they didn't have other shit arranged, they met here, just came on the off chance when they were bored or whatever. Sometimes, Bestie didn't turn up, like earlier when Nathan had ended up going to see Mrs Larkin.

That had worked out well, the grooming. While Larkin had gone inside to do a crossword, Nathan had yanked the brush through Herbie's fur so the animal would cry out. Larkin had come back out to see what was wrong, and Nathan had told her there were more knots than he'd thought. Satisfied, she'd gone in and closed the door.

By the time Nathan had brushed the hound so half its fur danced on the grass in tufts, Herbie looked a lot better. There was no way Nathan would walk it in its previous state, that would be embarrassing.

Herbie was good on the lead, obedient, and it pissed Nathan off because he didn't have an excuse to kick him for bad behaviour. At the oak tree, he'd sat on the ground, Herbie flopping on the grass between his legs, far too trusting, and Nathan had parted the fur on his flank and stabbed him with one of Mam's diabetes finger-prick wotsits. Herbie's yelp had been hilarious, but the blood was an issue. It stained the fur, so Nathan had taken him to the brook so he could wash it off.

Herbie forgot about the pain and dived in, paddling and splashing, having a great time, launching himself out of the water to come and lick Nathan's fingers, then dashing back into the brook again. In a way, Nathan envied him. What must it be like to forgive your tormentor so easily?

Nathan had let the dog have his fun for ten minutes — he could probably do with the wash anyway — then took the long route back to Larkin's, confused by the fact he quite liked this little animal now, how it gazed up at him every so often and seemed to smile. For the first time, guilt kicked Nathan up the arse. What if he made friends with Herbie instead of hurting him? What if he gained power another way, by making the dog adore him so much he didn't like Larkin anymore?

Nathan smiled. There were many ways to get what you needed, and it didn't necessarily have to be through pain. He saw that now.

A whistle drew him out of his thoughts. He stared at the trees ahead, spotting Bestie, who had a new tracksuit on, the one Nathan had said he liked when they'd been in Sports Direct. Fucking hell, Bestie always did that, one-upping him all the time. Nathan bet Herbie wouldn't deliberately upset him like that.

"Come on, people to rob, money to earn," Bestie said.

Nathan sighed. Yeah, they were going back to the pier, but to be honest, he didn't feel like it. "Why did you get the tracksuit? You know I really liked it."

Bestie shrugged. "It's not my fault you have to hand money to your mam. Why not skip giving her a night's takings and go and buy yourself one?"

"Because she's skint."

"Then she should go out and get a fucking job."

"She's too poorly at the minute."

"So she says."

Nathan didn't like this side of Bestie. His pal knew what Mam was like, how she bullied Nathan, hurt him like he hurt the cats — he'd learned the hard way about the pain you could get from a BB gun. Maybe he should have turned to self-harm instead of hurting moggies, taking his anger out on himself, not them.

Or maybe I should just kill Mam and be done with it.

One day. He'd practise on Larkin first, then he could take Herbie home to his house, see what it was like to be nice to him, to have a devoted pal.

Yeah, he'd do that, but there was no way he'd be calling him his fur baby.

CHAPTER TWENTY-FIVE

Train Carriage

Sofia was on the return journey home. She'd had a wonderful day, seeing the sights, taking a bus tour, and generally getting a feel for the place. She'd mainly wanted to see if it felt like home, that bustling London welcomed her, and with the added bonus of so many people, she'd disappear there, become one speck out of millions, a part of the masses.

It was ideal for her after she'd—

Let's not go there.

A Google search had given her the perfect place to eat. She'd lunched at the Connaught, supremely expensive but worth it, choosing a black truffle pizza with fontina cheese, something she'd never eaten before, and the white wine had been crisp and cold.

Her legs and feet ached from so much walking, but again, it was worth it. She'd seen and done so many things, wanting to cram it all into one day, because on her next visit she'd check out the residential areas, although it wouldn't be in Mayfair, she couldn't afford the prices. She'd find a job and rent at first, get a sense of the area she'd eventually choose, then look at buying. Money wouldn't be tight, she'd see to that, and she could enjoy life to the fullest.

A man in the seat to her right, sitting closest to the aisle, leaned towards her, brown hair on the cusp of turning grey at the temples, giving him a distinguished look. He was around forty, give or take a couple of years. He had a kind air about him, unlike those perverted types. He reminded Sofia of the man who'd dumped her.

"Would you like a sweet?" He held up a bag of lemon drops.

Sofia smiled to stop a laugh from tumbling out — of all the things he could have said to chat her up. "I would, but I don't know you from Adam. People get their drinks spiked in clubs all the time, so why not sweets?"

"True, although I assure you, that's not one of my pastimes. I prefer tennis or squash."

She laughed with him and dug into her bag to pull out a packet of Jelly Babies. "I'll stick to my own, thanks."

"Are you going back home?" he asked.

She stared at him quizzically.

"Your accent . . ." he said.

That put paid to her thinking she'd blend in with the Londoners. She'd have to practise, see if she could change the way she spoke. "Yes, I'm going home, and *your* accent says you're travelling *away* from home."

"You've got me there. I have a conference in Newcastle the day after tomorrow."

"Ah, you've got a way to go after I get off, then."

"Hmm. So what have you been doing in the city?"

"I could have got on at any of the stops along the route, so how do you know I was in London?"

"Err, I got on at the same time as you . . ."

And there it was, her inability to flirt, to sound like she had any sense in her head. She hadn't spotted him boarding, too busy thinking about her exciting day, yet *he'd* seen *her*. Did that sound promising? Something she could build on?

She rolled her eyes at herself. "I wasn't taking any notice of who got on with me."

"I know. Away with the fairies, weren't you?"

Oh God, how long had he been watching her? He didn't seem like the stalker type, but they didn't exactly walk around with a lanyard announcing it, did they? "You sounded a tad creepy there."

His eyebrows rose. "Did I? That wasn't my intention. I'm not creepy, I promise."

"I'll have to take your word for it. Are you staying over in Newcastle?"

"Yes, although I could hold that off for tonight if you're up for a date. Where you go, I'll follow." He winked, but it wasn't the leery kind, more him trying to convince her to say yes.

"I'm from Scudderton."

"Oh, the seaside. Nice."

"It is. And as long as it's *just* a date . . ." She couldn't believe she'd said that. She didn't even know this man. But what was it she'd once read? *If you don't take a leap of faith, you remain standing still.* She didn't want to stand still, she wanted to fly, and maybe, maybe, this was her chance to have some fun before she moved to the Big Smoke. Then again . . . "So you live in London, do you?"

"I do."

"And I assume, because you've asked me out, you don't have a wife or a girlfriend. That would be a dealbreaker, just so you know. I don't do cheating."

He held up his ring hand, which didn't have a mark where he might have taken a wedding band off. "Nope."

"Okay, then, meet me in a pub called the Little Devil at eight. It's opposite the marina. We can eat, then we can go on the pier if you're up for it."

"I'm up for anything. Where do you suggest I stay?"

"The Beachfront, it's a hotel."

He took his phone out and Googled, staring at a photo on his screen. "Let's hope they've got a vacancy, eh?"

She smiled while he spoke to the receptionist on speakerphone, resisting hugging herself, because she had a good feeling about him, and if they hit it off . . . well, maybe she wouldn't have to find a place to rent after all.

CHAPTER TWENTY-SIX

The Lord

With the news from Richard about the lads on the pier, the team had gone down an alley and hit a dead end. The working day had drawn to a close, so with no leads, evidence with forensics, and nothing new to report from Rib regarding Clem's post-mortem, Carol had declared their shift over.

She'd checked the whiteboard before leaving. Lloyd had added a section regarding CCTV and his findings, and Katherine had written down one sentence that had slumped Carol's shoulders: *Neither Clem nor Frank have been found on social media.* Given their ages, some would say they were unlikely to be on there anyway, but many older people enjoyed interacting online, just not these two. June had an account for her chippy, but it was clearly business only. Michael had got in contact with everyone who'd worked with Frank, and he'd nipped to see a couple of people who weren't on shift today, visiting them in their homes. No one had any idea why someone would want to kill Frank.

Tesco had sent the promised CCTV, and Lloyd had cross-referenced the drivers' alibis with the footage. All of them had told the truth about when they'd left the supermarket, although it could have been a cover, a deliberate alibi.

No one else had come forward, after hearing about Clem on the grapevine, to say they'd seen anybody walking along that road late at night. Nothing nefarious had been discovered in the woods by Clem's place, and from the initial exploration, his home hadn't been breached by the killer. Fingerprints and trace evidence could prove otherwise.

Carol sipped some of her white wine, thinking how nice it was now she didn't have to sit on pins and needles, waiting for her ex to come in and strike up one of his weird-as-eff conversations about storage boxes. It was his favourite subject along with keeping a house orderly, and he'd always interrupted her downtime with Dave. At least now he was in prison, she could relax and not have to look over her shoulder.

As Carol hated cooking and Dave didn't much like it either, they tended to eat in the Lord most nights. The prices weren't hideous, usually about six or seven quid for something like a curry or pie and mash. She'd quashed her earlier need for fish and chips, and they'd had lasagne instead.

"Do you want to talk work?" she asked Dave.

"I was just thinking the same thing. I stopped myself from having a guilt trip over being in here with a bevvy when two men are dead, but if we don't rest, we're no good to anyone."

"I agree, and uniforms are doing a lot of the legwork. The next shift will be bright-eyed and bushy-tailed, so the canvasing on Coldwater will be done and dusted by about nine tonight. If anyone saw owt, we can go and speak to them tomorrow."

And with that, Carol sipped her wine and chatted to Dave about having a conservatory put on the back of her cottage. She didn't expect him to contribute financially, but with the money saved up from renting out her caravan, by the end of next summer, she could put down a deposit to have it done.

It was good to have goals, ones her father couldn't shoot down.

* * *

It was a sad yet jubilant affair, scattering the ashes. Sad for all the obvious reasons, but jubilant because Mam was finally where she should be, at rest in the sea and on the ledge of the promontory, plus Carol had sprinkled some outside the master gunner's house when no one was looking.

Few had come to say goodbye with her. A couple of women who'd lived in Larch Lane at the same time as Mam had got on the minibus Carol had provided — she'd put a notice in the local paper, not expecting anyone to bother turning up. Frank had ambled onto the bus, patting her shoulder as he'd passed, and Carol had taken it that he was still watching out for her after all this time. Dave was with her every step of the way too, as was Rib.

Her two wingmen left her to contemplate things on the promontory ledge, the others visiting the ruins of the castle while they had the chance. Carol said her silent goodbye, thanking Mam for being there for as long as she could, telling her not to blame herself for what had happened after her death.

Carol turned and walked along the grassy path to the gunner's house, entering to find two sets of stairs — one going up, one down. She peered over the banister directly ahead to a storage area below — boxes on the elbow of the stairs, a picture in a black frame propped against the wall, and yet more boxes beside the bottom step. She felt it was disrespectful to use that area as a dumping ground. The house had history, and it was wrong to abuse it in this way.

The first floor was now a space for exhibits. She wandered around. Instead of fully taking in the prehistoric tools and pottery, the replica of a Bronze Age sword found on the site, she imagined the house as it might have been when people had lived here. She turned to look out of a window. Wooden picnic tables sat on the stretch of grass out the front, a modern blot on a beautiful landscape. She faced the room again and saw Mam everywhere, a ghost flickering between other tourists and exhibit cases, and she had to walk out. It was too much.

She found a room downstairs with wooden tables and chairs, a framed black-and-white picture of the castle above a brick fireplace. People must come here when it rained to drink their "hearty Yorkshire tea" from the café shack beside the house. She caught another gauzy glimpse of Mam standing in the corner, so she rushed outside and sucked in the fresh air.

A wren swooped and landed, and she'd swear it was the one in the garden at Larch Lane, but that was just her airy-fairy mind messing her about. Yet it stared at her the same, hopped closer and tilted its head. Then it was off, heading for North Bay, and Carol was content to imagine Mam had come back, telling her she was flying now.

She was free.

CHAPTER TWENTY-SEVEN

Nathan's House

Nathan had stolen enough cash to give to Mam but had also come up trumps with a credit card that actually had the PIN written on the signature strip at the back. He could withdraw a wedge and use the contactless option in shops. He'd take the day off tomorrow and go to Leeds, hoping the missing card wouldn't be noticed — knowing his luck it would be. He'd nicked it then popped the purse back in the woman's bag while she'd waited in the queue for a hot dog.

He'd parted ways with Bestie in town, saying he wanted to be alone, but he'd put his hood up, pulling it low over his face, and dipped his head at the ATM so the camera would only see his mouth and chin. He did a balance check. Blimey, there was eight grand in the account. Even if he only managed to withdraw this initial three hundred quid, he could still have a good spend in Leeds. There were so many shops there it boggled his mind, and he loved Kirkgate Market — it reminded him of going there with Nan when he was little. He'd buy a tracksuit, a better one, and maybe some trainers, too.

At home, he went straight to the living room.

Mam sat on the sofa and glared at him. "Did you keep out of trouble?"

"Yeah."

"Good, because I don't need the police sniffing around." She held her hand out.

He placed the two hundred and ten quid he'd pickpocketed on her palm, sickened by her smug smile. No wonder he hated her — what normal person sent their son out to steal cash? What normal person treated her son like a skivvy and her daughter like a princess? What normal mother shot her kid with a BB gun if he didn't behave?

"I heard you've made friends with Mrs Larkin." She tucked the cash into her handbag beside her.

"So?"

"She's got a fair few antiques, that one."

"No, I'm not nicking off her for you. It'd be obvious it was me."

"Fair enough." Mam sulked and reached for a Buns 'n' Bread bag, pulling out a Chelsea bun. She stuffed it in her ugly face.

Nathan turned away, despising her, especially because she wasn't supposed to be eating so much sugar. He walked upstairs, the ATM money burning a hole in his pocket. He couldn't wait to get the train to Leeds, to wander the city and use the card. He deserved new togs.

He deserved a better life, too, but he hadn't had one. Mam had seen to that.

CHAPTER TWENTY-EIGHT

Parsley Avenue

Madeline had left a sleeping Poppy in bed. Her child had believed her when she'd said the injections were for her health — she'd been doing it for a long time, so why would she question it?

It was a relief to get out of the house. Her next victim would be asleep, but that was okay, Madeline had a key, one Kevin didn't know about. She hadn't visited his mother for about a fortnight, and it had always been a secret since he'd left her; he'd wanted a clean break, although in Madeline's eyes, it had been decidedly mucky.

Gail would be pleased to see her. She'd been Madeline's ally ever since Kevin had walked out. The woman couldn't understand why her son had been so heartless. The end of a marriage she could comprehend, but not shirking his fatherly responsibilities. Mind you, Gail hadn't lifted a finger to help with Poppy either, claiming her arthritis was stopping her from living her life, from getting a taxi to Madeline's and sitting with her grandchild. Gail did phone regularly, though, so that was something, but as a punishment for her lack of care, Madeline hadn't brought Poppy here — why should *she* make all the effort?

Madeline stood at the bottom of Parsley Avenue in her boiler suit, putting on her gloves, Kevin's toolbox between her feet. She watched the silent street for any signs of activity. No one was outside, although some people were up indoors, light seeping from behind closed curtains. She walked quietly in her old, soft-soled nurse's shoes, remaining vigilant all the way along, turning up Gail's path and inserting the key.

She let herself in, closing the door carefully, her handbag strap hanging across her body. She needed the tools in there close to hand. The house stank of cabbage and boiled bacon, one of Gail's favourite dinners, and Madeline confirmed the woman had eaten that as her last meal by going into the kitchen and peering in the fridge. A second plate covered in clingfilm sat on the top shelf, likely Gail's tea for tomorrow.

Except she wouldn't be eating it.

Gail had washed up — so her arthritis didn't bother her *that* much. She always leaned on her affliction in public, and Madeline had secretly suspected she danced around the house while alone.

Well, she wouldn't be dancing anywhere tonight except in hell.

Madeline giggled and closed the fridge, but her laughter soon faded, as did her smile when she thought about Gail's part in this. She'd encouraged Madeline to marry Kevin, overly enthusiastic to be honest, eager for a grandchild, and although she'd tried her best — so she'd said — to get Kevin to visit Poppy, she hadn't tried hard enough. Gail was partly to blame for Madeline shacking up with that useless, lying piece of shit, and she had to go.

It would hurt Kevin. He loved his mother above anyone else, even himself, which was saying something.

She opened the back door and checked the houses at the bottom for anyone watching. All the windows were dark, so she tiptoed down the slabbed path in the middle of the grass to the shed. It was never locked — Madeline had been inside once to get some pruning shears to help Gail with her rose bushes out the front — so she opened the door. She turned to spy on the backs of houses in Gail's row, checked that no one was watching, then went inside the shed and deposited the toolbox on the floor so it'd be spotted easily.

Eyeing the dark shapes of Gail's gardening equipment, she snatched up the pruning shears and a trowel. They were important, another link to Kevin; the police would hopefully think he'd come here to kill his mother and had stolen her shears for the next victim. She dropped them in her bag and returned to the house, leaving the door unlocked to give the impression Kevin had been so incensed after the kill that he hadn't been thinking straight.

She crept upstairs, glad this place was detached so no neighbours would hear the creak of the two dodgy steps. Gail heard it, though.

"Who's there? Is that you, Kev?"

"Only me." Madeline paused on the third step from the top.

"Maddy? What on earth are *you* doing here at this time of night?"

"I needed a chat. Couldn't get to sleep."

"What about Poppy? Is she alone? And why didn't you just phone me?"

Because I don't want the police to see I did that, you silly cow.

Madeline went along the landing and entered Gail's bedroom. The older woman sat up in bed, the lamp on the nightstand emitting a soft glow. Gail didn't like the dark, but that was okay, there were plenty of flames in hell to light the way.

"What's wrong? Is it Poppy?"

Madeline sighed and sat on the edge of the bed. "Her and Kevin, yes."

Gail sighed, too. "This is a merry-go-round, duck. You need to get off. It's not doing you any good keep going over and over this. Kevin's proved he's an unfit father. It's a bitter pill to swallow, but face it, nowt you do is going to change his mind."

"He's disgusting. Poppy's in a wheelchair all the time now if she leaves her bed. Her legs have minimal feeling, you know that, so why doesn't he care?"

"It's a sad fact, but I think he's ashamed of having a daughter who . . ."

"Who's disabled?"

"Yes, much as I dislike it, that's the conclusion I've come to."

"But she wasn't disabled when he left, she just got poorly, so that theory has gone out of the window. Why can't you admit he didn't want the responsibility?"

"Because it hurts and I'm ashamed."

Usually, Gail's honesty went some way to mollifying Madeline, but it was too late now, she'd made up her mind about her ex-mother-in-law. "I suppose you've met his latest piece, the redhead, the one he's installed in that big house."

Gail looked abashed. "She came here with him last week."

"And?"

"She isn't you, that's for sure. I doubt she'd come to see me twice a month like you do. Too interested in going to all the ChatSesh bashes he's been putting on."

Madeline had seen them online, photos of him on a red carpet like he was some celebrity. Anger burned inside her at this new ginger bitch getting all the good parts of being with Kevin, when Madeline had suffered through the slog of scrimping and saving, helping him to develop his business. It wasn't *fair*.

"Did you hear about Old Clem?" Gail said. "Shocking."

"Hmm, Frank West was murdered, too." Madeline had no idea if this was common knowledge yet, but it wasn't like her mentioning his death mattered. She slid her hand in her bag and clutched the slim handle of one of the tools.

Gail gaped. "Oh God, *what*?"

Madeline brought the tool out and stood. "It's your turn now."

She stabbed the chisel in Gail's throat, leaving it there while she took a rubber-ended mallet out of her bag. Gail thrashed around, stupidly yanking the chisel out, red spurting from the slit in pulsing arcs and flooding down to settle on her collarbones, drenching the low, frilly neck of her nightgown. She choked out sounds that might have been words, but they were too garbled for Madeline to understand.

She snatched the chisel out of Gail's shaking hand, amused now by the woman touching the handle. It would muddy the waters for the police. Would they believe she'd killed herself?

Not likely after what I'm going to do next.

Madeline let out a roar of laughter and held the tools in one hand, dragging Gail down the bed with the other so she lay flat.

"There's no point in trying to talk, Gail, your voice box is fucked."

Madeline positioned the end of the chisel between the woman's eyes. Gail chose that moment to have a fit, or maybe it was a heart attack, her body bucking. Madeline waited patiently for her to finish being ridiculous — this was such an inconvenient waste of time — and, once Gail stilled, she put the chisel back in the correct spot. Using the mallet, she walloped the end — hard — and narrowed her eyes in spite at the woman who'd said she'd had her back but hadn't really. If she had, she'd have talked Kevin round. And she certainly wouldn't have entertained the ginger one.

Gail's eyes bulged, and blood dribbled to cover them in a scarlet sheen. The chisel blade had gone in farther than Madeline had anticipated and she couldn't pull it out, it was held fast, but she'd been leaving the weapons behind anyway, so it could bloody well stay there. She placed the mallet beneath Gail and stared at the deceased.

"You tried, I'll give you that, but it didn't get me or Poppy anywhere."

She sighed. This one had been a difficult decision. She supposed it was harder to kill someone you cared for. But the damage had been done with Gail dropping the ball, and really, it had been done when she'd poked her nose in, pushing for the wedding. With so many people urging her to marry Kevin, Madeline had been swept along on a tide of happiness, ignoring any pitfalls and red flags.

The only happiness she'd get now was when number four was dead and Kevin sat behind bars. She planned to convince him to let her and Poppy live in the posh cliff house while he served his time. It was the least he could do.

She swiped some of Gail's blood onto a fingertip and went back to the shed. A quick smear of it on the pale handle of another hammer, then she was off down the street, dipping into a stand of trees around the corner to take off her outfit. If a copper didn't spot that blood on the tool, she'd have to hope fate gave her a hand in them suspecting Kevin.

She didn't know what she'd do if he wasn't arrested.

CHAPTER TWENTY-NINE

The Pier

Sofia had enjoyed her time in the Devil with the man from the train. She'd added the clip-in extensions, always did if she didn't want anyone knowing her business, the others in the pub, for example. He'd complimented the extensions, saying she looked like a different person from when she'd been on the train, and she'd held back the urge to tell him that was the point. She'd realised, when she'd sat at a corner table, that she hadn't even known his name. Nigel Vanquis, like the credit card. She hoped he had a lot of credit himself, well able to take care of her if things went to plan. It seemed he did, as he'd paid for the meal and drinks with cash from a large wedge in his wallet.

Sometimes, fate sent you the right person at the right time.

She must remember not to be so trusting. To not know his name was a slip on her part, but she'd been so taken by him, it hadn't seemed to matter while they'd been on the train. She'd imagined him as a Robert or Samuel — Nigel was a bit of a gormless name if you asked her, although that was because she associated it with that kid from school who'd been as thick as two short planks and stared at everyone like he had sawdust in his head.

She must also remember not to associate things with other things, a habit that had held her back in life. At significant points in her timeline, she'd twinned food or music with an upsetting event, even what had been on the telly, and she'd avoided them ever since. But it was silly to do that. A song shouldn't be ignored or switched off just because it was a reminder. The name of a beautiful man shouldn't put her off the man himself. Especially because he clearly wasn't dim, and he certainly didn't possess a vacant stare, more like a comforting one that told her she might become special to him.

On the pier, they'd already been on the Ferris wheel, and it had been odd to pay someone else instead of Clem. She'd heard about his murder, and Reg had gossiped with some old duffer from Norfolk who'd come here for his holiday. Nigel had won her a teddy from the Shoot the Tin stall — she'd chosen a small one so it fitted in her bag — and they'd stood and watched the sea for a while, a brisk wind buffeting them every now and then. The best part was the talking, getting to know one another, and she was surprised they had so much in common: books, films, dramas on the telly.

He didn't once hint that she should stay in his room tonight at the Beachfront — she'd have told him to get lost on that score — and it was nice to see he was a gentleman, although she knew some men pretended, then changed once they'd got you under their spell. But she was alert for any signs, and if he ever displayed odd tendencies, she'd break it off.

Assuming he even wanted to see her again after tonight.

The time came to say goodbye, and she held her breath, waiting for him to offer her his phone number with a view to meeting up some other time. He did, she gave him hers, and her heart almost burst with her happiness.

"I can walk you home if you like. Or would you prefer a taxi?" he asked.

"No, no, I don't live far away, so you get off now."

He didn't kiss her, instead holding her hand for a long time and staring into her eyes. She had to glance away it was that intense, her cheeks heating. Then he was gone, up the steps of the Beachfront, disappearing inside, and she made her way home, thinking about him, smiling, and hoping he was true to his word and would contact her tomorrow.

At her house, she let herself in and went straight upstairs, shedding her clothes, putting the extensions beneath her mattress, getting into bed, and staring at the ceiling, her mind not on Nigel but *her*, the woman who'd forced Sofia's former man away.

The redhead who'd wrecked her life.

The plans were complete, and now all Sofia had to do was kill her.

And the others.

CHAPTER THIRTY

Dr Johann's Office

Seeing Dr Johann again hadn't been what Madeline had anticipated — Ian looked so distinguished now. She liked to imagine things in her head and play them out before the actual event, standing at her full-length mirror in the bedroom so she could see herself how others would. She'd have a pretend conversation with the other person, acting like they stood in front of her, taking note of how she appeared when she laughed, how her hair glimmered beneath the lights. How attractive she was.

Or wasn't.

God, Kevin had done a number on her self-confidence.

Would Ian fancy her? She'd like to think he would. Or was she too drab now, not to his liking? There was a time when she'd thought of being with him, giving it a go in a relationship, but she'd already married Kevin, so she'd stuck with him. She'd kept an eye on what Ian was doing over the years, though, asking his mam how he was. Last week, she'd found out he hadn't started working at this hospital until long after she'd left her job to care for Poppy, and she had the silly feeling he'd done that on purpose. Why, she wouldn't like to say.

The session with Ian wasn't going right at all. None of her practise conversations had featured, where they'd greeted each other in a mad flurry of silly squeals and hugs. She became annoyed then worried she'd lost her handle on things — or she'd offended him, although she couldn't remember when that would have been. Having done what she had with Poppy, it was imperative she stuck to the script so no one suspected her, but with other people involved, it had a habit of going haywire. She couldn't control them like she could herself, and it was frustrating.

They were supposed to laugh about the past, but Ian was aloof, somewhat brusque, and rude at times. At least that's how she took it. There was no need to be stuffy with her, was there? They'd been friends once upon a time, for goodness sake! He wasn't the lad from university anymore but a psychiatrist, a serious man who seemed to have lost his spark. Maybe he had a wife who'd drained the life out of him, like Kevin had done to her.

He decided, during the hour Madeline and Poppy spent with him, that her child was "normal", if a bit quiet and vague with her answers, shyness perhaps. One of his colleagues took her off to a play area outside Ian's office so he could talk to Madeline alone. He started off on the wrong foot: he had no idea what he could do to help as he didn't believe it was a psychiatric issue for Poppy, stressing the word Poppy. *He even intimated she hadn't put the poo on herself but that someone else had.*

"What are you suggesting?" Madeline snapped. "She only lives with me, I'm a single mother, so are you saying I did it?"

He didn't grow flustered like so many did when she spoke with that tone. Then again, he never had. He was calm, maybe confused by her outburst. "Not at all, but perhaps someone at school? This might be why she's so quiet, why she doesn't want to engage with me, because she's being bullied and feels she can't say."

Madeline relaxed. While the therapist angle had been thwarted, as had her getting Ian to fancy her, as had the supermarket refusing to give her a payout regarding the raw chicken sandwich, she could certainly go down the bullying route. Complain to the school that those in the medical profession had a theory another child was deliberately putting shit on her daughter's cuts and the grazes on her knees. The grazes were from Poppy appearing so clumsy, but Madeline had bought her shoes a size too big — for her to grow into. It wasn't to ensure she constantly tripped over at all, giving Madeline a broken section of skin on which to apply the faecal matter.

No, that would be cruel.

So, according to Ian, in a nutshell, Poppy was so traumatised by bullying she wouldn't tell Madeline who it was. If the school didn't do something about it, she could still go to the papers, still get herself in the spotlight. She could become a campaigner for bullying, going on rallies and getting her face on the telly in the news. Maybe she'd be asked on breakfast TV, and she could sit on the couch and tell the country how her child was being treated.

"So you don't feel she needs any therapy sessions," she said.

"No, I don't."

"How can you tell after only one hour?"

"She's withdrawn, maybe even depressed, and that's not my forte. She'd need a different therapist. I specialise in sessions for those who self-harm, and I don't think your daughter is doing owt to herself. It was obvious when I asked her that she has no clue how it happened. She isn't faking it — surely you can see that."

"I can see it, yes, she's my baby, so I know her best. I didn't think she'd do such a thing, but one of the nurses suggested it was a psychological problem, and as you can imagine, as a parent, I want to do everything I can to help, which is more than I can say for some people."

"This isn't the right place, Mrs Cotter . . ."

Oh, so she was Mrs Cotter now, was she?

She glanced at his ring finger. A gold band. Maybe she could get Kevin jealous by going with someone else, no matter that Ian was married. "What have you been up to since uni? I remember you went to live in Scotland for a while."

He flinched. "I'm at work, Madeline . . ."

He was so confusing, calling her that after he'd used Mrs Cotter. Mixed signals. Was he playing a game? He'd better not even think about it, not with the knowledge she had about him. She could fuck his life up just like that.

She wanted him. Needed him. "Shall we meet up later for a drink, then? Have a laugh about old times?"

"Old times? Err, that's not for me. Raking up the past isn't something I'm prepared to do, and I don't think my wife would appreciate me going out with another woman."

He stood and opened the door, waiting for her to leave. How strange that he wasn't the same, how he'd changed so much. Had

Madeline? Was that why Kevin had been having affairs? Wasn't she the woman he'd married come the end?

She'd had postnatal depression, and yes, that had altered her, but she'd worked hard to hide it, to remain who she'd been before the pregnancy — vibrant, vital, alive — but life, it had dragged her down.

She didn't bother saying goodbye, didn't even offer the sourpuss a smile — she'd sort him out some other time when he least expected it. How dare he brush her off like that, when . . .

She waltzed off, collecting Poppy, and thought about the drugs she'd stolen, the ones that would deaden Poppy's legs.

"Let's see how Kevin reacts to that!" she muttered and tugged Poppy along beside her.

"What did you say, Mammy?"

"Nowt, love."

"But I heard you talking about Daddy."

"It isn't owt for you to worry about."

"Will we be seeing him today?"

"I don't think so, but I'll tell him you went to see Dr Johann."

"I didn't like his questions."

"No, neither did I, but it's okay, you don't have to see him again." She grimaced about all those wasted scenarios she'd put her time into and whispered, "More's the pity."

* * *

Ridgebrook Close

Kevin didn't give a shiny shite about the therapist, proving to Madeline he wasn't interested in them at all anymore. She'd injected Poppy's legs in discreet spots while she napped, then checked her medical books to see if the drug would show up in blood tests. After a few hours, it would be out of Poppy's system, but the muscle weakness would remain for a while.

She'd make a doctor's appointment, claiming her child's legs wouldn't function and what should she do? By the time she got a hospital appointment, which would likely be months, she'd have practised administering the jabs and perfecting the timing so no matter what the doctors and nurses did, they wouldn't know why Poppy couldn't put weight on her legs.

Madeline smiled, thinking about all the tests — it might be a long stay in hospital this time, so extra attention — and how she'd strut out of there pushing Poppy in a wheelchair, curious onlookers staring at her in sympathy, thinking what a good mother she was for keeping a child who was clearly not right.

Kevin would have to care then, wouldn't he?

* * *

Ward 7

"There is no discernible reason why your daughter's muscles have weakened, Mrs Cotter," Dr Felshaw said.

She loved people calling her that. She'd refused to go back to her maiden name after the divorce. Why should she? She hadn't chosen to lose her surname, that was Kevin's idea.

Dr Felshaw sighed. "As you know, we've done test after test."

Madeline smiled. "How strange. What do you suggest, physiotherapy?"

He nodded. "Yes, then we'll go from there. She hasn't got a muscle-wasting disease, they look perfectly normal on the scans, so we really are stumped."

"That's the thing with the human body, new ailments crop up all the time."

"Hmm, but this one is a right puzzle."

Madeline left the ward pushing a sad Poppy down the corridor in the wheelchair provided by the NHS. "You're going to see someone soon who will try to fix your legs. Won't that be good?"

Poppy didn't answer. She'd become so sullen since Kevin had gone, moody, and she wasn't at all into board games or role play with her toys. All she wanted to do was watch the telly.

"School will help you," Madeline said, waiting by the lift.

"I don't want to go to school like this. Everyone will laugh at me."

A new idea popped into Madeline's head. "Then you can stay at home, and I'll be your teacher." She'd inform the school that because of the bullying, she was forced to remove her from their care. She was sure there was some kind of body she needed to inform and they'd give her the syllabus for home schooling, but it would be fine.

She stared at the steel doors of the lift, her daughter's reflection murky, marred by scratches. It resembled Poppy's new personality, obscure on one hand and pitted by feeling sorry for herself on the other, but this was how things were now, and Madeline wouldn't back down. Kevin had to learn to step up to the plate, and short of killing Poppy, Madeline would jolly well make sure he toed the line.

No matter the cost.

CHAPTER THIRTY-ONE

Leeds

The city was buzzing, even though it was early. So many people compared to Scudderton. Nathan had used the card twice so far, and the machine hadn't declined the sales. It was a Santander card, and they were a bugger for asking for PINs every so often after a flurry of contactless payments, so he paid for the next lot of stuff by using the keypad.

By half nine, he'd spent five hundred quid.

He stopped for breakfast at a café, shocked at it being served in a polystyrene container instead of on a plate. The sight of the plastic knife and fork was another stunned moment, but he supposed it saved on the washing up. Still, it was weird, but the full English was nice enough, only it wouldn't set him up for the rest of the day. He left there and went into Greggs, buying a sausage and bacon baguette and a cup of tea. He sat outside and ate, feeding the waiting starlings, contemplating life and the two roads open to him at the moment.

It felt good to be by himself, no Mam, no bugging sister and no Bestie. He'd definitely be leaving Scudderton, he was going stale there, but time wasn't on his side at the minute. He'd have to stay for a while longer.

The moment of clarity with Herbie had given him another option. Hurting animals was the easiest way to assuage his pain, but he hadn't considered an alternative route. Of shirking the cycle of abuse and being a kind person instead, not becoming a version of Mam but being better than her, showing he *could* make something of himself even though she'd said he couldn't.

He'd still have to pickpocket, keep her happy for a while yet, but once he could walk away, he'd be doing it. Maybe he could reach out to Dad and get to know him. He lived in Leeds . . .

Could Nathan leave Scudderton sooner than he'd thought?

He took his phone from his pocket, the starlings wandering off now his baguette was all gone, one of them bold enough to walk right into Greggs only to get shooed out by a customer. He plugged Dad's work address into Google Maps, studying the route.

Would Dad welcome him, though, that was the thing. Mam had said he was a waste of space, a loser, but Nathan only had her word for it. He couldn't remember a time when Dad had lived with them, he'd only been three when he'd walked out, but surely he'd want to see his kids if they turned up on his doorstep, wouldn't he?

Nathan found a public toilet in the Trinity shopping centre and put on the new tracksuit and trainers. At least he'd make a good impression then. Dad would be at work, he was a "fancy-arsed solicitor", and his office wasn't far away.

Nathan was going to do it, break free from Mam, and his only sadness at leaving Scudderton was not being able to see his new pal, Herbie.

How weird that a dog he'd wanted to hurt had so quickly and easily snuggled into his emotions.

* * *

Dad didn't look like the photos Mam had of him. He clearly had some money, and they sat in his Porsche in the office car park, both of them staring out of the windscreen. It was a tad odd, not knowing the bloke, but Nathan would pretend he was at ease, that he was a good kid, someone Dad would want around.

"I'm glad you came," Dad said.

"She doesn't know I'm here."

Dad laughed wryly. "I bet she doesn't. I take it you didn't want to face her bawling you out if you'd told her."

"No."

"You don't have to stay there, you know. There was always the option to come to me."

"She never said that. She reckoned you didn't want to know."

Dad sighed. "I see this every day in cases at work. Some women like to play games, to control, and they use their children to do it. Did you know we had shared custody but she never let me take you off for weekends?"

Nathan hadn't known that, but something bothered him. "You're a solicitor, so you know how it works. Why didn't you take her to court?"

"She became ill. I didn't want to add to the burden."

"So you walked away? Took the easier option?"

"I'm ashamed to say I did. Can we fix that now?"

Nathan nodded. "I'll never forgive you for not pushing, for not getting us taken away from her. She's off the charts with how mental she is."

"In what way?"

"She's got me stealing off people at the pier."

"*What?*" Dad twisted in his seat and gawped.

"I've been doing it since I was about eight. And she shoots me with a BB gun."

"Jesus Christ! You poor kid. I had no idea."

"To be fair, you wouldn't. You weren't around."

Dad winced. "I deserved that."

"Yep."

"What about Chantal?"

"She's the golden girl, always has been. She doesn't know half of what goes on now she's in her own flat. I look like you too much, so Mam takes her shit out on me."

"You're coming home with me, I'm not having this. She can say whatever she likes, but it has to stop. I thought . . . look, I thought she was caring for you properly. Had I known she wasn't . . ."

"I get it." Time for a confession. "My life is shit. I've been bad." Nathan wanted to test him, to see if he was still wanted if Dad knew the truth.

"Bad?"

"Killing cats and stuff."

Dad paled. "Fuck, *you're* the Cat Killer?"

Nathan shrugged. News must have spread from Scudderton already. "It was just . . . I couldn't . . . I didn't have any control."

"What, of whether you killed cats? Or in your life in general?"

"Both."

"You need help. Will you let me get it for you? No one needs to know about the cats, okay?"

Nathan thought about Herbie. "There's this dog . . ."

"Jesus, please don't tell me you killed that as well."

"No, it's mine. Well, it's a stray." *Liar.* "I've been feeding it, looking after it. I'd need to go back and get it."

"Then I'll take you this afternoon."

"Don't you have to be at work?"

"Some things are more important."

Like me? For the first time, Nathan knew what it felt like to be the number one priority. Tears fell, and he cuffed them away.

"All right." He sniffed. "What's this help you were on about?"

"Therapy."

"God . . ."

"I know, but you need to get seen. If you like killing animals, that's not good, you know that, don't you?"

Nathan nodded. The problem was, he liked it a bit too much and wondered whether therapy would even work. Could someone as broken as him be fixed?

CHAPTER THIRTY-TWO

Seaview Heights

Kevin had got up early so he could go and see Mam before his ChatSesh meeting. Life was all go at the moment, his social media platform having taken off big time, vying for the top spot. Eliza, his girlfriend (one in a long line of many, admittedly), was a keeper. He'd decided on that once he'd taken her to Mam's and they'd got along so well. Plus, Eliza didn't mind how much time he spent with his mother, whereas women in the past had complained. He'd moved Eliza into his new house, saw no reason to wait. When you knew, you knew, and he was madly in love. She was so different to Madeline and the others, eager to try everything life had to offer, and she wasn't interested in holding him back or clipping a ball and chain to his ankle.

Unlike his ex-wife, the lying bitch.

Christ, she'd put him through the wringer after Poppy had been born, all that depression she thought she was hiding, but it'd stuck out something rotten. Gone was the effervescent woman, exchanged for some kind of emo. She'd moped around, moaned about everything under the sun, so no wonder he'd gone elsewhere for a bit of light relief. At first it was to have sex, something she'd declined to do, claiming the stitches down below were the culprit and she was too tired from looking after a newborn Poppy and the house, which was a joke, because as far as he saw, she hadn't done much cleaning.

Their home had been a state, and she hadn't bothered showering, although he couldn't fault her with the baby, who was always bathed. A few months later she'd bucked her ideas up, and he couldn't disagree with her statement in court, she *had* helped him build his business, which was why she was entitled to that lump sum, and he paid her a top-end wage for doing nothing, to ensure she didn't go without.

It was a good job he *did* pay her really. She couldn't work, she'd had to give up her nursing career, what with looking after Poppy, who was a massive bone of contention between them. She'd become ill after he'd left — and his reason for leaving hadn't been to get his end away whenever he wanted to, despite what Madeline claimed. He'd had a DNA test done on the quiet, and Poppy wasn't his. Yes, he paid child support and had set up a fund for her — which in hindsight he shouldn't have done — but after a few months of visiting her and taking her out, he hadn't been able to stomach the deception. He'd been playing the father role when it was someone else's responsibility.

He'd confessed this recently to Eliza, who'd told him off.

"It doesn't matter that you're not her biological father, she *thinks* you are. It's not her fault, yet she's been punished for it. Can you imagine how she feels?"

"I know," he'd said, "but I can't stand to look at her. She's *his*, and it's so obvious."

That was who he suspected, anyway. Poppy resembled that man so much. Every one of her features was his; she even had the same hair colour. The truth had slammed him in the face one night when Madeline had been drunk, drinking a whole bottle of wine to herself while he was out. Kevin had been to the Devil for a few, coming back quietly so he didn't wake his wife or child, but Madeline hadn't been asleep, she'd been on the phone, slurring her words.

* * *

"I think he's going to leave me. He's cheating, I know it, and if he does go, you need to do your duty."

Kevin paused at the kitchen doorway, watching her through the gap by the hinges. She tugged at her hair, her face showing either anger or desperation, he couldn't work out which. His heart thudded too hard, and he tried to fathom what she'd meant by someone doing their duty.

"What are you on about, you don't know what I'm saying? Ian, she's yours, you prat. I'm surprised you never twigged . . . When was it? Can't you even remember? The last night of uni, that party . . . You did not wear a condom, so don't you even go there, you bastard."

Ian Johann? Fucking hell.

The last night at uni. Kevin had sensed something was off about her when she'd got back. They'd been married a year by then, and he'd known her since they were teens so had a fair idea of her moods and what they meant. She'd come home, acting shifty, having a shower, which was unlike her. Normally, she fell into bed if she'd had a few and didn't surface until lunchtime the next day.

"So you're not interested in helping to bring her up? Because I can tell you now, if Kevin leaves, he'll make sure there's a wedge between us, an excuse not to see Poppy. He's never really taken to her. What do you mean that's a stupid name? You cheeky shit!"

Kevin reeled, flattening himself against the hallway wall. It made sense now, why he hadn't bonded with Poppy. They weren't even related, and yes, it was a stupid name, he'd never liked it.

"So not only don't you care that you weren't in her life, you don't care whether Kevin is either?" A pause. "Of course I couldn't tell you back then, Kevin would have found out." Another pause. "No, it won't be awkward, and he won't know why you're coming round. We were friends and can be again. I'll make out you're here as a mate. That way you can watch her grow up. I'm not going to be telling her who you are, but you can guide her, be part of her life."

Kevin felt sick.

"What do you mean, you should have been given the chance earlier? How was I meant to do that, eh? What, you expected me to just walk up to Kevin and announce I'd shagged you behind his back? Ha, that would have gone down so well . . ."

Kevin swallowed. He was guilty of messing around so could hardly talk, but he hadn't started doing it until the child had come along. Madeline had done it way before that, and he didn't like how that truth stung.

He'd have to go. Leave. Make a clean break after a few months of being gone, easing out of Poppy's life bit by bit.

He couldn't bring up another man's child.

* * *

"Are you okay?" Eliza came to stand beside him at the kitchen island and rubbed his arm, her concern evident by the way it twisted her eyebrows.

Kevin bit back his anger. It still hurt even now, Madeline's deception, but he wouldn't take it out on his girlfriend. She didn't deserve to have him ranting and raving about a woman he couldn't stand. Eliza was so mature for her age, showing him the other side of many coins, making him a better person, trying to help him come to terms with what had happened. Eliza was right — ignoring her was unfair and would likely have a detrimental effect on her well-being. That was no longer his problem, but the guilt still prickled. He saw her from time to time, from afar, Madeline pushing her along in a wheelchair — that poor kid hadn't fared well in life — and all he saw was Ian's face, his eyes, his mouth, his nose.

"I was just thinking about . . . about her," he said, hating himself for once again visiting a past he couldn't change. ChatSesh's mantra was to look to the future, eyes always forward, and he could do with taking his own advice.

"Which one?" She rested her head on his chest and wrapped her arms around him.

He propped his chin on the top of her head, loving how she was always so affectionate, never shutting him out. "Both of them really, but mainly Madeline. It's just struck me how sick she is, taking Poppy to see Ian of all people. Firstly, it wouldn't be ethical for him to treat his own child, so what the hell had she been *thinking*?"

"Maybe you need to tell Madeline you know. This is eating you alive."

"What, and get into a slanging match with her? It'd end up being my fault as to why she went with Ian. There'd be some excuse. I did go to the pub a lot, granted, but so did she. We had no child then, we still had friends of our own we went out with. She'd find some way to lay it all at my door."

"From what you've told me, she sounds a bit unhinged, if I'm honest."

"That's an understatement."

Eliza's phone bleeped, and she took it out of her pocket and accessed the message. "God . . ."

Kevin's heart jolted. "What's the matter? Is it another hate email?"

"No, a text this time."

"I knew people would come after us because of ChatSesh. I said so, didn't I? What have they said?"

She sighed. "Well, it seems you were right when I got the emails, they *don't* like me being with you."

Eliza turned her screen around so he could read it.

I'm watching. I'm waiting. He's mine, and you're going to die, you ginger bitch. The hourglass is almost empty . . .

"Bloody hell!" Kevin snatched the phone and called the message sender back, but the phone was switched off. Then a snide thought blindsided him. "This has *got* to be Madeline."

Eliza laughed. "What? No! Why would she care if we're together? She didn't bother any of your other girlfriends, did she?"

"No, but . . ."

"Listen to me. It's just some weirdo who managed to get hold of my number. This is my work phone, remember, and it's on the ChatSesh website. Anyone could find it."

Kevin calmed a little. She was right. Eliza was his secretary and on the masthead. “Okay, fine, but if you get any more, tell me, and I’ll get hold of the police.”

She kissed his cheek. “The world is full of nutters, babe.”

“I know, and that’s what I’m worried about. My ex-wife is one of them.”

* * *

Parsley Avenue

Kevin used his key and entered Mam’s. The first thing that was iffy was the heating on full whack and there was no smell of bacon and eggs — she always made him a full English when he visited — and second, the silence. Worried she was ill, because she tended to get up at about six and clearly wasn’t now, he went straight upstairs.

He paused at the top. “Mam?”

Her bedroom door was shut, so he knocked. With no sound, no voice telling him to come in, he opened it. A waft of hot, putrid-smelling air hit him in the face. He automatically glanced at the window, which wasn’t open, and that explained the higher temperature in there. It had been a warm night for autumn, and with the door closed, the heating on . . .

He switched his attention to the bed.

“Oh God! Fuck! *Fuck!*”

Bile rose, and he flung himself back against the rails on the landing, the hard edge of the banister digging into his spine. Staring at the bed, he couldn’t get his mind to accept what he was looking at. Blood, loads of it, dark, not bright red. Mam, completely still. Something sticking out of the space between her eyes.

Was that a *chisel*?

He didn’t go in, couldn’t bear to be near the blood, and he *hated* himself for it, that he didn’t have the balls to check for a pulse, his phobia of blood taking over. Sweat broke out, sending his body clammy, and he had to get away, from the sight, the stench.

He staggered along the landing to the end, leaning on the wall beside the bathroom and patting his pocket for his phone, his mind whirling with what must have happened. Someone had broken in and killed her. Was it his fault? Someone angry at him for ChatSesh rising so quickly and almost taking over the other platforms?

He pulled his phone out, and the stupid thing didn't recognise his face. He relaxed his screwed-up features and tried again. This time, it let him in, and he prodded the phone icon in the bottom panel, selecting the keypad. It seemed to take for ever to dial 999, each poke in slow motion, and when he lifted it to his ear, the phone weighed a ton.

Someone spoke to him, and he answered, although what he said, he didn't know, he couldn't hear himself over the rushing in his ears. He sank to the carpet, knees apart, elbows propped on them, and listened to the person talking, then he replied, all the while listening to the sound of an angry sea swirling in his mind, the image of a chisel in his mother's head paramount.

"Take a deep breath, sir . . ."

Kevin puked.

CHAPTER THIRTY-THREE

Parsley Avenue

Carol thought about Joy's suggestion — older people being targeted. It was the same initial theory as with the Mason Ingram case, but it hadn't quite turned out to be true there. But here? A look into her details showed Gail Cotter was sixty-five, she wasn't *that* old.

She remained on the landing with Dave. Inside the horrific bedroom, the stink of death awful, the heat finally dissipating since someone had turned the thermostat off, Rib stood on a step on one side of the double bed, Todd on the other. A photographer snapped images of the bedside table — blood spatter, most likely. It had painted the walls with freckles, once red, now almost black. Todd and his team would be able to determine where the killer had stood, perhaps how tall they were.

"I was only joking when I said a chisel would be next," Dave said. "I didn't actually expect one to be sticking out of her."

Rib chuckled. "If I didn't know you better, I'd say *you* were the killer."

"Oh, behave. He was with me," Carol said, "so shut your cakehole."

Rib tutted. "Like I'd ever really think it was our Dave."

Todd sighed, groaning at the same time. "Someone's definitely going through a toolbox."

"Not necessarily one person, though. Gail could be unrelated to the others. Have you looked underneath her yet?" Carol asked.

Rib shook his head. "No, I was waiting for the photos of her in this position to be done. I'll put her on her side now. I'm going to lift her nightshirt and check her skin for other wounds, so look away if you like."

She did, turning her back to stare at a large pine-framed print on the wall halfway up the stairs. A view of the sea from the beach at Cove if she wasn't mistaken, one of the hidden bays, the rocks crowding either side of the canvas, on the right a familiar crag topped with high grass and a splodge of gorse. It had been done in oil paints, the style where a palette knife could have been used to create a 3D effect. The waves stood out, the paint thick below the white spume of each crest.

"All done," Rib said.

Carol faced the room, aware she ought to be leaving soon. The son, Kevin Cotter, waited for her with the neighbour next door. Richard was doing door-to-door enquiries with a couple of other uniforms, and a private carer called Yasmeen, who came to massage Gail twice a week due to arthritis, had been refused entry by Kevin after he'd phoned for help. She currently sat in her car.

Rib held Gail, who now rested on her side.

"A mallet," Dave said. "Aww, fuck, I bet that was used to hit the chisel."

Carol zeroed in on the bed. The mallet had a newish-looking wooden handle and a black rubber rectangle on the end. It would have to be weighted with something inside for the chisel to have gone so deep. Only about an inch of the blade was visible. She imagined someone raising the mallet high, bringing it down, and a chill wiggled up her spine.

Were the tools a clue, or was it a simple case of someone opting to use them because they were close to hand? Like she'd intimated to Todd, there might be two killers, and the fact they'd happened to choose tools was a coincidence.

Todd removed the mallet and bagged it, and Rib returned Gail to her original position.

"So she had the chisel wound to the neck first?" Carol couldn't see any other wounds.

"I'd say so, Bird. Rigor has set in, although we could have a skewed timeline here — this room was hot, and with the door and window shut, temperature can affect things. Heat provides a good environment for the bacteria, see, so everything speeds up . . . Also, if she struggled with her killer, as indicated by the bottom sheet being ruffled, rigor could set in immediately."

"How come?" Dave asked.

"Cadaveric spasm."

"Well, that helps me a lot . . ." Dave's sarcasm hung heavy.

Rib laughed. "Okay, I'll explain it for you. At the moment of death, had she been fighting for her life, her muscles would have been depleted of oxygen, bringing on instant rigor."

"Any signs of owt beneath her fingernails?" Carol asked.

"No, but she does have blood on her palm as if she held something bloody. Going back to what we were discussing, her age is a factor, too. Rigor progresses swiftly in the elderly and children. In short, the time of death with all of the victims so far is a broad estimate. In Gail's case, we might not have the usual two hours on top for rigor to get going. The factors here all point to a faster onset — heat, age, a possible struggle. From the feel of her, though, I'm saying yesterday evening at some point."

"Right." Carol imagined a neighbour must have seen someone if it was early enough. Evening was from 6 p.m. onwards. People would have been coming home from work around then, but if it was later . . .

Rib continued. "Gail and Clem weren't discovered until the next morning, and post-mortem hypostasis showed they'd remained in place since death." He must have clocked Dave's frown. "Lividity, the pooling of blood at the lowest point — they died in the position they were found. Gail has it on her back, her buttocks, the backs of her legs. Clem's was on his front. The blood spatter patterns here already tell us she died in this bed, but the lividity confirms it."

Carol thought about that for a second. "So she either didn't have time to get out of bed and run or she was placed in it prior to death."

Todd nodded. "Whatever happened, it's sickening."

Carol agreed. Who wouldn't, apart from the killer?

Dave nudged her. "Maybe she let the person in. She could have known them, but then again, she might not have and they forced their way in once she'd opened the door."

Carol blew out a long breath, creating heat inside her mask. "Was owt stolen, Todd?"

"We don't know yet. I said to the son we'd show him pictures of the rooms. He might be able to tell from those. I made an appointment to do that with him later. He's a tad distraught at the minute, as you can imagine. The vomit on the landing is his."

Carol would like to have said "Poor bloke" but wouldn't until she'd spoken to him, got a feel for him. The tools *could* be a coincidence and this case was nothing to do with Clem and Frank. Maybe this Kevin fella had got pissed off with his mother and decided to kill her.

She sent a message to the incident room to get the team to find out about any life insurance policies. Money was a good motive.

Carol mentally prepared herself to visit Kevin, but first, she'd speak to the carer.

* * *

Yasmeen Hollington was around thirty with wide blue eyes. Her bright-blonde hair perched on her crown in a bun, curly tendrils swaying by her cheeks in the breeze, and she folded her arms over a light-blue nurse's tunic and leaned against the driver's-side door of her red Ford. The street had been cordoned off close to Gail's home, the tape far enough away either side so neighbours couldn't hear any conversation between them.

"Tell me a bit about Gail," Carol said, scuffing her freshly bootied foot on the road.

She'd removed her protective clothing at Gail's front door and placed new shoe covers on so she didn't contaminate the street. SOCO were working out here, looking for blood spots or any other evidence the killer may have left behind as they'd fled the scene.

Yasmeen pulled a pained face. "She's got arthritis, finds it difficult to move, so I'm here today and Thursdays every week to massage her joints. Kevin pays me. He also pays me to visit his daughter, although that's mainly babysitting while she's asleep, and his ex-wife contacts me directly for that."

"What's up with the daughter?"

"She's been sickly, had a few issues with bacterial infections — I didn't ask for specifics — and now she's in a wheelchair. Something to do with her legs."

That pinged Carol's "quirk of fate" radar, although a few people in Scudderton used a wheelchair. Then the surname hit her. Cotter. Margaret or something, wasn't it? She'd introduced herself on the pier. "What's the ex-wife's name?"

"Madeline."

That's it. "Did she have owt to do with Gail since the divorce?"

"Not that I know of. Kevin left Madeline to, err, mess about with other women. I only know that because Madeline said. I don't like being told private things, but she's one for getting her point across about him."

"Has she got a gripe with him?"

"Only the sort that goes on when you get divorced."

Carol understood that. Dave had gripes with his ex. "Did you babysit for her last night?"

"No."

"The night before that?"

"No."

Didn't Madeline say she'd been to the Devil the night Clem died?

Carol shrugged internally. So what if she had? She could have taken her daughter with her. She'd find out more regarding Madeline's relationship with Gail from Kevin.

"What's Madeline like in general?" Carol asked.

"If you're wondering whether she'd have killed Gail, the answer is no. She's never said a bad word about her to me, and besides, she's not the type. She's devoted to Poppy and spends all her time looking after her. I doubt very much she'd leave her alone to come here and do *that*."

Satisfied with what she'd said, Carol finished up the conversation and jerked her head at Dave for him to follow her to Gail's next-door neighbour's place once he'd finished filling Yasmeen in on procedure.

Carol waited for him on the pavement, gearing herself up to have the difficult conversation with Kevin. If he wasn't the killer, he'd have had a dreadful shock at seeing his mother like that. No wonder he'd been sick.

Or was that guilt, the trauma of coming back to the scene when calmer, seeing what he'd done?

Dave approached. "What about sending a uniform round to Madeline Cotter's to get her alibi on record."

"Good idea, it saves us doing it when we've got a lot on our plate today." She called Richard over and asked him to arrange that. "Maybe send Alan?"

"Will do." Richard lifted a hand then dropped it at his side, a sign of defeat. "Early news about the neighbours is that no one saw or heard owt."

"What a surprise . . ."

"I've had a look at Kevin's phone and car GPS. All seems fine there."

"Thanks."

At the neighbour's door, Carol knocked, Dave beside her. A woman of about seventy answered and, upon seeing their ID, she gestured for them to go inside.

"Two seconds." Carol slipped her booties off, taking Dave's from him then handing them to a forensic tech who'd caught her eye from Gail's garden. They had spare pairs in their pockets for when they came back out. Who knew whether the killer had hopped over the garden divide and left anything behind.

Carol followed the lady into a neat, all-beige living room with freshly polished floors, and kept her attention away from Kevin, who sat on the sofa. She left it to Dave to assess him visually.

"Would you like tea?" their host asked.

"Sorry, I didn't ask your name." Carol smiled.

"Olive Earl."

God, for a second there, I thought she said olive oil. "Thanks, and yes, tea would be lovely."

Olive appeared awkward. "Do I leave it by the door or . . . ?"

"That would be great. Just give us a knock and pop it outside."

Olive wandered out, closing them in, and Carol finally turned her gaze to Gail's son. He was dark-haired, broad in the chest, and she recognised him. The man who owned ChatSesh. She cursed herself for not registering his name. He'd been on the news recently as his platform offered much more privacy compared to others, and he'd signed an agreement that his bots would never target users' browsing history to throw adverts at them, nor did his company listen in to private conversations via devices, something other platforms strenuously denied went on. But maybe he was the same as them, a liar, saying all this to lure people away from their current social media preference, thinking his was better.

Carol sat on a leather armchair with a flowery throw cushion, big pink pompoms all around the edge, one of them pushing into her back. Dave remained by the door. She'd say he was on tea watch, but he preferred to block any exits if he felt the need. Today, he clearly did. Kevin was a beefy man.

"Kevin Cotter?" she confirmed.

"Yes." Kevin cleared his throat. "Have you caught them yet?"

Carol had to stop herself from laughing wryly. How quick did he imagine the police worked? "An investigation like this takes time." She didn't tell him it could be days, weeks or months. "We have to speak to a lot of people, build up a picture of your mother and her movements. As she was killed last night, the person responsible could be miles away by now. Sorry to sound harsh, but I won't sugar-coat owt, it isn't fair to give you false hope."

"I appreciate that."

She smiled, glad he didn't bark at her and moan that while she was here talking to him, time was ticking by. "Tell me about yesterday."

Kevin frowned, his lips pursing. "What's that got to do with owt?"

Carol linked her hands. "Not only do we need to build a picture of your mother, but we also do it for people close to her. Olive will be spoken to as well. You own ChatSesh, yes?"

He paled. "Oh shit, you don't think . . . ?"

"It's possible, yes, that someone got to her because of you. *However* . . ." She held up a hand to stop him asking numerous questions. If his clouded face was anything to go by, he had a few sitting on his tongue. "We're also working on two other murders, and your mother's death could be linked to those."

Kevin processed that, his forehead crinkling. What must it be like to contemplate his mother was possibly one of three?

"I heard about Clem." He relaxed, sitting back in a slump.

"Did your mother know him well?"

"No. Everyone round here *knows* him because of the Ferris wheel, but we didn't have owt to do with him socially. Mam never told me any stories about him like you do when you're friends with someone. Who's the other one?"

"Frank West from the Odeon."

"Bloody hell . . ." His cheeks inflated, and he pushed air out, shaking his head.

"Something wrong?"

"No, it's just a shock. Who'd kill *him*? He was too nice to be bumped off."

Carol wouldn't argue with that. "Did you or your mother have much to do with him?"

"No. At least Mam never said owt. I knew him because of the sweets."

"We heard about that. A kind man. Okay, so, back to yesterday. What did you do?"

He scraped a hand down his face. "I know what you really want to ask, so why not just come straight out with it?"

"Fair enough. Where were you last night?"

"At a ChatSesh charity ball in Robin Hood's Bay."

"Where exactly?"

He gave her the address. "I got there at five and stayed until around two in the morning with my girlfriend and other members of staff cleaning the function room up a bit. I'd paid for the cleaners at the hotel to do it, but I didn't like the amount of mess left behind."

So he has a good heart? "What made you do that?"

"Mam was a cleaner for years." He shrugged as though no more words were needed.

"I see. So you wanted to make life easier for them."

"Yes. It was a pig state, it wasn't right to leave it like that."

"What time did you get home?"

"Half past three." He bit his lip.

Carol worked out the timing. It was dodgy. "You said you stayed at the hotel until around two . . . The drive home, given that the roads would have been empty, is around fifteen minutes, so what happened to the other hour and fifteen?"

He blushed. "We, err, we stopped off."

"We?"

"Me and my girlfriend."

"Where?"

"A lay-by."

Carol had an idea, but she needed him to say it. "For . . . ?"

He grunted. "Christ. Sex. Will I get into shit for it? I can't be doing with that sort of publicity."

"We won't be announcing it to all and sundry if that's what you're worried about, but a prominent man such as yourself . . . I'd suggest not visiting lay-bys again unless you've broken down."

He flushed red.

Carol felt for him, but bloody hell, for someone like him to take a risk like that . . . "Which lay-by was it?"

He explained, and Carol smiled internally. ANPR cameras were on that road, so they'd be able to find out if he was lying. "Excuse me for one second."

She used her phone to message Michael and get him on that job.

She gave Kevin her focus again. "Where do you live?"

"Seaview Heights. It's on one of the clifftops."

"I know it. I've been there. A beautiful house."

Her mind drifted to Gary Cuttersby. His wife had been killed. He'd lived at the house after her death but had now moved away. She made a mental note to get someone to speak to Willy and Lise next door, a quirky pair who'd been chatty when questioned before regarding the Cuttersby case. If they'd seen Kevin and his girlfriend arriving home, they'd be more than happy to say so.

"So, you went to bed," she prompted.

"Yes, me and Eliza."

"Your girlfriend? What's her surname?"

"Morris. I got up at eight. I have a ChatSesh thing this afternoon so wanted to nip and see Mam before that. I arrived at around nine, my GPS will confirm it because I have a new gadget installed that tracks all of my journeys — so I can claim mileage back. All my employees have one. I don't want them shelling out on petrol when it's to do with work."

Carol was warming to him more. A good boss was hard to find. "We'll want to take a proper look at that for elimination purposes."

"Someone already has. Think his name was Prince?"

"Okay, that's great, but I'd prefer to have someone go over it again."

"Do whatever you need to."

"So you arrived here and . . . ?"

He told her what had happened. "But I have no idea what I said to the woman on the phone. My mouth was working, but it was like my brain had taken me away from it all — make sense?"

"A coping mechanism. It's amazing what the mind does to help you manage the shock. Do you remember much after the call?"

"Yes, I went downstairs and straight outside, like the lady told me to. Yasmeen turned up, she's a carer, and I told her to stay back so she didn't get owt on her. I didn't go into the bedroom, so I don't think there was any blood on me, but I sank down the wall on the landing and was sick, so . . ." He gestured to the paper suit he had on. "Someone called Todd took my clothes and shoes."

"Right. Did you make any other calls?"

"No, that Prince fella checked my phone, so you can confirm it with him. I haven't even had a chance to tell Eliza what's happened."

Oh good. "I'd like to take your phone, too. Are you okay with that?"

"More than okay."

"Are you still going to the ChatSesh thing this afternoon?"

Kevin sighed. "Absolutely not. I'll send one of my managers."

"So you'll be home after you leave here?"

"Yes."

"What about Eliza?"

"She'll stay with me. She won't want to leave me on my own after this."

Carol moved forward. That bloody pompom was getting on her nerves. "Then we'll send an officer round to speak to her."

Kevin seemed puzzled. "What for?"

"To confirm your alibi." If Carol actioned it now, because Kevin claimed he hadn't spoken to her yet, he wouldn't have been able to coach her on what to say. Carol didn't believe he'd done anything, his account had been given sincerely, but she'd keep an open mind all the same. She glanced at Dave to let him know he could do the honours.

"There's something else that might be relevant." Kevin ran a hand through his hair.

Carol held her finger up to stop Dave leaving the room. "Go on."

"Eliza got a weird text message this morning, just before I came to Mam's. It went on about an hourglass, someone watching and waiting, and that she'd be dead."

Uneasy about this turn of events, Carol said, "We'll need to speak to her about this. It could be linked to your mother."

"That's what I'm worried about."

A knock on the door heralded the tea.

Dave opened up and brought a tray inside, placing it on the coffee table. "I'll just get someone to go and see Eliza."

Carol nodded. "Tell them to remain at the house for her safety until we get there."

Dave left the room.

Alone with Kevin, Carol asked, "Do you have another property you can stay in other than at Seaview?"

He nodded. "I have a few caravans. I think one of them is empty at the minute."

"Do many people know you own them?"

"No, only the park owner."

"Then after we've taken you home and spoken to Eliza, go and stay in one, and don't tell *anyone* where you are. Use a hire car. I'm concerned about that message, so better to be safe than sorry."

"Okay."

"What can you tell me about your ex-wife?"

He bristled with contempt, his top lip curling. "What about her?"

"How did she get along with your mam?"

He chuffed out a sound of derision. "She hasn't spoken to her since we split up. I thought Madeline would have kept in touch, they'd always got along, but no, she cut ties. In a way, I was glad. I didn't want Madeline nosing around, putting Mam in a difficult position."

"Any animosity there?"

"Absolutely not, on either side. They got along well."

"I meant with you."

"Oh. Well, I'd be lying if I said we'd parted on good terms."

"Would Madeline kill your mother to get back at you?"

"No, I can't see it, sorry."

They drank tea and discussed any enemies — for Gail *and* Eliza. Gail had none as far as Kevin knew, but it was clear *someone* had an issue with her. The question was, were the murders linked? The use of tools was the only common denominator here.

And another hole, the one in Gail's neck.

Katherine and Michael would be busy trying to find a strand that joined the deceased together, but what if nothing turned up?

"Eliza's a lovely woman," Kevin said. "I've never heard anyone get funny with her. At first, I thought the message was from some nutjob and they got Eliza's number off our website, but now Mam . . ." His lips quivered. "Christ, I can't believe she's gone."

"Do *you* have enemies?"

"Probably. Madeline hates me, but like I said, I can't see her doing this. And anyroad, where would Clem and Frank come into it?"

"I don't know. Maybe your mother's case is separate." She paused. "Who are your enemies?"

Kevin shrugged. "Take your pick. ChatSesh could draw any number of people."

Dave came back when the chatter had turned to Kevin's business, and they remained with him for another ten minutes while they drank their tea. She told him to stay put and they'd come for him soon.

Kevin appeared genuine, one of life's kinder people — his face had lit up whenever he'd spoken of his team and how he paid a full wage for a three-day week because he believed people coped better with lots of downtime, their concentration at its peak for the three days they were in the office. But as with all people she dealt with who'd committed hideous crimes, he could be a good actor.

He wasn't off the hook yet.

* * *

Outside, Richard called her name and waved her over to Gail's front gate. "We've found a toolbox in her shed," he said quietly. "There's blood on it."

Dave remained in the street while Carol followed Richard through to the back. She stood inside the doorway to the shed and inspected the toolbox without touching it. Pictures had already been taken, and a SOCO loitered, ready to bag it and take it down to the lab. The blood smear could have been deliberate, but it looked like someone had gone to take a slender hammer out then changed their mind. From the shape of the stain, a tech would be able to determine what had happened, but until then, she'd have to wait for any results. She'd bet her last quid the blood belonged to Gail, though.

She took a picture of the box, planning to show Kevin. She wanted to know if any tools were missing.

* * *

Carol stood on the street with Dave and Todd, going through what they'd learned so far.

"No forced entry on either the front or back door," Todd said, "although the back was unlocked."

"So the offender could have left that way," Carol said.

"Prints will determine that, but if they've got any sense about them, they'll have worn gloves." Todd gazed across at neighbours standing by the cordon, gossiping. "The blood on the hammer in the shed hasn't got fingerprint whorls, so yes, gloves. Any progress with the son?"

Carol stuck her hands beneath her armpits. "I doubt it was him. He was upfront with everything, even down to his antics in a lay-by, if you catch my drift."

Todd bobbed his head. "Richard checked Kevin's GPS and phone. All seems above board, but we can take the car and phone in for forensics if need be."

"Yes, do it," Carol said. "Best to cover our backs. I've already told Kevin anyroad. Oh, and I'll message you an address to visit him with the photos once I know it. There's been a development, and he won't be at home for a few days."

"A development?"

"Hmm, it seems his girlfriend might be another target."

* * *

Kevin encouraged everything the police were doing. If it meant finding out who'd done this to Mam, he was all for it. He could use his work phone for now as his personal one had been handed over to an officer. He wasn't going into work for a couple of days, needing time to come to terms with what had happened. His top-class managers knew how to run things, so ChatSesh was in safe hands. Some time holed up in a caravan would be perfect, although it disturbed him that they had to go. What if Eliza was in danger? What if *he* was?

He rested his head on the back of Olive's sofa, a sudden wave of lethargy coming over him. Probably the aftermath of the adrenaline rush.

"Can you tell me owt about this toolbox?" Wren showed him her phone.

He jolted from the shock. "Err, that's an old one of mine. What's it doing in Mam's shed?"

"Isn't it supposed to be there?"

"Um, no. I was *sure* I left it behind when I split with Madeline. Poppy was being a pest, following me around everywhere, and I just needed to go, so I didn't bother picking it up. Maybe I'm wrong. I'm trying to work out whether Mam asked for tools or owt and I dropped them off . . ."

"Is there owt missing from it?"

Kevin studied it closely, raking through his memory for the tools he'd bought during his marriage. "I barely used any of it, I'm not much of a DIY person, but Mam said everyone needed tools, just in case, so I went out and got them all in Homebase. There was a bigger hammer than the one in this picture, the claw type. And a wrench, the large kind. Oh, and a mallet. Wooden handle, rubber on the end." A great whoosh of nausea flooded his system. "Oh God, there was a chisel . . ." Panicked, he looked from Wren to her partner. "It wasn't me, I swear it. I haven't seen that toolbox for ages. Can you check with Madeline? Maybe she brought it here?"

"Is that likely?" Wren asked, thumbing a message on her phone.

"I don't know with her. Maybe she dumped a few things here after we split and Mam just didn't say. She wouldn't have wanted to upset me."

"You realise what this looks like, though, don't you?"

Kevin nodded. "I do, but Jesus Christ, why would I kill my own mother? Or *anyone's* mother, not to mention Clem and Frank."

Wren stared at him a bit too hard. "That's what we aim to find out."

"So am I going to be arrested?" God, this could ruin ChatSesh and everything he'd worked for. All those users who'd found a safe place to talk and share their lives might move on, not wanting to be associated with him. He'd started the platform to help people, and now it could all go tits up.

"We don't have any evidence it was you." Wren walked to the window. "Contrary to popular belief, we can't just go around arresting people willy-nilly. We have to wait until we have something that will stick. To be honest with you, just because your toolbox is in your mother's shed and some tools are missing, it doesn't mean you've been out on a rampage, does it? Where were you when Clem and Frank were killed?"

She gave him the times, and he told her where he'd been — ChatSesh events among hundreds of people. Both were being filmed for a documentary, so he was safe.

"I'm telling you, it wasn't me." He rubbed his temples, a headache forming.

"No, I don't think it was," Wren said.

He wondered whether she was supposed to say that out loud because she looked like she could bite her tongue off to stop herself from saying more.

"Come on, we may as well give you a lift home," she said. "As well as talking to Eliza, I want to speak to your neighbours."

He nodded, beyond caring about that when a murder charge could have been on the table. He stared though the window, tears falling, his heart breaking because his lovely mam was gone.

CHAPTER THIRTY-FOUR

Mrs Larkin's House

Nathan had asked Dad to park a couple of streets away, saying he'd be back as soon as he could. Head down, hood up, gloves on, he walked down the side of Mrs Larkin's house to her rear door and knocked on the glass. The old biddy looked up from her little dining room table, squinting. Herbie spotted him and ran up to the door, standing on his hind legs and smiling at him.

Tears pricked Nathan's eyes. Like Dad, Herbie was pleased to see him. It felt good to be wanted, and even though he'd have to go to therapy, his new life would be better than this one.

Mrs Larkin beckoned him in, so Nathan opened the door and bent to fuss a manic Herbie who whined and licked his face.

"You're early." She sounded grumpy today.

"Yeah, I had some spare time so . . ."

"You know where the lead is." Larkin returned to her crossword book.

Nathan seethed over her gruffness and walked into the hallway to collect the lead off the hook by the front door. He returned to the kitchen and clipped it to Herbie's collar, then took the dog out into the back garden and tied him to the leg of a wooden bench. He was unable to ignore the kill-burn inside him. Why had she been so off with him? He was fed up of being treated like a second-class citizen. Larkin couldn't live. She'd tell someone he'd stolen her dog, and the police might come looking for him.

Inside, he shut the door. "I'll make you a coffee before I go."

"Right."

He poured from a carafe and added milk and sugar. With his back to her, he spied a screwdriver on the worktop next to a blue roller blind in its packaging. Was she going to put it up herself? Or was she waiting for someone to come and fit it?

Shit, he'd better get a move on.

He pulled on a pair of thermal gloves he carried in his pocket, picked up the screwdriver and held it down by his side as he took the cup over to her. She didn't even say thanks. More anger surged. Behind her, he plunged the tool into the base of her neck beside what he imagined was her spine. Her scream was too loud, and he panicked. Nathan wrenched the screwdriver out and stabbed her back repeatedly, but she wouldn't shut up, garbling weird noises this time, groaning and whimpering. He had blood on his new tracksuit, and it really pissed him off, but thank God no one would see it on the black fabric. His lovely white trainers, though . . .

For fuck's sake, he couldn't have *anything* nice.

Larkin twisted, looking at him over her shoulder. He moved to stand at her left, and she followed his movement with her head. He jabbed the tool into the side of her neck — there was an artery or vein there, he was sure of it — and at last, she stopped making a racket. The screwdriver had plugged the hole, only a bit of blood trickled, so he yanked it out, jumping away to ensure he didn't get sprayed. Blood pumped, and he stared as it arced out and spattered on the floor. He tossed the tool onto the table and rushed to the sink, plunging his gloved hands into the sudsy washing-up water in the bowl. Then he legged it out into the garden, untied Herbie, and pelted down the side of the house, the dog yipping in excitement.

Nathan kept his head down and ran home, shitting himself at seeing a police car parked outside that weird woman's house, the one with the daughter in a wheelchair. He secured Herbie to the washing line pole out the back then stepped inside. Mam would be in the living room, and he had to pass it before he could go to his bedroom. She might see the blood on his trainers.

He risked it and jogged past, ignoring her question about why he was home and going upstairs. He took the tracksuit and trainers off, stuffing them in a backpack, annoyed he'd let his urges overtake him at Larkin's because now he'd ruined a really nice new outfit. Maybe he could wash them at Dad's when he was at work.

He changed, shouldered the backpack, and returned downstairs, pausing in the living room doorway.

"I'm going to live with Dad."

Mam laughed, a bag of peanut M&Ms beside her jolting with the movement, a couple of yellow sweets rolling out and settling in the gap between the seat cushions.

"You're going to kill yourself by eating all that sugar, and I'm glad," he said.

"Fuck the sweets. I'm more interested in how you think that waste of space is going to take you in."

"He's waiting for me in his car. It's a Porsche."

She snorted with derision. "A likely story."

"Whatever."

He strolled out, collected Herbie, and found Dad. Nathan opened the back door of the car, and Herbie hopped inside, circling then settling down. In the front seat, Nathan buckled up, stowing the backpack between his legs in the footwell.

"Ready?" Dad asked.

"Yeah."

"I see you changed clothes."

"Yeah, she took them to sell. And the trainers."

Dad shook his head. "She's a piece of work. I'll buy you some more."

His father drove away, and Nathan smiled. He wouldn't wash the tracksuit or trainers, he'd keep them at Dad's, tucked away somewhere. What would the blood smell like when it had dried?

Therapy. It wasn't going to do a damn thing in turning him around.

CHAPTER THIRTY-FIVE

Ridgebrook Close

A smug Madeline smiled at the officer sitting at her kitchen table. He'd been with her for a quarter of an hour so far and had interrupted her chat about the weather by going to the window and nosing outside. Now, he'd finally got to the point of his visit.

"A toolbox?" she said. "Kept here? Err, no. Kevin took everything he owned with him, apart from a few clothes." Things were going according to plan. She'd hoped the police would go down this route once they saw the blood on that hammer in the shed. They must have discovered it had belonged to Kevin. And they must have found Gail. She forced herself not to crack up laughing. "Why do you need to know?"

PC Alan Pitson stared at his notebook. "When was the last time you spoke to your ex-husband?"

"Oh, ages ago." She flapped a hand to dismiss it. "He's not interested in me and my daughter. He left us."

"Right. How do you get on with his mother?"

"Gail?" She hiked her eyebrows up so he'd think she was surprised he'd asked. "She's lovely."

"When did you last see her?"

Madeline pretended to ponder that. "It was before we split up. I didn't think Kevin would appreciate me going to visit her." She was safe from any prying eyes with Gail's neighbours. Madeline popped a hood and sunglasses on whenever she went there, Gail's idea. Neither of them wanted Kevin to find out about their chats over a cuppa. Gail had felt it would create strife.

Pitson consulted his notebook again. "I have it down here when you divorced. Was it an amicable parting?"

"Would *you* feel amicable if you found out your partner was having affair after affair? No, I was angry, but I've come to terms with it."

"How do you feel now he has a permanent girlfriend?"

"It's none of my business. If he wants to flit around with all those young redheads, I'm better off without him."

"Redheads?"

"Yes, he likes a ginger nut." She sipped some tea, wishing she had a different kind of ginger nut to dunk into it. A biscuit would go down well at the minute. "Am I allowed to say that these days?"

Pitson ignored her question. "Do you know of anyone who'd want to harm Gail?"

Madeline's tummy went over. This was all so exciting. They *must* have found her. "No. She's kind, hasn't got a bad word to say about anyone."

"Where were you last night?"

Having expected this question, she released a laugh, liking the way it sounded wry. "I'd like to say I was out dancing, having fun, but I was here with my daughter, as usual. She can't do owt without my help — she has to use a wheelchair — so me leaving her isn't a possibility."

He frowned. "I checked the files before coming here, and you told an officer that you visited the Little Devil the night before last. Did you have someone come in to sit with your daughter, seeing as you don't like leaving her?"

Oh God, she hadn't factored that in. "She went to a friend's for the evening. Um, why are you asking about Gail?

Has someone upset her? It'll be that ChatSesh, drawing all the crazies."

"Mrs Cotter was murdered last night."

Madeline had practised this bit in the mirror. "What?" She concentrated so her face didn't go red, thinking of other things to stop a blush forming. Rain drumming on an umbrella. A snowy landscape. "Oh my *God.* Was it Kevin? Did *he* do it?"

Pitson perked up. "Why would you think that?"

Now was her chance. She couldn't wait to spill the lie. "I remember him saying once that she was a pain in the backside, always butting her nose into his business, and he wished she'd . . . well, he said he wished she'd fuck off. I didn't agree, Gail was just being a concerned parent, but Kevin said if she died it would do him a favour."

"I see. And when was this?"

She told him. "Maybe he's been planning it all this time. Letting it fester."

"Where were you yesterday, around lunchtime?"

"In town. I had a carer here for Polly and spent some time browsing the shops. I'm sure I'll be on CCTV somewhere." She rushed on so he didn't dwell on that. "You mentioned his toolbox. What does that have to do with owt? Did he batter Gail with a hammer?" She trilled out another laugh. "Sorry, that was horrible of me."

Pitson cleared his throat. "What have you been doing today?"

"I've been here."

He asked her a few more questions about her movements, then thanked her for her time.

"Not a problem."

She saw him out and leaned on the closed door, chastising herself for not thinking things through properly. She'd almost messed everything up by telling the police she'd been to the pub. She'd been too desperate to give herself an alibi, but it might have backfired if she hadn't been quick on her feet and diverted the conversation with Pitson.

What if he came back and asked which friend Poppy had gone to see?

Shit.

Madeline got her coat on and grabbed her handbag. Poppy was out for the count. She'd been taught to inject herself for naps now, Madeline telling her it was medicine to fix her legs. She wanted her child to be more self-sufficient, and in a weird way, if Poppy was doing it to herself, Madeline couldn't get the blame.

But you're supplying her with the drugs . . .

Piss off.

Madeline had time to take a walk and get some fresh air to clear her head. She wrote a note for Poppy, telling her she'd be back by seven, and rushed upstairs to place it on the bedside table. Poppy wouldn't be able to get out of bed by herself, so that was okay. She had the remote control, so she could switch the telly on if she got bored, and if she wet herself, fine, that was what the nappies were for.

Yes, a long walk at Cove would sort Madeline out. The sea air had always given her clarity.

CHAPTER THIRTY-SIX

Seaview Heights

Sofia watched the ginger bitch from behind some bushes in Kevin's back garden. The ground floor had bi-fold doors which were closed, but Eliza sat in the dining area, putting on make-up in front of a mirror with bulbs all around it. There was a ChatSesh do later, so she was probably getting ready for that. Was the camera crew going to be there? It had been announced on the ChatSesh website that a documentary was being filmed about Kevin's rise to stardom, as it were, and she supposed he was lapping it up. She hated him for throwing her over, leaving her for redhead after redhead, finally settling on Eliza. He was disgusting the way he'd slept around, but Eliza had ensnared him. He seemed happy with her though. He must be if he'd stayed with her for the past six months.

Fancy shagging your secretary.

Sofia had memorised what she needed to and would come back later when she had perfected her plans. Kevin would need to be home, she wanted him to get the blame for it, but it was going to be difficult to kill his girlfriend if he interfered.

She hoped the text message had shit the silly cow up. Sofia had bought a cheap pay-as-you-go phone with money from the jar in the cupboard, topping it up with a tenner. She'd switched it off after sending those cruel words, then an hour later had turned it on again to see one missed call. Either Eliza or Kevin had phoned her.

Eliza stood and wandered upstairs, taking the mirror and make-up bag with her, and Sofia left the garden, careful to keep her head down as she walked along the street past two other large houses. She entered an estate and kept to the outskirts, planning to catch a bus home. She had to change her clothes. Nigel had texted to ask if she'd like lunch in Whitby, and at first she'd declined, but she'd agreed in the end.

She could do with something to take her mind off things.

CHAPTER THIRTY-SEVEN

Seaview Heights

Carol would never get used to the opulence of this place, how awe-inspiring it was, how the view was perfect no matter the weather: the stretch of sea out the front, the expanse of sky. If she concentrated hard enough and narrowed her vision while looking at the vista, she could almost believe she was alone here, not on business but taking a holiday.

It was a rich person's house, the kind she'd never live in unless she won the lottery, all open-plan space and mod cons. The downstairs was one big room sectioned off into living, kitchen and dining. The glass ceiling at the front of the ground floor was the best feature. It must be lovely to stare at the stars.

The PC who had come to check Eliza's alibi had gone. Carol walked to the dining area at the back and sat at the table with Dave, Kevin and Eliza, coffees on coasters and a plate of shortbreads beside a black sculpture of an armless, hairless woman in a dress. Carol dreaded to think how much it had cost and worried she'd knock it somehow and break the bloody thing.

She put her hands in her lap, tucking her elbows in. "First, can I have the address of the caravan you'll be going to, please, so Todd Butcher can visit you with the photos of your mam's house later? It's important we rule out a burglary gone wrong at this stage. With the back door open, we can only assume she forgot to lock it and the person entered that way."

"She was always forgetting, said her street wasn't the sort scallies came to, but now we know different, don't we?" Kevin sniffed. "I warned her time and again, told her she was vulnerable living alone. I even offered to buy her a place with better security, but she said she didn't want that, preferring to stay there. I wish I'd put my foot down now, but that would mean forcing her, and I just couldn't do it. If your mam's been good to you, you don't get nasty with her, do you?"

Carol didn't remember much about her mother, only highlights, the memories fading over the years, but she did recall how nice she was, and no, she wouldn't have been nasty to her either. "I'm so sorry. It sounds like you were lucky with your mam."

"She was the best," he choked out.

Eliza reached over and held his hand.

Carol pushed on. "Would you know if owt had been taken?"

"Yes, she asked me to help her with the cleaning from time to time, and I lived there during my childhood, so everything's familiar. She wouldn't even let me get a cleaner in for her, said she'd heard about a theft from some woman with Fox in her name, and she didn't want it happening to her."

Carol wasn't going into that. The thief in question had outwitted the team, and it still rankled. "How come she let Yasmeen go there, then?"

"It took a while for me to persuade Mam, but once Yasmeen had been, she said she felt much better." He paused. "Will the photos show the inside of the cupboards, too?"

"They will."

He gave her the address of the caravan, and she messaged it to Todd with an explanation.

"Okay, Eliza, let's crack on. I need to see that text, plus I want the phone number so we can try to trace where the SIM was purchased."

Eliza handed it over. "I've removed the passcode. It's my work phone, so I'll need it back soon." She glanced at Kevin. "I'll have to email the documentary people."

"I'll need to speak to them too." She asked Eliza for their details, and Dave jotted them down. "Going back to your phone: you can keep hold of it as long as you don't delete anything. Actually, even then, digi forensics will be able to retrieve it." Carol wanted them to know that if they were hiding something, it was pointless.

She opened the offending text.

I'm watching. I'm waiting. He's mine, and you're going to die, you ginger bitch. The hourglass is almost empty for you . . .

"Lovely," she said dryly. "So, let's dissect this for a moment. The first two sentences are obvious. Have you seen anyone hanging around or felt like you're being watched? Either of you?"

Kevin laughed, but it was obvious he didn't find anything funny. "I've had a film crew following me around for a while now, so yes, but as to anyone outside of that environment, no, everything's been normal."

Eliza nodded. "The same for me. We're too busy to have noticed owt like that, always flitting from one place to another. We hardly get time to breathe."

Carol sipped some coffee. "Kevin, I'm going to need a list of women you've been with since you left Madeline. Addresses, too."

"Err, there are a few."

"It doesn't matter. They all need speaking to. One of them could have sent that text."

He turned to Dave and reeled off ten names and where the ladies lived. Dave wrote them down, got up, and walked to the front of the living area. Carol assumed he was phoning Richard.

She moved on. "Right, would any of those have it in them to want to kill Eliza?"

"No! They weren't long-term affairs. I took them on dates, got to know them for a bit and realised they weren't for me. All were nice enough."

"So none of them displayed any behaviour that brought up red flags?"

He shrugged. "A couple were whiny when I finished things, and one was persistent in sending me texts to get me to change my mind." He told her one of the names. "But they certainly weren't red flags, just emotions getting in the way. What I don't get is, I've been with Eliza for six months, so why is someone doing this now?"

"Maybe *because* it's been six months. She could have waited to see if it fizzled out like the others. When it didn't, it tipped her over the edge." Carol called out to Dave, "Can you send that phone number so the team can get on with tracing it?"

He nodded.

"Now to the last bit, about the hourglass." Carol looked at Eliza. "You realise what this implies, don't you?"

"Yes, which is why I'm more than happy to go to the caravan and stay there."

"Is that the only message you've had?"

"By text, yes. I've had a few emails."

"Can I see them?"

Eliza took her phone back and accessed her email account. She passed the mobile to Carol, who noted they'd been put in a folder called "crackpots". They were from various addresses, people telling her she was a gold-digger and only after Kevin's money. Lots of cruel name-calling.

"Are you okay with giving us the details to log in so our digital department can try to get some idea of who sent these?"

Eliza nodded but turned to Kevin. "Are you all right with that? There's sensitive information in there to do with ChatSesh."

"I don't care. If it means getting answers . . ." He glanced at Carol. "No one will copy any of the info, will they?"

"Not unless it pertains to the hate mail. All other data will be safe. We'll probably print the emails, and of course, someone will try to track them."

"Fine."

"Just write it in my notebook." Carol passed it over. "Along with the web address we need to go to. Do you have enough supplies here to take to the caravan with you?"

Eliza gazed at the ceiling in thought. "Yes, we'll be fine."

Carol thought about the logistics of travel. "Are you okay with an officer going with you to collect a hire car?"

Kevin drummed his fingertips on the table. "If you could drop us at the van, we won't need a car. I plan to stay there for a while, not just a couple of days. We can always get the bus if we need to go into town, but I really don't want to. I'll arrange for one of my security men to stay up there with us. He won't say owt about where we are."

"That makes me feel better." Carol handed him her card. "Ring me if there's any trouble, doesn't matter what time it is. I'll need a number for you, so I can contact you while digi have the other mobile."

He recited it, and Carol wrote it down.

"Oh, and if I can take a picture of that text message . . ." That done, she took three large gulps of coffee then stood. "While you pack, we'll nip to see your neighbours."

Kevin knuckled his eyes and yawned. "Sorry, I'm exhausted. Willy and Lise's lights were on when we got back in the early hours, so they might have seen us or at least heard the car pull up." He propped his cheek in his hand.

"Okay, we'll be back soon."

Carol left them, Dave following, and walked across the grass that joined the two properties.

Twenty-something Lise had changed slightly from the last time Carol had seen her. As she answered the door, Carol thought her Botoxed lips looked a bit bigger, her enhanced chest higher and her brunette hair longer, possibly extensions.

Willy, close behind her, had more white in his beard and sideburns, but he was still bald, and he sported the same rings in his nostril and eyebrow. Carol had mistaken the couple for father and daughter at one time.

"Oh, thank God you're here!" Lise dramatically slapped a hand to her chest.

Alarm crept inside Carol. "What's the matter?"

"I swear that house is cursed." Lise jerked a thumb at Kevin's place. "Someone was in their back garden earlier, behind the *bushes*." She'd whispered "bushes" like it was a dirty secret.

"Who?"

Willy fiddled with his medallion, on display because of his V-neck jumper. "We don't know her, do we, Lise?"

"No, Willy, we don't."

Carol had forgotten the odd way these two spoke to each other. "So it was a woman. Do you have a description for me?"

Dave got his notebook out.

Lise scrunched her heavily kohl-lined eyes. "Well, if she was trying to stay incognito, she wasn't doing a very good job, was she, Willy? She had bright-yellow *hair*."

"What about her height and build?"

"She was skinny," Willy said. "We saw her run out of the garden and walk down the road. She kept her head bent the whole time, and her hair fell forward, so we didn't get a look at her face, but she had dark clothes on. Leggings, a long T-shirt and a puffa jacket, although it was much too big for her, wasn't it, Lise?"

"It was." Lise nodded. "Now, you know I don't like to be catty, but . . ." She glanced up and down the street. "She appeared *homeless*, a right bit of rough baggage."

"Scruffy, you mean?" Carol asked.

"No, more that she couldn't afford a nice haircut and her face tweaking." Lise grimaced.

Willy stroked her upper arm. "Not everyone can afford surgery or to go to the hairdresser, lover. Remember what we talked about? Compassion." He looked at Carol. "We're working on that, aren't we, Lise?"

"Yes, Willy. Not everyone is rich like us."

Carol scratched behind her ear. These two . . . "Which way did she go?"

Willy pointed down the sloping road. "I expect she's from the estate, although why she'd be in Kevin's garden, I don't know. Maybe she's one of them paparazzi people."

"So no vehicle, then?"

"We didn't hear one, and we would." Lise poked a finger above her head. "We have sliding doors in our bedroom, don't forget, and we had the back doors and some windows open as well."

Dave tapped his pen on his pad. "How tall was she?"

"About the same as Lise," Willy said. "Minus her heels."

Lise took off her shoes, black platform numbers.

"About five-four, then," Dave mumbled to himself.

"Did you notice her arriving?" Carol shuddered at the idea of some woman watching Eliza. A journalist or not, it was still wrong.

Willy shook his head. "No, but she left a minute or so before you turned up."

Ugh, we must have just missed her. "That's excellent, thank you."

"So glad we could help, aren't we, Willy?"

"We are, Lise."

"Did you happen to notice when Kevin and Eliza got back during the night?" Carol asked.

"I did." Willy smiled, pleased with himself. "I had to get up for a wee, and they parked about half three."

"Thanks." Carol ended the chat and left Dave to it, going farther down the slope to the next house.

"Carol, Jim and Sonya aren't in," Willy called as Dave strode to Kevin's. "Do you not remember me saying before that it's their holiday home? They spent the summer here then buggered off."

Carol wandered back up the pavement. "You did say that, yes."

"Will we need to go to the station and repeat what we said like last time?" he asked.

Carol sighed. "I'll let you know."

"Brilliant. Tarra now."

He closed the door, and Carol met Dave outside Kevin's.

"Bloody hell," he muttered.

"I know. They're an acquired taste." She knocked on the door.

Kevin let them in and pointed to a black bag on the floor. "That's all my clothes I was wearing when Clem and Frank got . . . Well, in case you need them. You can match them to camera and photo footage from the events I attended."

Carol arranged for someone to collect them before they left for the caravan, to preserve the chain of evidence as much as possible. That Kevin had offered up his clothes wasn't lost on her. He wanted to prove he hadn't been involved, and she was happy for his things to go through testing so she could officially scrub him off her list.

Shame there wasn't anyone else on it.

But could it be the blonde in the garden?

That reminded her . . . "What colour hair do you usually go for, Kevin?"

"Same as Eliza's."

"Do all of your ex's have red hair?"

"Um, yes. Why do you ask?"

"A woman was in your garden earlier, albeit a blonde." Carol caught sight of Eliza coming over from the kitchen.

"What?" Eliza stroked her collarbone.

"Did you see anyone?" Carol asked. "The couple next door said she was in the bushes." She walked over to the doors that overlooked the patio. "Probably down there."

Everyone else came closer.

"An easy place to hide," Dave said.

"Oh God, I was sitting right here doing my make-up." Eliza pointed to the dining table. "What time was this?"

"Just before we arrived with Kevin," Carol said.

"I'd gone upstairs to put my mirror and make-up away, so she must have left then." Eliza turned to Kevin. "Who the hell can it be?"

He appeared concerned. "Honestly, they were all nice women, and I didn't date blondes, so unless one of them has dyed it . . ."

"One of them has lied to you," Carol said. "We just have to work out which one it is."

CHAPTER THIRTY-EIGHT

Undisclosed Location

Unforeseen circumstances had put a massive spanner in the works according to Boss. The plan had hit a pothole in the road, but Desmond thought it had played right into their hands. It was going to be easier now.

And death would be quick.

Desmond explained his thinking to Boss. "Do you see?"

Boss snorted down the phone line. "I do. I knew there was a reason I employed you."

"I'm not just a pretty face."

"No, clearly not."

Desmond slipped his phone away, conscious Boss had probably tapped it so he could listen to everything he said in Target's presence. Which was why Desmond never took it with him.

He switched it off and placed it in the drawer beside the bed. Desmond had stayed here since he'd started this mission. He hadn't put any of his clothes away, preferring to live out of his suitcase for an easy escape. The only thing he didn't like was not knowing *when* he could leave. Still, he had his new name, passport and credit card, and he could book a last-minute flight quickly enough. He'd dump the car Boss had loaned him and hire one to go to the airport.

Maybe tonight would be the night, then it would be goodbye Scudderton.

Goodbye England.

CHAPTER THIRTY-NINE

Whitby

Sofia had never been to Whitby before. It was a lovely place. She sat in the Ditto restaurant opposite Nigel, who'd said he'd pay for the meal. Good, it was a bit too expensive for her pocket at the moment. She ordered beef shoulder, salsa verde, mash and parmesan, nothing like the food she ate at home. It was wonderful, and they chatted about anything and everything so easily, like they'd known each other for years. He was her dream person, much better than that bastard Kevin, especially as Nigel offered her the chance to have dessert, something Kevin had never done. She opted for lemon posset with meringue, white chocolate and strawberries, glad she hadn't had a starter. She was full, uncomfortably so, but a coffee helped her food settle.

It was time to go, and with Nigel going to Newcastle, he promised to phone her tomorrow after his conference.

"I need to see you again," he said. "Can you come back to London with me? I have a spare room. I wouldn't expect you to do anything like . . . you know . . ."

Did she have time to kill Eliza and one of the other redheads before then? She wanted to murder the lot of them to be honest, but maybe two would be enough to assuage her anger. The thing was, she couldn't flee for good until other factors came into play, and if she wasn't around, it would look suspicious. She'd have questions to answer because of her previous association with Kevin — they might think an irate woman from his past had a score to settle, and she'd have to disabuse them of that notion. Or they *could* warn her that she might be next on the killer's list.

"Maybe another time," she said. "I still don't know you very well."

"That's fine by me. Can I phone you, though?"

"Text me, and we'll work something out."

The ride back to Scudderton went too quickly, and Sofia wished she could stay in his company for longer, but no, she really did need to finalise things, as tonight she'd be going back to Seaview Heights and doing the business.

She asked Nigel to drop her off in town, and he made to move across and kiss her cheek but changed his mind. Maybe he thought he was being too forward.

"Thanks so much for the lovely lunch," she said.

She got out and walked towards the Devil, her hair swishing across her face. She left it there and went down the alley beside the pub, quickening her steps through Coldwater, hoping she wasn't seen.

She really didn't need that complication.

CHAPTER FORTY

Incident Room

Kevin and Eliza were safe in the caravan with the bodyguard who'd met them there. Preston Brown was head of ChatSesh security and had assured Carol he would take care of the couple. Richard had gone to speak to Kevin's ex-girlfriends either at their homes or places of work — hopefully, he'd get their measure and one of them would need looking at more closely. The team had eaten lunch, and two o'clock had rolled around with everyone searching for clues and links. Digi were working on Eliza's emails.

Michael cleared his throat. "Okay, ANPR corroborates Kevin's movements. I also contacted the documentary people, who confirmed he was present and on film. They're not keen to send any footage but will if they have to — as in, if we get a warrant. I suppose they think they've got a blockbuster on their hands and we might send it to the competition." He tutted.

"Their word will do — for now." Carol sat at the spare desk with a can of orange Fanta. "Did anyone get owt from the phone number I sent in, the one used to contact Eliza Morris?"

Katherine held her pen up. "The SIM was activated two weeks ago and was bought at the big Tesco. I'm waiting for some help on whether more messages or calls were made from that number, but that could take a while. The service provider is one of those who likes to drag their heels, even with a warrant."

"Progress, nonetheless. So the offender purchased it in order to contact Eliza. They've thought this through." Carol smiled at Lloyd. "What have you been up to?"

"Doing background checks on all of Kevin's women in case Richard needed to know. None of them have records. All of them are a lot younger than him, not that it matters, but I was thinking more along the lines of whether their age is a factor when killing someone. Like their physical fitness."

Carol pulled her phone out. "Hang on a second, that's reminded me I need to check in with Alan." She selected his number and waited for him to answer. "Hi. How did it go with Madeline Cotter? We've reason to question all the women in Kevin's past."

"She came across okay to me, if a bit of an oddball, like she doesn't get to speak to people much. I was just going to ring you anyroad as I've finished my report. She spoke about Kevin and how he once said his mother was, and I quote, 'a pain in his backside, always butting her nose in, and he wished she'd fuck off'. Now, that bit I can get on board with, my mam used to drive me batty, but Kevin apparently said that if his mam died it would do him a favour. It was a while ago, but she said he might have been letting it fester."

"Bloody hell. He didn't give me that impression at all."

"Well, he wouldn't, would he? Her first response after I told her about Gail's death was to ask if Kevin had done it, then a bit later she asked if he'd battered her with a hammer. I think she said it because I'd mentioned the toolbox, but I wanted you to know. I suppose if she'd said a chisel, I'd have had alarm bells ringing, but if I think of a toolbox, I think of a hammer first."

"So do I."

"She gave me alibis — the Devil when Clem was murdered, in town when Frank was. She mentioned being on CCTV, which was a tad odd, but I took it that she was worried I was accusing her, which wasn't the case."

"What did she say about this morning?"

"She was at home. I checked with neighbours either side, and neither of them saw her going out."

"Doesn't mean she didn't."

"I don't think she's who we're after. She's harried, too busy looking after her daughter. Said she rarely leaves her alone."

"What about when she went to the Devil?"

"She took her to a friend's house."

"Did you follow that up?"

"No . . ."

"Can you?"

"Yep, I'll give her a ring now."

"Thanks." Carol put her phone on the desk and sipped her drink, then told the team about Madeline. "Bugger, I must phone Richard." She did that, explaining Alan had already dealt with her.

"That's good, because I was on my way there."

"Saves you a trip. Any news from the others?"

"I've spoken to six, and all were normal human beings as far as I could tell. None of them had met Gail, and they've moved on with other people."

"Thanks. If any of the others seem iffy, let me know, especially if one of them has blonde hair and a black puffa jacket. Someone's been spying on Eliza, Kevin's girlfriend. A woman was spotted leaving the property earlier."

"Christ."

"Before I forget, I need a couple of officers on the estate behind Seaview Heights, asking if anyone saw a woman of that description."

"I'll get on it."

Carol ended the call, popped her phone down again and addressed Michael. "Have we got owt back on the possible height of the killer? Forensics will have had time to work on the spatter patterns by now."

"Nowt as yet." Michael pinched his bottom lip. "I've popped some info on the whiteboard for each victim and suspect, so we know at a glance where we are. There's so many people in play, I thought it was best I did an overview. I also had a go at a geographical triangle to determine where the killer might live."

"Thanks." Carol got up and went over to read the board.

She must remember to look over Rib's notes, then there was Frank's post-mortem results to check. There couldn't be anything she would need to know because he would have phoned her by now if there was.

Carol read the info about Asher Welding, who had a red cross beside his name to indicate he'd been ruled out. Then came Madeline and the other women Kevin had been seeing. Carol filled out the information Alan had given her about Madeline, but she'd have to wait for the others until Richard had filed his report so she could get better details. Eliza Morris, Yasmeen Hollington and the names of the staff at the Odeon followed, all with question marks beside them and their information beneath.

None of them appeared suspicious.

She went to her office and accessed her emails. Rib had sent one about Frank. As she'd thought, the initial observation at the scene in the yard was correct — cause of death was the hammer blow to the forehead.

She returned to the incident room and the board. The geographical map showed the three murder sites, so the killer might live inside the triangle, but it wasn't giving any secrets up yet.

She approached Dave. "We're going to have to go and ask Kevin about what his ex-wife said. It could be done over the phone, but I want to see his face."

Dave stood and shrugged his jacket on. "I thought you didn't think it was him."

"I don't, but you know me, I like to cover my arse." Her phone rang — Alan. "Hello, you."

"Madeline said the friend moved away this morning, which is why Poppy went round there. A goodbye party. I checked the address five doors down, and it's empty. I'm on my way back to the station now, so do you want me to ping an email over with the address so Michael can look into where the family have gone?"

"Please, and thanks for doing that."

She let Michael know to expect information from Alan and left the room, thinking of all the twists and turns the case had taken so far. It felt like it centred around Gail, Kevin, Eliza and Madeline, Clem and Fred having been put to one side, but she couldn't ignore this avenue — the cases might be linked.

Sometimes, she wished she had a clone.

* * *

Sunshine Caravan Park

Carol's caravan was up here, but she avoided going near it today. A family had rented it this week, and the last thing they'd want while on holiday was the owner nosing through the windows to make sure everything was okay.

She walked with Dave over the grass between vans and knocked at Kevin's double-wide. A dark shape approached the leaf-patterned glass, and the door opened to reveal Preston Brown.

Carol smiled. "Sorry to disturb you. We need a quick chat."

"Not trying to tell you what to do, but in this situation, could you phone first?" Preston asked. "That way, I won't panic."

He'd made a good point.

"Sorry, I should have thought of that myself."

"Is that Carol?" Kevin said. "Let her in."

Carol and Dave stepped inside. It was one of the more modern vans, no built-in seating but a proper three-piece suite, a fireplace and vertical blinds instead of curtains. They were closed — sensible. Anyone would recognise Kevin if they glanced inside, and none of them needed the press arriving en masse, revealing the hideout.

"What's happened?" Kevin stood from a cream leather armchair, his eyes red raw. He must have let his emotions run free after they'd left him here earlier.

Preston closed and locked the door. Eliza, curled up on the other armchair, gnawed her top lip. Was she anxious about the emails and whether they'd found the sender? It would be awful if Eliza knew them personally.

"A query, that's all," she said, "but first, has Todd been here yet?"

Kevin hugged himself. "He left about five minutes ago. Nowt was stolen as far as I could see in the photos."

"Has anything come of the text and emails yet?" Eliza asked.

"I'm afraid not." Carol gave her a look of apology.

Kevin sniffed. "So what's the other query?"

Carol repeated what Alan had told her about Madeline, hoping she'd got the wording right.

"She said *what*?" Kevin rammed a hand into his hair and held it tight. His jaw clamped, and he closed his eyes. A tear leaked. "I swear to God, if that woman doesn't leave me alone . . ." He snapped his eyes open. "I'm going to go mad, and I mean literally. I can't cope with her. She's off her tree." He let his hair go and poked at a temple. "She's in here, won't get out, and despite the divorce and time passing, I still keep thinking about her and what she's done."

Eliza got up and rubbed his arm. "Tell them."

"Tell us what?" Carol didn't like having things kept from her during an investigation. People thought information wasn't relevant when it could be, and time was wasted chasing the wrong leads.

"I'll make us some tea." Eliza wandered to the fancy kitchen area.

"None for us, thanks," Carol said. They'd not long had a drink at the station, and she'd forgotten to have a wee before they'd left.

Preston stepped forward and took Kevin by the elbow. "Sit down, pal. Don't let her get to you. This is what she wants. Don't play into her hands."

Kevin sat. "Cheers. I know you're right, but . . . How can I let this go when she makes shit up like that? *More* shit?"

"I don't know," Preston said, "but try, otherwise she'll ruin the rest of your life."

He moved back to stand by a dining table with six chairs around it. Dave took a seat there and brought his notebook out.

Carol opted for the sofa, thankful there were no cushions with pompoms on them. "We have to check everything."

Kevin nodded, flopping back, hands on his thighs. "I know, I get that, but you have no idea what she's put me through."

"Then why don't you tell me?"

He went on to explain about his discovery. Poppy wasn't his. Now Carol thought about it . . . When she'd seen her on the pier, no, she hadn't looked like either Kevin *or* Madeline, so she must favour her real father, who was apparently a therapist at the local hospital called Ian Johann.

"Is there any proof she's his?" Carol asked.

"There's proof she isn't mine. I had a DNA test done."

"Did you tell Madeline or Poppy?"

"No, I didn't think it was fair to upset the child so I eased out of her life. I still make sure Poppy wants for nowt. I pay Madeline a lot of money every month, plus Poppy has cash in a trust for when she gets out from beneath her mother's thumb."

"That's kind of you."

"I couldn't let the kid suffer financially when I had the funds to help her. No, she isn't mine, and no, I haven't been seeing her, haven't for yonks, but that's not her fault." He raised a hand. "And before you say it, Eliza's already given me 'the talk' about Poppy."

Eliza handed the teas out on a tray. "At least tell Madeline you know, then it's up to her to explain herself to Poppy. Or not."

"No, I don't want to see her. She drives me round the bend, just can't let things go — that much obvious by what she's said about me wanting my mam dead." He blew on his tea and sipped. "We were together since we were younger. Looking back, we were pushed into marriage. Loads of people said we were the perfect couple, and we kind of ran with it. We did get along at first — until she had Poppy, then it all went downhill. Madeline had depression, couldn't seem to get the monkey off her back, even with antidepressants. I felt for her, tried to help as best I could, but I ended up walking out and going down the pub most nights to get away from her. Not my finest hour. When I found out about Poppy not being mine, I had to make a choice." He shrugged. "I'll admit I slept around. I wasn't a good husband in that regard. Too young, too stupid, and I regret being so underhand. She's never let me forget it. I haven't seen her for ages, not even in town or whatever, so I thought she'd finally moved on. Now she's said what she has, she's proved she still can't let it go. What annoys me is I was faithful for years, and she was the first one to step out, with Ian. She's harped on about me shagging behind her back, when she'd done it, too. She'd done it *first*."

"Has this changed your opinion on whether you think she could have killed your mam?" Carol asked.

"No, I still can't see her killing anyone. Causing trouble, being spiteful, yes, but she's so wrapped up in Poppy, I don't know when she'd find the time." He looked at Carol with pain in his eyes. "You don't think I said that shit, do you?"

Carol shook her head. "No. What I want to know is *why* she said you did. Sounds to me like she wants to fit you up for your mother's murder. For kicks? Who knows." She sighed and glanced over at Dave. "I think we need to go and have a word with her ourselves."

CHAPTER FORTY-ONE

Ridgebrook Close

Ian came round for a visit a year after Madeline had dropped the bombshell. What a cheek, waiting this long, like Poppy didn't matter. He seemed awkward, out of his depth, and Madeline supposed he would be. His face when he'd looked at her, though . . . Had he seen himself? Poppy's hair was his exact shade, and she was lucky she hadn't inherited the ginger gene from Madeline, who hated having pale skin and freckles that she had to cover with make-up. Kevin was dark-haired, too, so the ruse had worked, although he'd never queried why Poppy didn't look like either of them.

Ian sat on the sofa but didn't glance at his daughter again. "Listen, this isn't going to work. It's weird."

"Of course it isn't. You're my friend, and that's all people need to know." She had to be careful, because Poppy was clever and might realise what was going on if Madeline said too much. "I just want you to see" — she pointed to the back of Poppy's head and mouthed "her" — "once in a while. So you've had a chance to watch the flower grow."

"I didn't even know there was a flower. I understand why you kept it from me, but why bother phoning me about it when you didn't from the start? I've got family commitments of my own now, this isn't going to work."

Poppy rested on her stomach, colouring in on the floor. She used a blue crayon to fill in a peacock's tail.

Madeline wanted to explode. "I told you why I kept it to myself for so long. But then he left, just as I predicted. He doesn't even see her these days. She's got no male figure in her life. My dad's dead now, did you hear about that? And my mam, well, you know she died while I was at uni."

"Sorry about your dad."

"Shit happens. A lot of it, in my case. Poppy hasn't been well. She's been in the hospital a few times now."

He didn't seem to have heard her. That or he was like Kevin and didn't care. "What if I said I'd need a test before I committed to coming here? I mean, you must have been with Kevin the same time as me. And what if I wanted shared custody?"

"Err, no, that's not on the table. And for your information, I hadn't done owt with him for a month before you, we were too busy and tired, and I had to instigate a session because of what me and you had done. You don't have to give me any money either, Kevin's doing that side of things."

His mouth flopped open. "You haven't told him, even though you're not together anymore?"

"God, no."

"You're not right in the head."

"Oh, are you analysing me now? Like I'm on your couch and you need to fix me? How was Scotland by the way?"

"Mam said you'd been asking about me, which, to be frank, is creepy. It was okay, but I'm back for good now."

"Why did you go in the first place?"

"You know why."

"I bloody don't!"

He sighed. "The constant phone calls, you turning up at Mam's house and staring up at my bedroom window after . . . after we'd . . . and it was weird. Too much. You were married, and we should never have done what we did. I had to get away."

"Didn't your mam pass on that I was having a baby?"

"No."

"What did you think when I phoned you?"

"Disbelief. You've always told fibs."

That was a bit rude. "Did you only come back because I don't work at the hospital anymore?"

"Of course not. A position became available, and I wanted to come home, it was as simple as that."

"Aren't you going to do some colouring with Poppy?"

Ian stood, shaking his head. "This is stupid. Let me know if you want the test done."

"This isn't the last time you'll be seeing me, Ian," she called to his back.

He walked out, and Madeline stared at the seat he'd occupied, asking herself if she should go down the test route. If she did, Ian would have rights, then she'd lose the money Kevin paid out. No, she didn't want Ian to have any claim.

It was time to make Poppy poorly again. The lack of attention was draining.

CHAPTER FORTY-TWO

Blanche Crescent

Richard had one more woman left to interview. It was nearly the end of his shift. The days had been hectic recently, and he dreaded tomorrow in case they woke to another body. But he'd plough on, as usual, although he was concerned about the spate of murders in Scudderton lately, like the town had been cursed.

He knocked at number seven, wondering what he'd face this time. He'd phoned ahead, and Fiona Quinn had said she'd leave work early and meet him at her place.

A redhead answered, although it wasn't the sort from a bottle, more strawberry-blonde. A natural, then. Could she be the one in Kevin's garden? He showed her his ID despite his uniform, and she led him into a minimalistic lounge that reminded him of a show home rather than the average, lived-in house.

"Would you like a drink?" She smiled, nervous.

"No, thank you."

She pointed to the grey suede corner sofa, and he sat on one end while she chose the other.

"Will we be talking long?" she asked. "Only my boyfriend doesn't know I was with Kevin and I'd like to keep it that way."

"Any particular reason?"

"Well, with Kevin being famous like that Facebook fella, it's just something I'd rather not mention. There'd be questions, and honestly, I only went out with Kevin three times, so there's nowt to tell really. Why do you need to talk about him anyroad?"

Dave had asked Richard not to mention Gail's death but to concentrate on the woman hiding in the bushes at Seaview.

"Sorry to sound like I'm accusing you of owt, but if you could just bear with me and answer my questions, I'll be out of your hair."

"Okay . . ."

"Where were you today?" He stated the approximate time Dave had given him.

"At work from eight. I'm a secretary in Whitby."

"Did you drive there?"

"Yes."

"Did you stay there all day?"

"Yes, and I didn't even get a lunch break. I work for solicitors, and there's a big case tomorrow, so it was all hands on deck. I stayed at the office until I left to meet you." She picked her phone up from the coffee table and swiped the screen, jabbing it a few times. She held it out with a phone number on the display with the name Peter Kellogg at the top. "My boss. Ring him."

Richard declined to take the phone. That number could go to someone she'd asked to lie for her. He preferred to do the research himself. "What's the practice called?"

"Kellogg and Whittaker."

"I'll be sure to contact them." He wouldn't be surprised if Kellogg backed up Fiona's story, but he wouldn't apologise for not trusting her.

"I understand. So what is it you think I've done?"

He ignored that. "Do you know any of Kevin's other former girlfriends?"

"Not personally, no, but I heard he's had a few."

"Do you know his ex-wife?"

"No. We didn't really talk about ourselves in that way. More like what we enjoyed doing, stuff like that."

"Do you know Eliza Morris?"

"Most people do, if only because she's in the papers and social media. She's his girlfriend. Started off as his secretary, if the stories are to be believed."

"Have you ever met her?"

"No."

"And how did you feel when your relationship with Kevin ended?"

Fiona shrugged. "It wasn't really a relationship, just a few dates and . . . sex." She blushed. "Sorry, I don't like talking about things like that. When he said he didn't think we were compatible, I agreed. Besides, he worked too much, and I knew I wouldn't get a look-in when it came to his time. When I was seeing him, he was devoted to ChatSesh and helping people have a better online experience, and I doubt that's changed. He used to be on the phone during our meals. His goal is to make his corner of the web a safer, nicer place to be. He's actually a lovely person, we just didn't gel."

"So you're not jealous of Eliza?"

Fiona laughed. "Why would I be? I'm really happy with my boyfriend."

Richard stood. "Thank you for your time."

She rose and showed him to the door. "You didn't say what this was about."

He smiled. "No need. Just following procedure."

In the car, he phoned Carol. "She's a redhead but leans towards being blonde. Saying that, I don't think she's done owt. I'll check with her boss, but I expect he'll confirm she's been at the office in Whitby all day. ANPR will show she drove there."

"Did any of them have proper blonde hair? One of the witnesses said it was bright."

"Nope."

"So if it isn't any of the exes, who was it?"

"Do you expect me to answer that?"

"No, it was rhetorical."

Glad about that, Richard said, "Right, I'm off to the station to file my report, then I'm going home."

"Okay, have a good evening."

"You, too, if you manage to get one."

She laughed. "I live in hope."

CHAPTER FORTY-THREE

Ridgebrook Close

Madeline seemed eager to speak to Carol and Dave. Like on the pier, she came across as hyped, a chatterbox, which married with what Alan had said about her maybe not having much social interaction. Yet she'd been to the Devil so must involve herself with people sometimes. Maybe being cooped up with her daughter meant she went overboard while in company.

They sat in her living room. Poppy was upstairs having a rest. Carol wanted to get this episode cleared up so she could check in with the team, and if they weren't getting anywhere, they may as well pack up and go home.

"When PC Pitson was here earlier, he mentioned Gail had been murdered. Why was your first instinct to ask if Kevin did it?"

Madeline smiled. "Because of what he said to me once. Plus there was the query about the toolbox. I just added the two things together. Why ask about that if it's nowt to do with the murder? It's a logical assumption, isn't it?"

Carol supposed it was, like a hammer being the first thing most people thought of. "Kevin doesn't recall saying those things regarding his mother."

Madeline scoffed, and her expression changed. A hint of annoyance passed over her face. "Well, he isn't going to admit it, is he? Would you? I mean, imagine if *you'd* said that, then the person wound up dead!"

Carol hadn't said it, not out loud, but she *had* thought it — and her father *had* ended up dead. But she hadn't killed him, and she didn't think Kevin had killed Gail either.

"Could it have been a throwaway comment?" Carol asked. "He was annoyed with his mother at the time, and the words popped out in anger?"

"Oh no, he meant it all right. I could tell by his eyes. They go darker when he's thinking of nasty things. He may come across as Mr Nicey-Nicey, but believe me, behind closed doors he's someone else."

"What are you implying?"

"He can say some cutting things when he has a mind."

"Like what?"

"Oh, like I'm a boring cow, that I'm not who I was when we met. Of course I'm not! I was younger, I hadn't had a baby and postnatal depression."

Calling someone a boring cow wasn't nice, but it didn't make someone a killer. People got wired, words were said in the heat of the moment, but Kevin could have been frustrated, and he *had* said the period of time he'd been cheating wasn't his finest hour, that he'd been young and stupid.

People grew into their personalities over a number of years, and they *could* change, become a better human. From what Carol had seen, Kevin was a nice bloke, and if he'd said things to Madeline while their relationship had been so up in the air, it was kind of understandable — she was sure Madeline must have blasted him with vitriol herself. No, Carol didn't condone bullying, but she did acknowledge it was a fact of life, and it didn't make someone evil.

Madeline's shoulders stiffened. "He cheated on me several times, always bringing me flowers afterwards, promising not to do it again, then when the next redhead came along, oh look, his trousers happened to fall down to his ankles all by themselves."

Carol wouldn't usually probe into someone's private life, but she wanted to hear it from the horse's mouth. "Did *you* ever cheat?"

Madeline's bounding puppy manner shrank back along with her shoulders, and a different one took its place. Frosty. "I don't feel that's pertinent, do you?"

"Well, yes, that's why I asked. When we're dealing with murder cases, nowt is off the table. Often, people's pasts reveal clues for the present. Like you telling us about Kevin and what he said. So, did you have an affair?"

Madeline squirmed, and her eyes darted left and right — was she thinking of a suitable answer to get her out of this? Was she wondering how they knew about the father? Finally, her gaze levelled on Carol. "It *wasn't* an affair. An affair is a long-standing thing."

"Okay, then, I'll rephrase it. Did you have sex with someone else while with Kevin?"

"Has Ian been talking?"

"No, we haven't had the need to speak to him, although we might have to." *In case you two worked together to kill Gail.*

"God, it was just one time." Madeline blushed. "At uni. We got drunk and . . . Things happened."

"And you found out you were pregnant."

"Yes. Who told you if Ian didn't?"

"I won't disclose that."

"But that means someone else knows, that Ian might have been blabbing. I can't have anyone knowing."

"By that, do you mean Kevin?"

"And Poppy."

Time to move on. "What are your feelings towards Clem Talbot?"

"I heard about his murder. Terrible. It'll be strange not seeing him at his wheel."

"What about Frank West?"

"Who?"

"He worked at the Odeon. PC Pitson mentioned him to you earlier, so I'm surprised you asked who I meant." *Is her mind addled because we know about Ian, or is she trying to act innocent?*

"Oh, yes. Sorry, you just threw me for a loop, knowing about . . . about Poppy's father. I only knew Frank like everyone else does. The man who handed out sweets before films. He was so kind to Poppy whenever we went to the cinema." She paused. "Someone's obviously got a vendetta."

"Why would you say that?"

"*Three* people have been killed in quick succession, so it's obvious, isn't it?"

Carol wouldn't usually divulge case-sensitive information, but in this instance, she had to. "They were all killed with tools, hence us being interested in the box found in Gail's shed. It isn't clear enough yet why that box was in there. You say Kevin took it when he left; he says he forgot to take it. Why would it even be at his mother's anyroad?"

"He went there when he drove off, the day he ended things with me. He stayed there for a bit until he found a place of his own. Stored things in her shed. I bet there are other items of his in there that will prove it."

"How do you know this?"

"He told me. Went on a rant about having to move in with her, like he was a failure in life if he had to resort to going back to his childhood home. Ask him. See if he denies *that*."

"Why would he move into his mother's when he had the money to rent a house?"

"Don't ask *me*!" Madeline laced her fingers around a knee. "Do you believe me, that he said and did those things?"

Carol glanced at Dave, then back to Madeline. "We'll leave you be now. Thank you for your time."

Outside, Carol phoned Kevin. He admitted he had stored things at his mam's, had lived there until he'd bought a house and he *had* said what Madeline had claimed, but he wondered what it had to do with his mother being killed. Yes, there was probably some old stuff still in the shed, but all it did was prove he might have also taken the toolbox but had forgotten.

What if the tools used in the murders turn out to be his?

* * *

Madeline had panicked a couple of times during that conversation. Who the hell had told them about her fling with Ian? *Had* he been gossiping? Had he told his mother? Yes, it could have been her, she was one for letting secrets slip, but why would she have been spoken to by the police?

Maybe she was friends with Clem or Frank.

Madeline was pissed off about Kevin recalling that he hadn't taken the toolbox. She'd thought he'd have forgotten in all the confusion, but it sounded like he was sticking to his guns.

What if the police didn't have enough evidence to arrest him? Did fingerprints deteriorate after time? Would those forensic people be able to tell how long the prints had been there, which would rule him out from using them recently?

They might think he had gloves on and still charge him with murder.

She sighed, going over and over the police chat. Had she come across as spiteful towards Kevin? That she was trying to frame him? It wouldn't do to be seen as desperate. At least they hadn't mentioned the friend Poppy had supposedly seen when Madeline had gone to the Devil.

If they looked into that, they'd know she'd lied.

* * *

Incident Room

"So where are we with things now?" Carol sat at the spare desk, exhausted from her mind being so full of unanswered questions.

Michael pulled his notepad closer. "I can't find where Poppy's friend moved to so we can confirm she was there when Madeline went shopping in town. They can't have had time to register elsewhere for council tax and the like, or maybe they have and it hasn't come up on the system yet. I found a few names and phone numbers of other neighbours, and the two I rang said a family moved out, but they don't know where they went. The family apparently kept themselves to themselves."

"Okay, it's not vital that we confirm it," Carol said. "Poppy's highly unlikely to be who we're looking for, and Madeline's odd, but if she's got alibis, we can't arrest her for owt. Katherine, what have you got?"

"Digi have had no luck whatsoever tracing the email account used to contact Eliza. What they did find is that it's hosted on a secure server. Likely accessed on a Tor browser. The email address itself, the company doesn't exist — searches were done for it. So it's not like Gmail or whatever where anyone can create an account."

"So whoever's sending those emails knows what they're doing." Carol sighed — she'd been doing a lot of that. "Do we think the emails are linked to the text message?"

"I'm not sure. There are other emails that *are* traceable, but they're just your usual weirdo complaints about ChatSesh."

"Like what?"

"You're rubbish, you're not as good as the other sites, Cotter's lying, that kind of thing."

"Lying about what?"

"The site poking into users' data or listening to private conversations through phones and laptops et cetera. That's probably why he went public with his company policy. Some of the emails are abusive, but not in the way the text message and the hidden account emails are."

Dave scratched his head. "Do people like Kevin always have to deal with those sorts of things?"

"Famous people get crap all the time," Michael said.

Carol nodded. "But why go after Gail? If they even did. She wasn't owt to do with ChatSesh, was she?"

Katherine smiled. "Well . . ."

Carol smiled back. "I *knew* you'd find something."

"I found a list of ChatSesh employees, and Gail is listed as one of them. I had her bank accounts pulled, as well as Clem's and Fred's, and Gail was paid quite a bit of money each month from the ChatSesh account."

"How much are we talking?"

"Ten grand a month."

"Bloody hell! Did she actually work for them, though?"

"No idea yet."

Dave tugged at the skin beside his mouth. "What if the hidden email and text sender is targeting employees? Contact has been made with Kevin and Eliza, but do we know if Gail received any threats? Or anyone else?"

Lloyd swung from side to side in his chair. "I've been through Todd's inventory of Gail's house. No digital devices that would be used to access emails. They didn't even find a mobile phone."

Carol took hers out and rang Kevin. "Sorry to bother you yet again, but your mother received wages from you. Did she work for ChatSesh?"

"Not technically. That money was more to pay her back for the life she gave me. She's down as my adviser, and she did give good advice, so it isn't a fiddle or owt."

Carol wasn't concerned about any fiddles at the minute. Murder trumped that. "Okay. Do you know if your mam had an email address? And did she own a mobile?"

"She wouldn't have owt to do with modern stuff. It was a big enough job getting her to switch to a flatscreen telly. No email, no mobile. Can I ask why you need to know that?"

"We're discussing things now, and we're wondering if ChatSesh employees are being targeted."

"None of my workers have come to me with anything like that. And what has that got to do with Clem and Fred?"

"The cases might not be related." *Oh, come on! The tools under the bodies link them.*

"Christ, this is all such a mess."

"It is. Well, we must get on. Thanks for confirming that for me." She said goodbye and let the team know what he'd said.

Dave snorted. "That's put *that* theory to bed, then."

Carol twiddled a paperclip on the desk. "Owt going on with people being questioned on the estate behind Seaview?"

Lloyd chimed in. "The officers have filed their reports — nowt so far. They've switched shifts, so two others have continued where they left off. No word from them yet."

The mention of the shift change prompted Carol to consider whether they continued plodding on or went home. "We're missing something. The murders are linked, I just can't see how. What's the motive? None of the deceased had owt to do with each other."

"The emails and text could be unrelated to Gail." Katherine leaned back and finger-combed her hair. "Just because we became aware of it while investigating Gail's death, doesn't mean it's all tied together."

Carol closed her eyes briefly. "No, you're right. With the blonde in the Seaview garden, I'm more inclined to think the Eliza situation is separate. Richard said none of Kevin's exes seemed off, and all of them have alibis. Has Kevin forgotten about someone he was seeing? Like, she's not even on that list? A one-night stand? Or are we dealing with a nutjob who fancies him?"

"A fantasist?" Dave asked.

"Hmm. He's famous, she might have a severe case of fangirl going on, and she's confusing reality with her day-dreams. She thinks Kevin should be with her, so she's taking it out on Eliza." Carol sifted through everything in her mind. The team had worked hard but had found no answers that would move the cases forward. They could sit here all night and still end up where they were now. "Let's call it a day." She slapped her thighs. "Until we get results back from forensics about the tools, we're treading water. Much as we hate waiting, we've done everything we can for now."

The team packed up, and Carol went to her office to check her emails in case Rib had done Gail's post-mortem.

He hadn't contacted her, so she closed her computer down and went to see the DCI. She gave him a quick appraisal, then returned to the incident room. Everyone had gone bar Dave.

"Fancy fish and chips at Cove?" she asked. "I feel the need to sit on the wall, get some sea air."

"Are we going to the Lord after?" He rose and put his jacket on.

"Yep, I need a glass of wine."

"Good, because a lager is calling my name. I might even have lime in it."

"Blimey, you're pushing the boat out. Lime is an extra fifty pence."

He shook his head, smiling. "Shut your trap."

She laughed, glad to be casting off the day and transitioning from copper to civilian. Except she couldn't while on a case. She might look like she didn't have a care in the world when she was off the clock, but her mind was always ticking in the background, reminding her she still had so much to do in order to bring the killer to justice.

She remained resolute. One person had murdered these people.

The burning question was, who?

CHAPTER FORTY-FOUR

Seaview Heights

Sofia had used a large stone from the rockery to break the kitchen window. The smash and tinkle of glass was on purpose — she wanted Kevin and Eliza to wake up and investigate — but so far, there was no sign of them. No alarm had sounded either, and it annoyed her how stupid it was to be famous but not have a decent security system, unless they'd forgotten to set it. She'd wanted to create a commotion that matched her inner turmoil and brought the pair running. She'd timed it so she could get away before the police came.

The excitement of it all fizzled to a smouldering anger.

Prior to climbing through the window after she'd reached in and unlatched it, she'd checked the house next door, but it stood in darkness, and when she'd come past, no windows or the sliding doors on the first floor had been open. Maybe they'd gone out.

That suited her.

She prowled the ground floor, the space disorientating because she lived somewhere that had inside walls. It was weird to have all the rooms as one, although they were clearly sectioned off into quadrants. She didn't like the fact she couldn't inspect each part individually like she would if they had been rooms. There was too much to scan at once, but she didn't detect Kevin or Eliza hiding anywhere.

The stairs stood in the middle, the landing and floors above creating the ceiling in the kitchen and dining areas at the back. She climbed, spooked by the glass ceiling in the other half of the downstairs — it felt like someone was watching her from the sky. A large knife from the kitchen drawer at home held tightly, she checked each bedroom.

Empty.

Where were they?

The master had T-shirts on the bed, and one of the built-in wardrobe doors had been left open. Some hangers were without clothes, so Sofia inspected the wash bin to see if the items were in there.

Nothing but pyjamas, socks and underwear.

She turned and spotted a suitcase beside the bedside cabinet. It was open, revealing a smaller one inside. Was there a bigger one that was missing? Had they gone away?

Angry that she couldn't kill the ginger bitch and show Kevin his chickens had come home to roost, she grabbed a photo of him and Eliza from the dresser and smashed it against the wall. She threw the frame on the bed and stabbed Kevin's face with the knife, the tip going through the backing and embedding in the mattress.

She walked out, fuming, and left the property via the bi-fold doors using the key already in the lock.

This was *not* how it was supposed to turn out.

CHAPTER FORTY-FIVE

Poisson Mort

Madeline and Kevin had wanted to do something different, bored of the pier as a way to amuse themselves, and had paid to go on Skipper Kinnock's boat when he and his crew sailed to catch fish. Madeline couldn't give two stuffs about learning to fish, she just wanted to be out on the open sea in the darkness of a winter morning, to feel the wind on her face and get a rush from the sway of the boat on the choppy waves. Skipper did what he called "tours", although he said he'd be packing it in soon because other people just "got in the bloody way".

His wife, Violet, came along and did the commentary, pointing things out and boring Madeline with irrelevant information. She wanted to be left alone, to hold Kevin's hand while they stood by the railings and enjoyed the thrill.

"Aww, would ye look at the pair of ye." Violet came to stand beside them, encroaching on their private moment.

Madeline seethed inside. Why did older people have to butt in all the time?

"Ye make a nice couple, so ye do." Violet's shape in the darkness was small and slight.

One push, and she'd be overboard easily. Madeline held herself back from doing it.

"When are ye setting a date?"

"I don't know if we are," Madeline said. "It's up to Kevin."

Violet laughed. "Well, come on, lad, give the girl an answer."

"Next year?" he said.

"That'll give ye time to plan everything." Violet leaned on the railing. "Ye know, ye remind me of myself and Skipper at your age. Holding hands, being close. A fine pair, so people said, and the same could be said for ye. Some folks are destined to be together. Don't let anyone tell ye about age, how young ye are. If ye love each other, then do it, get married. Ye won't regret it."

* * *

The Woodland

Madeline did regret it. She stood behind a tree in gloves and her killing outfit, staring across the road at Fisherman's Rest, a cul-de-sac. Skipper Kinnock was dead, but his chatty Irish bitch of a wife still lived there, probably still mourning him.

Violet had encouraged them even more on a couple of occasions — once at the summer fete, and another time in town when they'd bumped into her in Buns 'n' Bread. She'd gone on and on, pushing for a wedding, and it had given Madeline ideas. She'd wanted to stuff a cinnamon bun down Violet's throat so she choked and snuffed it. These people who'd offered their opinions, the memory of what they'd done, had got on her nerves so much after Kevin had left her that it was inevitable it had come to this.

Murder.

She crossed the road and made her way into Violet's back garden, all the other bungalows dark. She knocked on the glass, a blind blocking out the room behind it, and waited, her handbag containing the trowel and pruning shears she'd taken from Gail's shed.

A light splashed on and shone from around the edges of the blind.

"Who is it?" Violet asked.

Madeline didn't answer.

The blind rolled up, and Violet peered out, frowning. Then recognition dawned, and she twisted the key in the lock, swinging the door open.

"What are ye doing out here at this time of night?" Her long granny nightie swayed from the breeze wafting inside.

"I-I didn't know who else to t-talk to." Madeline ended it on a sob.

"Come away in."

Madeline stepped inside, sweeping her gaze over the kitchen. A ceramic slow cooker sat on the worktop close by. That would do.

Violet closed the door and came to stand in front of Madeline. "What's happened?"

"It's Poppy . . ."

"Oh God, is she hurt?"

"No, she's okay, it's just . . . She's being so difficult, and it's hard for me to care for her by myself. Kevin doesn't want to know. I feel like I'm going mad, and with my mam and dad gone, I've got no one."

"It's a fair old way ye've come from the other side of the estate. Did ye walk?"

"No, I got a taxi." Lie.

"I must say I'm surprised ye chose me. Sit down, and I'll make ye some tea."

Violet turned to walk towards the kettle, and Madeline snatched up the slow cooker. It was heavy, and she raised it high then brought it down on the back of Violet's head. The glass lid went flying, and the plug swung on the end of the cable. The stupid old cow screeched and staggered forward, the momentum sending her down on her hands and knees. Madeline took the pruning shears out of her bag and sat on Violet's back. The meddling fucker collapsed onto her front, arms sprawled above her bleeding head. Madeline grabbed her hair like she'd done with Frank and pulled it back, then to the right to expose the side of her neck.

She opened the shears and snipped the skin in the area of the carotid artery. Blades apart, she dug them into the wound and squeezed the handles together. They sliced through flesh, and blood oozed. She drew the tool out and smiled at the scarlet fountain squirting with each pulse. Violet gargled, weird sounds coming out of her, and Madeline reckoned blood was a better choker than a cinnamon bun any day. She got off and turned her over, watching for a moment. Violet's eyes rounded, and she convulsed, her hands slapping the floor, heels drumming.

Madeline pushed the shears beneath the body then washed her gloved hands at the sink. She took the trowel out of her bag and planted her feet either side of Violet's torso, the pool of blood forming beneath the head and neck growing bigger. Violet still breathed, still shook in some kind of fit, reminding Madeline of Gail, but she'd soon stop that.

Bending over, Madeline held the trowel with both hands and powered the tip downwards into Violet's open, blood-coated mouth. She leaned on the end of the handle until she was met with resistance from the floor. Violet's skin either side of her lips split with the force, and with one last splutter, blood rising in globules, the woman went limp.

Madeline swiped her face with her sleeve — some blood had landed there — and she stepped away from the body.

"*Ye make a nice couple, so ye do.* Wasn't that what you said? Well, guess what, you were wrong."

She walked out, leaving the back door wide open, and took one last look at the body. The mess. What someone else would see when they discovered her. It was enough to make anyone sick, but Madeline was used to blood from her time as a nurse, and it didn't bother her at all.

They were gone, the four people who'd put ideas in her head, ideas that she could have a long and happy marriage, that she'd be delirious because Kevin was "the one".

He was the one all right, just not how they'd thought.

He was the one who'd take the blame for this. Especially now gardening tools from Gail's shed were at the scene.

Let's see how you get out of this, *you bastard.*

CHAPTER FORTY-SIX

Sunshine Caravan Park

Kevin sensed someone nearby, but he was so tired from crying and grieving that he couldn't be bothered to open his eyes. It was probably Eliza, who'd gone to bed, getting up to see if he was okay. Or Preston, pacing the van, always on alert.

"I think someone's outside," Preston whispered to Kevin, his breath hot on his ear.

Kevin sat bolt upright from the nest he'd made on the armchair, blinking from the light of a nearby lamp. "What?"

"I saw someone with a gun."

"Jesus Christ! What time is it?"

"Half three."

"Did you phone Carol?"

"No. I went out there, and they ran off. I think we should go somewhere else. Looks like someone's leaked where we are."

Kevin's heart pounded far too hard, and he had trouble breathing for a moment, his chest tight, his lungs seeming to curl in on themselves. He managed to suck in a deep breath then stood, going dizzy.

"Careful," Preston said, steadying him with a hand to his elbow. "I've booked us into the Beachfront Hotel, all right? In my brother's name in case anyone goes snooping. I've told them who you are and that you need to remain incognito. They said you could pay cash on arrival."

"Okay, okay . . . We'll need to stop at a cashpoint, then."

Kevin rushed into the main bedroom and woke Eliza, who was understandably confused at first, then she woke right up after he'd explained and dashed about packing their things. Earlier, Preston had put his SUV in the car park near the front of the site, but it was outside now, between this van and the next, so he must have brought it here when he'd chased that person off.

He drove them away. Kevin clutched Eliza's hand in the back seat, his whole body shaking. He hated this side of being famous, the worry for their safety, how people always found a way to know where he was, mainly the press. That was why he'd bought Seaview so he could see anyone coming up the road and parking by the cliff edge to take photos, why he'd kept the caravans, so he had a bolthole. Now that secret had been discovered, and he felt like he wasn't safe anywhere, not even at the hotel.

* * *

The Beachfront Hotel

Preston parked around the back and hustled them in via a side door, then up some stairs and to a room on the second floor. He swiped a key card in the slot and pushed the door open, ushering them inside.

Eliza went straight to the window and lifted the edge of the curtain to peer outside. She took her phone out and prodded the screen.

"I thought you said we had to pay cash on arrival?" Kevin said. "How did you get this room and key card already?"

"It's my room," Preston said. "I'll go and pay for your suite now."

Kevin nodded, although he was confused as to why Preston stayed in a hotel when he'd given them a residential address when he'd started working for ChatSesh. "Why do you live here?"

"I had a flood at my place. The builders are in."

Kevin took his wallet out and handed over a couple of hundred quid. "Do the special knock when you come back."

Preston left the room, and the door closing felt so final — and creepy.

Kevin shook the clawing sensation away. It must be the man with the gun at the caravan park giving him the willies.

* * *

Desmond shrugged off his Preston persona and leaned against the closed door. He smiled, his bright idea of getting them out of the van going like clockwork. Boss would be pleased, but Desmond wouldn't be around to see it. He'd collect his suitcase later and leave, starting his new life.

He moved along the corridor so he wasn't seen through the spyhole. He'd sent an accomplice to pay for the suite on the top floor — Desmond had rung her outside the caravan while pretending to look for the fictitious man with the gun. She'd collected the key card and placed it on his SUV wheel arch an hour later.

Desmond waited ten minutes then did the special knock and opened his room door. Kevin shot up from his seat on the bed and came towards him.

Desmond held up the key card for the suite. "Got it. Come on."

Worry bled out of Kevin's features, and Eliza let out a sigh of relief.

The suite was posh, with two bedrooms, a living room and a large bathroom with a clawfoot tub. Desmond made a sweep of it for show, then allowed Kevin and Eliza to go inside. He ensured the door was locked and went to the window, peering into the street below to make out he was checking for them being followed.

"All clear," he said.

"Are you staying up here with us?" Kevin asked.

"I think I should. There's another bedroom, so . . ."

"Good." Kevin nodded. "I need to phone Carol."

"I suggest leaving it for now until we can speak to her in person. The leak could have come from the police station. We need to let her know she can't put our location in the database."

Kevin's shoulders slumped. "Fine. I see your point."

"Get some sleep. Everything will look brighter in the morning."

For me.

* * *

Desmond waited two hours until snoring rumbled through the adjoining wall. He left the suite and went to his hotel room, taking a gun out of its hiding place, then returned to the suite. In the master bedroom, he stood there for a while to let his eyes become adjusted to the darkness. He didn't want to shoot the wrong person.

The shapes of Kevin and Eliza in bed grew more defined. Eliza slept without a pillow, hugging it to her stomach instead, her side of the covers thrown back. Desmond moved closer, picked up a pillow Kevin must have put on the floor, then carefully propped it behind the man's head on top of the one already there. Desmond crouched to check the trajectory. The bullet would miss Eliza.

He raised the gun, a silencer on it, and placed the end an inch or so away from Kevin's temple. Trigger pulled, Kevin's body jerked, the shot somewhat muffled but still loud in the silence.

Eliza stirred.

CHAPTER FORTY-SEVEN

Fisherman's Rest

Another older victim. That it was Violet Kinnock was a shock. Carol and Dave had got to know her somewhat during the Mason Ingram case, coming here to speak to her after her neighbour, Ortun, and her husband, Skipper, had been murdered.

Violet lay on her back on the kitchen floor, the trowel sticking out of her mouth obscene and so wrong. Rib had already said there had been a pair of pruning shears beneath the body. He'd turned her to check once photographs had been taken of her in situ.

There were five bungalows in Fisherman's Rest. Callum Roberts in number two had found her. He sailed the *Poisson Mort* for Violet now Skipper was dead, and he'd come here this morning to tell her they'd be going farther out for the next fortnight, past the reef the crew had recently fished at, as he'd heard about another good one a mile or so away. Violet hadn't answered his knock at the front, so he'd gone round the back and found the door open, then spotted Violet. He hadn't entered the property, which was one less headache for SOCO, and he'd dialled 999, being sick on the grass afterwards.

Carol and Dave would go and speak to him soon.

"It was nippy last night," Rib said. "Well, compared to the weather we've been having lately, that breeze was a bit mad, so with the door left open, it's slowed down rigor. Despite that, I'd say she died yesterday evening."

Todd stood by the fridge. "There's diluted blood in the sink, so I'm guessing they washed their hands. Also a slow cooker there that has blood on it."

Rib nodded. "When I gave her a brief check after turning her over, I noted a head wound at the back. It's in a curved shape, the same as on the base of that cooker, so perhaps it was used to incapacitate her."

Carol glanced at it. The cooker looked heavy. "Poor cow. So she trusted the person enough to have her back to them?"

"Seems so," Dave said.

Rib coughed. "Excuse me. Got a tickle in my throat."

"Are you coming down with something?" Carol asked. "You had a frog in it before."

"I feel all right. Okay, so lividity is on her back; she died in this position. As with Gail, the blood tells the story. She was killed in this room."

"And it's the same killer because of the tool being hidden beneath her." No one had leaked that to the news, so it wasn't a copycat killer. The ages, though. It *had* to be important, didn't it? Every dead person was sixty-five or over. "We'll have to check with Kevin to see if he recognises the shears and the trowel. Are they from his toolbox?"

"Or were they taken from Gail's shed?" Dave suggested. "Either way, if they're Gail's, we've still got the question of whether this *is* something to do with Kevin. Yes, he seems a nice enough fella, but a lot of them do."

Carol sighed. "I've taken pictures on my phone, so he might be able to tell us something. It's unfortunate that the trowel is still in Violet's mouth — that's something you can't *unsee* — but it can't be helped. Then there's the blood on those shears."

"I don't have to tell you her neck was gouged with those, do I, Bird?" Rib asked.

"No, I worked that out for myself. Have you done Gail's PM yet?"

"No."

She glanced at the clock on the wall. Seven o'clock. Callum had arrived here at quarter to five — he tended to set sail early — and time had passed quickly with SOCO and Rib turning up, officers cordoning the cul-de-sac off and the tent being erected. Carol had only been told around six, the call getting her out of bed.

"We'll do house-to-house enquiries in the Rest," she said. "Richard's already out with officers in the nearby streets. I don't even know the residents here anymore apart from Violet and Callum. Since the Mason case, homeowners have changed. We'll do the others first in case they leave for work early."

Callum could wait until last. She doubted he'd feel like going anywhere.

* * *

The woman in Edward Fields's old bungalow had three kids and a little dog that wouldn't stop yapping around her ankles. Carol had a headache, and each grating bark set off the throbbing in her scalp.

"Is it possible to pop the dog in the garden?" she asked.

Bethany Swithin did that then returned to the front door, her young children peering at Carol through the balusters, their bums parked on the stairs. It reminded her of when *she'd* sat on the stairs in her family home, listening to Dad ranting and raving.

She'd already shown her ID and introduced them. "We're investigating an incident across the road at Violet Kinnock's, number five. Did you hear owt going on late last night?"

Bethany laughed. "You're joking, aren't you? I'm out like at light by nine with the kids. I'm a single parent and exhausted. I work long hours."

"Okay, thank you for your time."

The man at number three was gruff as arseholes, clearly having been woken up by her knock, but once he realised they were the police, he lightened up a bit. He hadn't seen or heard anything either, going to bed at ten to watch a film that had "loads of guns and shit" blaring through the speakers. The couple at four were just leaving as Carol and Dave approached, the man strapping a baby seat in the back, the occupant squalling, the lady rubbing her red eyes and sighing. They'd gone to bed at seven — their baby always kept them up from three until five — so they'd grabbed the chance for some sleep while the child was settled.

"Callum's, then," Carol said.

Dave followed her to number two. An officer opened the door, and they stepped inside, finding Callum at his kitchen table with a hot drink in front of him.

"How are you?" Carol asked.

"How do you think?" he snapped. "Sorry. I'm just . . . It's . . ."

"I know." She sat beside him.

He went through what had happened, adding that he'd been in the Devil until eleven last night, came home, and fell asleep in the living room with the telly on. "Violet, though. I heard about Clem and Frank an' all. What the hell's going on? If Mason was still around, I'd think he was at it again."

"There's also a Gail Cotter. Do you know her?"

"I know the name Cotter, but only because of that ChatSesh fella."

"As you've got quite close to Violet since taking over Skipper's boat, would she have told you if she was having trouble with someone?"

"Yeah, she would, but she never said owt. I don't get why someone would kill her. She's lovely."

As were Clem, Frank and Gail.

So who the bloody hell was going around killing nice people?

* * *

Carol left Dave chatting with the log officer and walked to the next street to find Richard, who was coming down someone's path, shaking his head.

"As usual, we've got nowt," he said. "Everyone so far was in bed."

"We've just had the same in the Rest."

"Is Violet linked?"

Carol nodded. "A pair of pruning shears left beneath the body. She had a trowel rammed in her mouth. The blade bit. Looks like it's gone right to the back of her neck. I didn't ask Rib if it had penetrated the skin."

"Err, I wouldn't have either."

"Sorry, I've just given you a horrible image."

"I'd imagined it myself anyroad. Christ, this is someone with a lot of rage. They've got to be angry if they're attacking people like that."

"I know, but with all of them being so well-liked, how we're meant to know who'd have a grudge that bad is beyond me."

"There'll be a reason, there always is. Might not make sense to us, but to the killer, it'll seem a good enough excuse to kill."

Carol would never understand the workings of a criminal mind, and no excuse would fly with her. Four good people were dead, but what had they done to the killer to warrant their deaths?

Or is it just random? Wrong place, wrong time?

Her phone rang, and she waved at Richard to end their conversation and moved away to answer. Joy's name sat on the bar across the screen, and Carol hoped one of the uniforms had come up trumps and they had something they could go on.

"Morning," Carol said.

"Morning. We've had a triple-nine call from the manager at the Beachfront Hotel. There's been a murder in the top-floor suite."

"Oh God. Any ID on them?"

"It's Kevin Cotter. Eliza Morris woke up and found him."

Carol's world narrowed to just a patch of sky and the breeze ruffling her hair. Selfishly, she thought about the shears and trowel. She had no one to show the pictures to now. "What the hell are they doing *there*? They're supposed to be at his caravan."

"I don't know. I've sent Mulholland and Grebe."

"Shit, Rib's with Violet Kinnock. Mind you, he might be finished soon, and Violet will stay in situ for a while yet anyroad as there's a lot for SOCO to do in her bungalow. Okay, we'll be there in about half an hour. I'll let Rib and Todd know."

"Good, I was just about to phone them. Err, have a nice day . . ."

"I'd laugh, but I haven't got it in me."

Carol rushed back round to Violet's, slowed down by having to phone Michael and Katherine to get in earlier than usual, putting booties on at the edge of the property, signing the log and telling Dave about Kevin. His "What the *fuck*?" said it all.

She entered the rear garden and remained at the back door, looking in at Rib and Todd. "Kevin Cotter's copped it at the Beachfront Hotel."

Todd groaned. "Okay, I'll get Ben over there with another team. I feel for them as everyone's been so busy. They'll be knackered. This lot here are hanging. Can't be helped, I suppose."

Rib stared down at Violet. "Sorry, love, but I've got to go."

Tears stung Carol's eyes. Murder affected so many, not just the family and friends left behind. Coppers, pathologists, techs, everyone was touched by it.

She only wished she could catch this bastard before anyone else died. But was Kevin connected, or was his murder to do with the messages Eliza had been getting? The woman hiding in the bushes behind his house?

Not knowing pissed her off.

* * *

To say today had gone tits up, all before eight o'clock, was an understatement. Head to toe in protective clothing — she felt like she'd lived in it the past few days — Carol stood on an evidence step next to the bed farthest from Kevin. She had a dilemma. Who was his next of kin now? Madeline was an ex-wife, Poppy wasn't his child, and Michael had added details to the whiteboard beneath Kevin's name which stated his father was deceased and there were no siblings. Were there aunts and uncles? Grandparents? Cousins? As a courtesy, she'd let Madeline know later so she could break the news to Poppy if she was still maintaining the ruse about her daughter's paternity.

The other suites on this floor had been vacated, the guests relocated on the lower floors. According to Mulholland, no one in the suites either side of this one had heard any noise that would alarm them.

Kevin had died from a gunshot wound to his temple. The sickening sight of a clean shape on the bed next to him where Eliza must have lain had Carol coming over queasy. There was even the outline of her hair where it had splayed on the mattress. Blood and brain matter would have landed on her, and to think she'd been oblivious gave Carol the shivers. How had she slept through the noise of a shot? Was she a heavy sleeper? No, more likely, a silencer had been used.

Carol glanced at the bedside cabinet on Eliza's side. A set of orange earplugs. That explained her not hearing the shot to a degree, but those things didn't deaden noise completely.

She imagined Eliza waking up, her hair matted and sticky, her face tight with dried blood. Turning to cuddle Kevin, only to find one side of his head had been blown off. Eliza was currently downstairs in an office. Mulholland had informed Carol that Eliza had been naked when he and Grebe had arrived, and he'd asked reception to bring up a dressing gown for her to wear while being escorted from the scene.

The woman must be in bits.

Dave grunted beside her. "All that money he earned, and there's no one to leave it to. No one to sell ChatSesh to."

"Maybe he had provisions in place. I'll ask Eliza."

Ben Asher came in and balanced on a step. "Photos have been taken of Eliza, for the blood spatter, so we can determine if they match what's happened at the scene."

"Thanks. That must have been embarrassing for her."

"Apparently, she wasn't bothered about having no clothes on, she just wanted it done so we can find out who did this to Kevin. The bullet lodged in that chest of drawers over there." He pointed.

Carol spotted a hole beside the handle.

Ben continued. "The rest of the suite's tidy, but we've got a bugger of a job on our hands. Despite the cleaners coming in here when guests leave, there's bound to be umpteen hairs and fingerprints that aren't owt to do with the killer. The fingerprints might not be on file either. Not everyone's a criminal."

"Then we'll go through the guest list, get their alibis and strike them off that way," Carol said.

Rib bent over to get a closer look at Kevin's temple where the bullet had entered. "Close range. Someone held the gun about an inch or two from his head. Seems to me like he was asleep when it happened. He's not in full rigor — he's actually still warm — so this is an early-in-the-morning murder. Say between five and eight."

"Surely staff would have been around."

"Not up here," Dave said. "Guests would still be asleep, unless they needed to move on for work."

"Downstairs, then. Staff would be up to get breakfast ready."

Mulholland called out from his position at the front door as log officer. "Grebe's checking all that now."

"Okay," Carol said. "So someone broke in, killed him and left."

"Unless Eliza did it." Dave scrunched his eyebrows.

"Are you kidding me?" Carol folded her arms.

"I mean she got someone else to do it."

Carol didn't think Eliza was the sort. "Didn't you see how she looked at him? She's well loved-up."

"Could be an act." Dave didn't have to say it, but Carol knew he was thinking about his ex-wife. He hadn't had a clue she'd been messing around behind his back, and she'd likely looked at him nicely, too.

"Okay, there's nowt more we can do here, so let's go downstairs. Hopefully, someone will offer us some coffee."

* * *

Eliza shook, her teeth chattering. She sat on a plastic chair in the hotel office, with a blanket around her as well as the dressing gown, and her arms wrapped across her middle. She glanced up at Carol entering, and tears filled her eyes.

"I'm so sorry." Carol went over to crouch by her and hold her hand.

"When can I . . . get this blood off me?"

"You can have a shower as soon as we've had a chat. You can't have any of your clothes, though, they're part of the crime scene — I noted your suitcase was open on the floor on your side of the bed, so the things inside will be . . . I'll get an officer to bring you a tracksuit from the station for now, then we'll drop you at Seaview to collect some bits and bobs. We'll have to put you somewhere else." Carol glanced around. "Where's Preston?"

"I don't know." Eliza clamped her teeth to stop them from clacking.

Carol stood and walked over to the door to speak to Grebe. "Can you find out whether Kevin's security officer is around, please?"

He nodded and left the room.

Carol closed the door. "Okay, first, tell me what you're doing here."

"Preston s-saw someone outside the caravan with a gun. He w-went after them, but they ran off. He said we should leave, that our location was c-compromised, and he booked this suite in his brother's name so no one would know we'd come here. Kevin gave him enough cash to pay for last night."

"So you came here, and then what?"

"Kevin wanted to phone you, but Preston said it could be a leak at the station. He suggested we tell you to your face so only you would know, and Kevin agreed. We went to bed, and Preston was in the second bedroom. Next thing I know, it's morning, and I sat up to get out of bed but didn't hear Kevin snoring. I looked over my shoulder and . . . Oh God . . ."

"Did you phone it in straight away?"

Eliza nodded. "Yes."

"Did you touch him?"

"No!" She shuddered.

Carol could understand it, her not checking for a pulse. With the exit wound, it was clear Kevin was dead. "So you didn't hear anyone coming in, nor the gunshot?"

"No. I wear earplugs."

"But surely you'd have still heard something."

"I didn't."

A silencer, then. "When you phoned the police, where did you do it? In your bedroom?"

"To begin with, yes, but I couldn't stay in there with Kevin like . . . like that, so I walked around trying to find Preston."

"Was he there?"

"No."

"Didn't you wonder where he was?"

"I assumed he'd gone out to do a recce. He's got a list of things he does every day, and making sure that the hotels we stay in are safe is one of them."

"Yet he hasn't come back."

"Oh my God, do you think *he* killed Kevin?"

"That . . . or whoever did it took Preston."

"Why would they do that?"

"He could have woken up and discovered them."

"Oh no . . ."

"It's okay, CCTV will help. I have to ask this. Do you know what will happen about Kevin's money and ChatSesh now, because with Gail dead, there doesn't appear to be a next of kin."

"We've only been together for six months, so it'd be rude to ask. It isn't any of my business. He has a solicitor. The one in town. James Abbott."

"Right, we'll get you a shower sorted, then we'll go to Seaview. After that . . . we'll work something out."

"If this is the person who sent me the text and the emails, why didn't they kill me, too?"

"Like I said, Preston might have interrupted them. Whatever the case, you're not safe until we catch who did this, so staying under the radar is important."

"Okay."

A full-body tremor took hold of Eliza, and she broke down crying, her sobs hard to hear. She'd be beating herself up for not hearing an intruder, for not saving the man she loved, and unfortunately, she'd have to live with that for the rest of her life.

* * *

With Eliza having a shower and an officer standing guard outside the room the hotel manager had assigned her, Carol checked in with Grebe about Preston Brown. No one had seen him leave, and CCTV at the front wasn't any help. He hadn't left that way, so the only other route was a set of patio doors in the dining room or the staff entrance. *Had* Preston done this? To cover all bases, Carol phoned it in as a BOLO and also asked her team to drag up any information about him. Was he a killer or a victim?

She left Dave to wait for Eliza and wandered out to reception to speak to the manager, who took her into another office.

"I need to know who booked that suite," she said.

"I've already looked into it for you. It was a Mr Spectre."

"Um, is that a joke?"

"Not as far as I'm aware. It was paid for in cash under that name."

"What, no one asked for photo ID? Surely you should have done that. When was this?"

He blushed. "We messed up there, and it won't happen again. I'll speak to whoever was on duty and reprimand them. It's policy to see ID. And as for when this was, it was during the night, at around half past two."

"Who came in to pay?"

"A young woman. I've isolated her on CCTV for you and taken a still." He handed a printed photo over.

Carol didn't recognise her. She had large sunglasses on, blonde hair — the woman behind the bush? — and a black beret. A trench coat straight out of a spoof mystery film was cinched at the waist with a wide belt. Black knee-high boots. Couple that with the name Mr Spectre, and this was taking the piss.

"Thanks. I'll need to take that CCTV."

He passed her a memory stick. "Thought you'd need it. One more thing. A second room was booked under that name. The gentleman has been staying here full-time for six months, also paying in cash."

"Again, without showing his ID?"

"I'd have to check the system to see."

"Deary me . . . What does he look like?"

"I also have a still of him." He fetched it from the desk.

Carol stared down at an image of Preston Brown. Shit. "Right, um . . ." Her mind spun with all the possibilities, but the main thing now was to get that room searched.

The manager gave her the room number and key card and she went out to her car, collecting two forensic suits. Back inside she asked the uniform in the lobby to send one of the others to wait for Eliza outside room ten. There, she stood with Dave until the officer relieved him.

"Preston had another room here." She handed Dave a suit and booties. "SOCO are stretched, so we'll do the initial search."

They found the room, and Carol opened the door, anxious in case Preston was hiding out in here. She proceeded with caution, alert, and checked the bedroom area plus the bathroom.

No Preston.

They set about doing a full search, Carol taking the wardrobe, Dave nosing through the bedside cabinet. Preston had cleared the place out.

"Carol . . ."

She turned. Dave had lifted one half of the mattress. She moved to his side and stared at the divan base.

A gun.

She smiled. Whatever had happened, Preston was a suspect now, not a missing person. The idea he'd had to leave here under duress didn't ring true. He was a trained security officer.

Or was he a trained assassin?

CHAPTER FORTY-EIGHT

Seaview Heights

Carol stared at the broken kitchen window. A large stone sat on the floor, glass shards spread wide, some bigger pieces in the sink. Eliza remained by the stairs, and Dave had gone up to see if anything had been disturbed.

Carol phoned Todd to see if he could spare a couple of SOCOs to go over the house. She was concerned that Preston's blonde accomplice from the hotel had broken in to steal things, knowing Kevin and Eliza were at the caravan. Had she come here to carry out the threat in the text? That didn't make sense. Preston would have been able to tell her the couple weren't at home.

"Carol?" Dave called. "Come up here."

Carol jerked her head at Eliza for her to follow — she couldn't leave her vulnerable down here on her own. She found Dave in the master bedroom and stood on the landing, looking to where he pointed.

A framed photo lay on the bed, a knife sticking out of Kevin's face. The blade stood upright, stuck deep into the mattress. Eliza gasped from behind her, and Carol moved across so she could see.

"Do you recognise that knife?"

"It's not one of ours. We have steel handles. Oh God, who's *doing* this?"

Eliza broke down, sitting on the landing, and Carol crouched to place a hand on her shoulder. "From the knife being in Kevin's face, I'd say it was a warning about what happened early this morning, that he was the target. While you were packing and we were next door with your neighbours, did you tell anyone about going to the caravan? Did he?"

Eliza shook her head. "No! Do you think we'd *want* them following us?"

"Of course not, I just wondered if you had any family or friends you'd want to tell."

"You told us no one could know."

"Come on, we'll go outside. Do you have any clothes elsewhere in the house? It's best we don't take any from this room."

"There's a double wardrobe in my dressing room."

Eliza got up and went through one of the other doorways, coming out with an armful of clothes. "My suitcases are in our bedroom."

"Just take them like that."

Carol led her downstairs, and she left her outside with Dave to wait for SOCO while she went to see Willy and Lise.

Willy opened the door. "Oh, hello again. Have you come to tell me we're needed down at the station for a statement?"

"No. I just need to ask if you heard owt going on next door last night. Kevin's had a break-in."

"Oh, bloody hell! I knew we shouldn't have gone out. We took a train to Leeds and stayed over. Caught a show. Only just got back. We left there early because Lise has a spa appointment this morning. She's there now, getting primped."

"Never mind."

"Is Kevin okay?" He craned his neck to look at Eliza and Dave.

"I'm afraid Kevin died this morning."

"Oh my days, that's awful! How?"

"I'd rather not discuss it. I'm sure it will be on the news today."

"Ah, some other murders were on breakfast telly this morning. Four of them, all *old* people." He'd said it like old was a dirty word, his face scrunched up, yet he wasn't exactly young himself.

"I seem to recall you mentioning working on compassion . . ."

She walked away with him apologising. Lise wasn't the only one who needed to watch what she said.

CHAPTER FORTY-NINE

Ridgebrook Close

Sam Larkin hadn't seen his mother for six months, staying away because his Polish wife, Uroda, deserved to be treated better. Mam hadn't liked the idea of Sam marrying "some foreign person who can't even speak English properly". He didn't blame Uroda for not trying harder to get Mam to see her for the wonderful woman she was. Why should she when Mam picked at her whenever she got the chance, poking fun at her accent, the way she dressed, everything she did? She'd even gone as far as accusing Uroda of marrying Sam so she could live in the UK. That was ridiculous, he'd been seeing Uroda for years before they'd married. He conducted business in Poland and had stayed at her flat, and she'd only moved over here last year. Uroda was a good woman, kind and generous, and if Mam couldn't see past her being Polish, then that was her problem.

He hadn't expected to see Mam like this — who the fuck would? Slumped over her little dining table, blood everywhere. What he *had* expected was another argument, her saying he was supposed to have come to fix the blind yesterday, not today, berating Uroda for keeping him away, then it would move on to Herbie and the state he was in. Sam had offered to take the dog to a groomer and pay someone to walk him, but Mam hadn't wanted to risk Uroda going anywhere near him if Sam was too busy to do it. She had the idea that Polish people ate dogs and Uroda would cook him, serve him up for Sunday lunch alongside a stack of roast potatoes.

He obviously wouldn't be putting the blind up now. How odd that he didn't feel anything but the initial shock. He'd never dreamed it would end like this, but no tears stung his eyes, no memories of good times crashed into him (there weren't any), and he didn't feel the need to go to her, to check if she was still alive. Not because it was obvious she was dead but because . . . sometimes, a mother shouldn't be a mother, and a dead one like this deserved all she got. Some women weren't born to have children, it wasn't their calling, wasn't in their make-up, and that was okay. Uroda didn't want kids, and Sam didn't think anything of it other than it was her right. Mam wasn't maternal, she should never have had Sam, she should have followed her instincts and declined to procreate, but apparently, Dad had forced her into motherhood.

It had been a mistake.

Sam found it difficult to feel anything towards the woman bent over the table. She'd made no bones about him being a pest, always in her way, preventing her from doing what she wanted. The fact that Dad had died when Sam had been two had been the mouldy cherry on top of Mam's shitty life cake, and she'd been stuck with a child she'd never wanted. Why the hell hadn't she put him up for adoption?

Sam hadn't gone inside. He'd rung the bell out the front and, getting no response, had come round the back, finding the door wide open and no Herbie, which was a concern. Then he'd seen her, and a sense of relief had gone through him. No more disdain, no more acerbic comments. Bar her funeral, he was free of responsibility now.

He sat on the wooden bench in her garden, legs stretched out, planning to phone the police soon, but for now, he'd take a moment to revel in his freedom. Maybe a good few moments. Another hour or so wouldn't hurt.

It wasn't like she was going anywhere, was it?

CHAPTER FIFTY

Ridgebrook Close

Eliza had been placed in a safe house with PC Helen May. Carol was glad to have the weeping woman off her hands, not that the crying got on her nerves, but she couldn't stand seeing her so upset. It drained her energy.

Now, she had Madeline to deal with.

"What do you need from me? I was just about to get Poppy's coat on upstairs and take her to the pier."

Carol remained standing in the kitchen. "I don't know how you want to play this with your daughter, considering what we know about her parentage, but I have some sad news."

"What is it?"

"Kevin died this morning."

"What?" Madeline shrieked. "*What?* Kevin, dead? How?"

"He was murdered. Shot."

Madeline sank onto a dining chair, elbows on the table, holding her forehead in her hands. "No, this can't be happening. He wasn't supposed to *die*!"

"What do you mean by that?"

"He's . . . Did he kill himself, is that it? Couldn't he stand the guilt of murdering his mother?"

"Kevin wasn't anywhere near Gail, or the others, when they were killed. His whereabouts are on film."

"What about the tools?"

"They're undergoing tests, but he couldn't have used them."

Madeline pinched at her cheeks. Alarmed at the woman's ferocity, Carol reached out and lowered her hands to the table.

"I understand this must be a shock, but I'm going to have to ask you where you were in the early hours of this morning."

"What, you think *I* killed him?" Madeline laughed hysterically. "I might detest the man for what he did to us, but I didn't want him *dead*."

"What about yesterday evening, later on in the night? Where were you then?"

"I was here with Poppy."

"Is the name Violet Kinnock familiar to you?"

"Of course, she was in the paper about her husband dying."

Carol recalled the interview Violet had done. "Do you know her any other way?"

"She was a tour guide on Skipper's boat a long time ago. Me and Kevin went out on the trawler."

"And that's it?"

"Yes." She clawed at her neck.

"The family who moved away down the street. The friend Poppy went to see while you were in town. Where did they move to?"

"I don't know. To be honest, I don't bloody care, not after what you've just told me. What am I going to tell Poppy?"

"That's for you to decide, but if she doesn't inherit Kevin's money or business, she might ask questions later down the line."

Carol made her a cuppa and left her to it. A domestic drama between mother and daughter wasn't something she wanted to witness.

* * *

Carol had phoned Michael to ask him to contact James Abbott, Kevin's solicitor, and let him know his client was deceased and to find out if there were any relatives they didn't know about. Now, she sat in Dr Johann's office, Dave beside her on a squidgy blue sofa, Ian behind his desk.

"I have ten minutes between patients," he said.

Carol studied him. He was nondescript, someone you'd pass by without bothering to look at him — nothing about him caught the eye. He was relaxed, showed no signs of distress and had a professional aura about him.

"How do you know Madeline Cotter?" she asked.

His demeanour changed. A scowl formed, and his back straightened. He tapped a pen against his cheek. "We went to university together."

"I'll come clean and tell you we're aware of Poppy."

"Right . . ."

She blasted him with a second shock. "Kevin died this morning."

His eyebrows hiked up, and he paled. "Oh God, she's going to want me to step in now there's no worry about him finding out."

"What do you mean?"

"She contacted me years after Poppy was born, asking me to come round as a friend so I could watch her grow up. Kevin had left her, and he wasn't seeing the child, so she wanted me as a father figure. I don't even know for sure if she's mine."

"According to Kevin, he had a DNA test that states she definitely isn't his."

"What? He *knew* about it?"

"That's why he stopped contact, although he paid money out for her."

Ian closed his eyes for a couple of seconds. "Christ. Does Madeline know he was in the loop?"

"Not that we're aware."

"How . . . how did he die?"

"He was murdered. Shot." She watched his reaction.

"Jesus. Who the hell would have a gun around here?" He appeared genuinely confused and shocked. "I don't know what to say. I didn't really know him, only from the brief chats if Madeline brought him to the student bar, which wasn't often."

"What's your relationship with her now?"

His cheeks reddened. "We don't have one. She . . ." He sighed. "She got fixated around the time we had sex. Kept turning up at my mam's where I lived and standing in the street, staring up at my bedroom window. I didn't go out there — uni had finished, so I didn't want to see her anymore, mainly because going with her had been a mistake. She was married to Kevin at the time. In the end, what with her constant phone calls and what I felt was general harassment, I opted to move to Scotland to do work-based psychology where I learned on the job."

"So you didn't hear about Poppy until . . ."

"She phoned me. She'd got my number off Mam. She was drunk and said she thought Kevin was going to leave her, then she dropped the bombshell. She rang me again a while later. I'd come back to Scudderton by then as I'd got the job here, although she wasn't aware of where I was working, and later, when I went round to visit her, she accused me of only coming back because she wasn't a nurse here anymore. I told her I didn't think it was going to work, me spending time with Poppy, and to be honest, like I said, I didn't even know if she was mine. I told her to get in touch if she wanted a DNA test done and left it at that, and I didn't see her again until a few months later."

"What happened at that meeting?"

"It was here. She'd asked for a slot so I could assess Poppy."

"What for?"

"Is this to do with the case you're working on? I'm thinking patient confidentiality."

"Yes, it could be relevant."

"Okay, then she brought Poppy here to see if she had mental health issues as she'd been in hospital on several occasions. Her blood had been poisoned by faecal matter, and Madeline was worried Poppy was smearing it into her cuts in order to get attention. Kevin had left her, so Madeline thought Poppy was crying out to be noticed. After speaking to the child, I could see straight away she wasn't doing it to herself. I implied Madeline was doing it, and her reaction seemed genuine — that it wasn't her either — so I told her I wasn't the kind of psychologist Poppy needed. Besides, if she's mine, it would have been unethical for me to treat her."

"Why didn't you check up on whether Madeline wanted a DNA test?"

"Believe me, if she'd wanted one, she would have said so. I took it that Poppy wasn't mine, Madeline just wanted a patsy to foist her onto, and that was that."

"Do you know her state of mind regarding Kevin?"

"We're talking quite a while ago, so no, I don't, not these days, and when I did see her, she didn't come across as having a vendetta against him, if that's what you're really asking."

"It is." Carol smiled. "I should have known better than to try to kid a psychologist."

Ian laughed. "I really don't think I can help you. I'm married now, I have children. I've moved on, and I suspect Madeline will have, too."

"That's debatable."

"Oh dear."

"Hmm. Okay, thanks for speaking with us."

They said their goodbyes, and Carol and Dave headed for the car park, her mind on why on earth Poppy would have been infected with faecal matter. Was that why she was in a wheelchair? Had the poisonings affected her in some way? It was a strange, mixed-up little scenario but not something Carol could poke into. Madeline and Poppy had alibis; therefore, looking into Poppy's medical records was off the table.

Besides, Poppy wasn't a suspect, so Carol's hands were tied, but curiosity was a persistent bitch, and she thought about the hospital stays all the way back to the station.

She walked in, and Joy called her over.

"What's up?" Carol asked.

"There's been another one."

"For Pete's *sake*!"

Joy looked at her with sympathy. "I feel your pain. It's a Mrs Rebecca Larkin. Elderly. She lives in the same street as Madeline Cotter. Number twenty."

"We've not long been there to see Madeline. Shit, did we just miss the killer or something?"

"I don't know how long she's been dead. There's a screwdriver at the scene."

Carol closed her eyes. Were they ever going to find this nutter? She hoped so, because the deaths were piling up, and whoever it was needed to be stopped before some other unlucky sod lost their life.

* * *

Ridgebrook Close

Protective clothing on, Carol and Dave stood on evidence steps in the deceased's kitchen waiting for Rib as he had to travel from the Beachfront, where he'd been attending Kevin's scene. Todd had left Violet Kinnock's bungalow in capable hands to come here with a small team of SOCOs. He was off doing a walkabout and taking notes.

Rebecca Larkin had several holes in her blouse where the screwdriver had been stabbed into her back. A cup had been knocked over, probably when she'd fallen forward, and the contents had spread on the table. So had she been sitting here with a drink when someone had attacked her? With no other cup around, it would suggest she hadn't made a brew for her "guest".

"Yet another older person," she grumbled.

Dave puffed air out, his mask inflating. "Changing the subject . . . I don't know about you, but I'm knackered."

"Same. It's not just gadding about questioning people, it's the mental angle that takes its toll. My brain hurts."

"Same."

Todd came back through from the hallway, using the evidence steps to move closer. "There's no visual blood anywhere else, but Luminol will show up owt we can't see. It doesn't look like a robbery — no sign of a disturbance. The water in the washing-up bowl has a pink tinge to it, so I assume the killer cleaned his or her hands. How's the son doing?" He glanced out of the glass in the back door. "Oh, he's gone."

"I asked Fisher to sit in his car with him," Carol said. "He doesn't need to see us standing by his dead mother, discussing her."

"No," Todd agreed. "Ay up, there's Rib." He nodded to the back door.

Rib sorted his booties then stepped inside. "I'm going to have no room left in my fridges at this rate." He grinned and raised his mask. "I've got a Home Office pathologist down at the lab. I can't be in all places at once. We'll be working together on Violet, Kevin and this poor soul here. Rebecca Larkin, yes?"

"Yes. Her son found her." Carol looked at the roller blind on the side. "According to Richard, Sam Larkin came to do a bit of DIY. We need to speak to him in a sec, but I wanted to wait for you to see when she died, because I need to rewrite the timeline in my head. Like, was she before or after Kevin?"

Rib got on with doing Rebecca's temperature via her ear. "This didn't happen today." He felt her arm. "Rigor is at the tail end, so an estimate is twenty-four hours ago." He glanced at his watch. "So around this time yesterday, maybe a bit later."

"Okay, thanks. We'll leave you to it, then." Carol paused on her way to the back door. "Oh, can you check if there's owt on her lap, a hidden weapon? With her hunched over like that . . ."

Rib bent to look into the gap her torso had created. "Well, there's no other weapon, but look at that neck."

Carol hadn't seen it from her position on the other side of the body. She shifted across to view where Rib pointed. A hole in the neck. "That'll be where the majority of the blood came from?"

"Yes." Rib indicated the floor. "Classic spatter pattern of a ruptured carotid. As for the hole at her nape and those on her back . . . The back seems to indicate a frenzied attack, so perhaps Rebecca affected the killer more emotionally than the others did."

"Let's hope we find out someone had a grudge against her. We need a lead."

"We do."

"Right, we'll get going. Bye for now." Carol dealt with her protectives and signed out of the log.

Dave wasn't far behind her. She walked out the front to a silver Saab, spotting Sam Larkin staring out of the driver's-side window. PC Fisher exited the passenger seat so Carol could take his place. Dave got in the back.

"Hi, Sam. I'm DI Carol Wren, and this is DS Dave Waite. I'm sorry for your loss. Apologies for getting straight to it, but can you tell me a bit about your movements today?"

He explained his morning up until now. "And the dog's missing."

That's the first time he's shown any emotion. "You said the back door was open, but was the gate? As in, he could have run away?"

"Yes, the gate was open, but he'd have stayed with Mam. The dog's devoted to her, though God knows why."

"What's that mean?"

Sam sighed. "Look, I'm going to sound nasty, but me and my mother . . . Let's say she should never have had kids. She didn't want me and made no bones about it for my whole life. We were kind of estranged. I stay away because she's rude to my wife, rude to me, and I've had enough of it. Just because she's my mam, doesn't mean I have to put up with it."

That hit home for Carol. She'd put up with her father when she should have walked away, cut him out of her life. Maybe if she'd had a boyfriend she'd cared about who Dad had been rude to, *she'd* have estranged herself, too. "I understand, I really do, and that isn't just lip service. So why did you come here today?"

"She needed a blind putting up in the kitchen. She only phones me when she needs stuff like that doing. The rest of the time I might as well not exist. I said no, that I'd pay for someone else to do it, and she said she couldn't trust other people to do the job properly and not steal her things."

"What kinds of things?"

"Her house is full of antiques, did you not notice?"

"I'm afraid I wouldn't know an antique if it slapped me in the face."

"She collects them. She used to leave me at home when I was little and swan off to fayres and auctions, sometimes leaving me overnight. I fended for myself a lot of the time. I must be one of the only kids who loved going to school because it meant I was with people who gave a shit, teachers and whatever."

"I understand that, too." It was eerie the way they had parallels. "Would you know if owt has been stolen?"

"No. I left home at sixteen, got myself a bedsit and a little job. I didn't come here much after that. Too busy with college, then uni, then starting my business."

"What is it you do?"

"I run a logistics firm."

"Would any of your employees or clients have killed your mother to get at you?"

"I doubt they even know I have a mother. I don't discuss her. I tried again with her when I first got married — you know, wanting to see if it could work. I had this stupid need to introduce her to Uroda — that's my wife — but Mam didn't like her, so . . . Christ, I wish I hadn't come today."

"So you wouldn't have been the one to find her?"

"Sort of. It's more because I had to experience the sense of relief I felt seeing her dead. I thought it made me a bastard."

Carol reached out and rested a hand on his arm. "If you've had the kind of life I suspect, it really is natural to feel this way. I've been in your position, and knowing they can't hurt you anymore is a massive weight lifted."

Sam nodded. "I didn't deserve being brought up by her. It wasn't my fault she didn't want me."

"Then you're in a good place mentally if you're thinking along those lines."

"I don't throw pity parties for myself. I prefer to put the past behind me and move on. Otherwise, I'd be depressed."

Carol's way of dealing with her situation had been to throw herself into work. "Okay, so despite everything, you didn't have a grudge against her?"

"No. I did once, but Uroda's made me a better person. She's shown me that Mam was . . . different, shall we say, and her issues aren't mine to carry. I'm apathetic, that's the word. I didn't care if she lived because I'd chosen to barely see her, and I didn't care if she died either."

Carol knew if he'd said this to any other officers, he'd be straight at the top of the suspect list. Those who hadn't endured a bad parent would never understand how someone could feel this way, and Dave was well aware of Carol's circumstances so would have empathy for Sam. "Do you know of anyone else who'd have wanted to do this to your mother?"

Sam laughed. "God, I imagine there's a few. She can be acerbic. Cruel with her words. I don't know any names, I'm just guessing people might have been offended by her. Neighbours."

"Was Uroda offended by her?"

"No. She's got this ability to brush things off. The way Mam treated her hurt *me* more than my wife. Uroda is . . . amazing; she's too kind to do owt like this. When was Mam killed?"

"About twenty-four hours ago, maybe more."

"Oh, then we were in Whitby. An all-day conference." He let her know the location.

"Can you give PC Fisher a description of the dog so the relevant people can keep an eye out for it? Was it chipped?"

"No, Mam didn't feel she had to follow the rules like that. Last I saw him he was matted — she didn't groom him or owt." He explained about offering to get it done for her and that his mother had refused.

"She sounds like she didn't want any help at all, barring you doing the blind."

Sam sighed. "My father insisted she have a baby — me. She's rebelled against being told what to do ever since. That's what Uroda thinks anyroad."

"Okay, that's handy. It lets us know what sort of person your mam was. We're going to get on now, and someone will be in touch for a proper statement soon. I realise the circumstances are unusual in your case, but will you be dealing with the funeral?"

"Yes, but I don't want to."

"I get that. It'll be a while before you can arrange it. We'll need to hold on to the body."

Dave took Sam's details, and Carol got out of the car to speak to Fisher about a statement and the dog. Next she moved along the street to talk to Alan Pitson, who chatted with Richard Prince.

"What time did you go and speak to Madeline Cotter yesterday, Alan?" She passed on the estimated time of death.

"I was with her around the eleven o'clock mark — I was just telling Richard I looked through her window and saw someone going into Mrs Larkin's via the back then coming out with a dog."

Carol's interest piqued. "Oh?"

"He had his head down so I couldn't see his face — well, I assume it was a he. Tracksuit, trainers, so maybe a teenager or young man. He was in there for around five minutes then left. I assumed he'd gone to take the dog for a walk."

"Did you see any blood on him?"

"No, the tracksuit was black."

"At least I have a sighting of someone going to Mrs Larkin's, which is more than I had two minutes ago." Carol smiled at Alan then turned to Richard. "Any news from residents so far?"

"A couple of others saw the same person entering Mrs Larkin's, and one claimed he'd been there before to take the dog out, so do we assume he just goes there to do that?"

It's plausible. "Hmm, Todd said it doesn't look like a robbery was committed, and her son claims she has antiques — surely they'd have been nicked if someone knew she had them. The lad might not have owt to do with it. I'd still like to find him, though, to rule him out."

Alan folded his arms. "But if he walks the dog, why hasn't he brought it back?"

Carol pondered that. "Maybe he did and no one around here saw him; she could have been stabbed after he'd dropped it off. The killer left the door and gate open. The son says the dog wouldn't have run, but maybe the killer frightened it." She glanced around at the uniforms. "I'll leave you lot to it, there's nowt we can do here that you can't. Before I go . . . did anyone hear her screaming?"

Richard shook his head. "Nope."

"I wonder if the lad was Asher Welding." Carol stared over at that house. "I'm going to check with his mother."

She waited for Dave, and as they walked towards Asher's, she filled him in on what Alan and Richard had said.

Her phone rang. Michael.

"Hi," she said.

"We've had the results back from Asher Welding's clothing. Despite the clothing being washed, there was a speck of diluted blood in the elasticated hem of one leg, but unfortunately, it wasn't Clem's. It's feline."

"Oh right. I didn't see a cat when we were at his last."

"Have you not heard?"

"What about?"

"Someone's going around killing cats."

"Oh, fuck me. We're just going to his house now with regards to Rebecca Larkin — have any of you found owt of significance about her yet?"

"Nowt that would mean someone would kill her, unless they're easily offended. Will you be back soon? Just so I can put the details on the board before you get here."

"Yep, we're nipping to speak to Heidi Welding, then we'll come in."

"Okay. The cat killings were picked up by the local news earlier when a journalist discovered they'd all been shot with a BB gun. Maybe Asher's involved."

"Maybe he bloody is. Thanks for that."

"Don't go yet. There's something else. In his tracksuit pocket was a debit card belonging to a Mr P Jackson, who'd reported it missing on the night Asher had been to the pier with his mother. The pocket was zipped, which is why it wouldn't have fallen out into the washing machine."

"The night Clem died."

"Yes. We're in the process of contacting the bank to see who he is."

"Okay, can you get Lloyd on the pier CCTV again to look a lot closer at Asher and what he was doing. If he's thieving, it might not have shown up as such — he could be good at it, nabbing purses and wallets in the crowd."

"Will do."

Carol said goodbye and slipped her phone away. She faced Dave. "Apparently, someone's killing cats."

"Bloody hell, that's rotten."

"And it could well be Asher. Feline blood was found on his tracksuit, and guess what? Heidi might have to eat humble pie, because it seems like her son isn't such an angel after all. He had a stolen debit card in the tracksuit pocket."

"Oh dear."

"I know. She's not going to be pleased."

* * *

"You fucking *what*?" Heidi screeched. "My son's a cat killer and a thief now? You'd better have proof, because I'm telling you, I'll go straight to your boss and let him know you're harassing us."

"I can give you his phone number if you like," Carol offered.

"Yeah, you do that."

Carol took one of her cards out and wrote the DCI's name and number on the back. She handed it over.

Heidi snatched it and slung it on the worktop. "Listen to me. My Asher is a good boy. First you say he's killed Clem, then he's being a shit at the Odeon, one of you lot came here and said he was skiving, and now this."

"We *do* have proof that there's cat blood on the tracksuit, and we *do* have proof a debit card was in his pocket. What we *don't* have proof of is whether Asher is involved, but that begs the question: why would either of those things be there if he hasn't done owt? As those two pieces of evidence have come to our attention, we have to follow it up whether you think Asher is a good boy or not."

"Asher loves animals. Well, dogs anyroad. He wouldn't kill them."

"Someone will need to speak to him about it, plus the debit card. Unless you know a Mr P Jackson who could have loaned him the card?"

"I don't know any Jackson apart from them singers, so no, he wouldn't have his ruddy card."

Carol smiled tightly. "Okay, well, Asher will be spoken to about both matters. We have someone looking closer at the CCTV on the pier, so if he's caught lifting someone's wallet—"

"You cheeky cow! You lot talk a load of old shite. Innocent until proven guilty, my arse."

Carol didn't want to respond to the name-calling. Heidi would probably use it as an excuse to do it even more. "We're also here on another matter."

"Oh my *God*! Seriously? What is it, then? Has he nicked the queen's tiara an' all?"

"Err, no. Does he walk Mrs Larkin's dog for her?"

"No he bleedin' well doesn't. I see what you're doing. Someone's already been round asking about her. She's dead, right? You want to pin her murder on him. Well, he was in school when it happened, so up yours."

"Was he, though? You mentioned skiving . . ."

"Get out." Heidi pointed to the doorway. "Don't you come back here until you've got proper proof."

Carol pinched the bridge of her nose. "Someone will be in touch, and you'll need to go down to the station. If you don't want to sit in on the interview, an appropriate adult will be appointed. Enjoy the rest of your day."

"Sarky bitch . . ."

Dave held a hand up. "Stop, Heidi. Take a breath and please refrain from speaking to my colleague in that way. It won't do you any favours in the long run. *If* Asher has committed any offences and it's proven he's done so, you *will* need to accept that there's a side to him you were unaware of. Preaching that he's a good boy who'd do no wrong isn't working out too well for you at the minute, because we already know he's on his last warning at the Odeon. There will be CCTV of him annoying Frank West there, and the camera doesn't lie."

"But he's so nice at home."

"Most kids are. It's what they do outside that's the problem." Dave lowered his hand. "I understand that you don't want to face the fact your child might have been bad, but he could have, and we all need to deal with it in a calm manner. Being nasty to DI Wren won't change owt."

Heidi swallowed and glanced at Carol. "Sorry."

Carol kept quiet, not wanting to brush it off or negate Dave coming to her defence. She bloody loved him for doing that. "Like I said, someone will be in touch."

Carol left the property, wondering how the interview with Asher would go, glad she wouldn't be the one doing it. She felt for the poor officers who'd have to deal with Heidi, because she didn't think the woman was sorry at all. No, she'd give them hell. Maybe an appropriate adult would be assigned after all if she didn't behave herself during questioning.

CHAPTER FIFTY-ONE

Incident Room

Carol read the whiteboard. Rebecca Larkin owned a mobile phone, and Carol had let Todd know so he could find it and get it looked at by digi with regards to any messages and calls. Richard had rung in to say he'd checked the records and Rebecca had had run-ins with a few of the neighbours over the years but nothing that would result in someone wanting to stab her with a screwdriver. It was the usual gripes: 1991, someone had dropped litter in her front garden and her dog had choked on it; 2002, a teen had thrown a rock and smashed her living room window; 2018, she'd chased someone up the street while wielding a broom, all because they'd given her a funny look.

Most saw her as a crabby woman who was best avoided.

There was nothing else that pointed to a reason for murder.

"Is Rebecca on social media, Katherine?" Carol asked.

"Yes, but she doesn't have many friends. She belonged to a few groups, though. Antiques. All contacts relate to buying and selling."

"Has anyone got owt else about our other victims?"

Michael sat back and swung his chair round to face the room. "I've informed Kevin's solicitor about his death and enquired about his estate on the off chance Mr Abbott might divulge something. Unfortunately, he wasn't prepared to say what was going on but that he'd contact the relevant party today. I let him know Gail is also dead, so it can't be her."

"I wonder who it is." Carol stretched her legs out at the spare desk. "I doubt it would be Madeline, but would he have felt some duty to Poppy? Although . . . no, he'd already put some money in a trust."

"Maybe he's got a best friend — there's no other family, by the way," Katherine said. "I'll go through his social media accounts and see if someone comments more than others. Shall I also contact his managers? Do you know which one he left the running of ChatSesh to while he was taking time out?"

"No, but phone Eliza, she'll know."

Katherine wrote on her pad. She picked up her hands-free desk phone and dialled, getting up to make the call outside the incident room.

Carol glanced around at everyone. Dave had his feet up on his desk. Lloyd stretched out much like Carol, his hands linked over his stomach.

"What have we got on Preston Brown?" Carol asked.

Michael cleared his throat. "We should really speak to Eliza to get some details about him — his National Insurance number, for instance. The Preston Browns in this area, none of them match his age. As for the whole country, yes, there are quite a few who could be him. One curiosity, though. There's a Preston from Scudderton who's deceased and would be thirty-one now if he'd lived. He died at seventeen, road traffic accident, so would have had an NI number. If we're looking at our Preston as the killer, could he have assumed that identity?"

"That's foul if he did." Carol got up and went out into the corridor, intending to also speak to Eliza on the phone.

Katherine had already ended the call. "I've got the main manager's number. A Travis Underhill. Eliza said he should be in the Scudderton office until around four, then he has to attend a meeting. She's already spoken to him about Kevin."

"Michael mentioned a Preston Brown, deceased. We're wondering if his NI number will match our Preston's."

"Way ahead of you. She said to speak to a Julia Grisham, she's on payroll."

"Okay, we'll shoot over to ChatSesh now." Carol went back into the incident room. "You all know what to do. We're off to ChatSesh to see if we can make sense of this mess. Michael, can you get hold of Joy so she can arrange for all of the employees to be spoken to today and tomorrow — there's likely to be a lot of people working there, and that will swallow up a lot of time."

"Will do," he said.

CHAPTER FIFTY-TWO

ChatSesh HQ

Carol had seen the facade of the headquarters, perched on the edge of Scudderton, on numerous occasions but hadn't really taken any notice of its beauty. If a building was always there it became invisible after so many years, much like the residents in Oxford probably ignored the presence of the universities. This place was much like one of those, and had a cathedral-like air about it. It had once belonged to nobility, then had changed hands over the years. Individual businesses had set up home there from time to time, many of them sharing the space, but now it was used solely by ChatSesh. Kevin must have been richer than she'd imagined if he could afford to rent the whole place. Maybe he'd even bought it.

She approached the gleaming glass doors. They didn't fit with the structure, too modern, the revolving type like at a supermarket, and she laughed at Dave having to wait for the next section to swing round because he hadn't been fast enough. The inside was sleek and contemporary. She went up to the desk once Dave had made it through, smiling at the manicured, dolled-up woman behind it. Her red-rimmed eyes told Carol that news must have spread about Kevin.

Carol held up her ID. "We're here to speak to Travis Underhill and Julia Grisham."

A badge proclaimed the receptionist as *Karen, Happy to Help You!*, although she was far from happy at the minute. "You need to take the lift to floor three. Travis is using Kevin's office, which is the first door on the left as you leave the lift."

"Thank you."

Carol and Dave ascended then stepped out into a foyer with doors either side. *KEVIN COTTER* seemed to call out to her from a gold plaque on his door. She knocked, and a man in his thirties opened up. Brown hair swept to one side with product, a fade cut, his suit clearly expensive. She'd bet his tie alone cost the same amount as her monthly mortgage payment.

Carol held up her ID. "DI Carol Wren and DS Dave Waite."

"Ah, come in. Eliza let me know you'd be here. Coffee?"

"That would be lovely, thank you."

Travis walked over to a sideboard and got busy with a Tassimo machine. He took a glass jug of cream out of a built-in fridge. Carol and Dave chose the two seats opposite the expensive desk.

"Awful news from Eliza this morning," Travis said.

"It was a shock, yes." Carol nosed at the room to get a feel for Kevin. A couple of photos on the wall appeared to have been taken in Africa. In one, he smiled for the camera in a crouch, several children around him. In another, he stood beside a red water pump with a white ChatSesh logo on the side, his fist in the air. She was saddened that such a kind man who'd obviously been helping people had died in such a violent manner.

Travis handed the cups out and sat. He leaned back and steepled his fingers. "What do you need to know?"

"Preston Brown."

"Head of security? He's been here for around six months and came highly recommended. He'd applied with several other people but stood out as the most adept. Eliza said he's missing. I have to say that's strange. Preston would never abandon his post, so I think something bad must have happened to him."

Not likely. He had a gun stashed under his mattress, pal. "Do you know him well? I mean, as a friend?"

"No, I don't mix business with pleasure. I have tried his work phone, but it goes straight to voicemail." He opened his screen, poked about, then wrote a number on his pad. He ripped the page off and slid it across the desk. "Thought this might help."

"Thank you." Dave copied the number into his notebook.

"Do you know a Mr Spectre?" Carol asked.

Travis frowned. "Sounds like something from James Bond."

"Hmm, it is a bit odd for a surname."

"No, I don't recall anyone called that."

"Did Preston give a proper residential address when he joined the company?"

"I should imagine so. Why?"

"He's been renting a room at the Beachfront. Under the name of Mr Spectre."

Travis laughed as if shocked. "What?"

"And the suite Kevin was killed in was also in that name."

"But that's insane! That's saying Preston . . . Oh God, no. It wasn't him, was it?"

"He *is* missing, so . . . Do you know if Preston has a girlfriend? Blonde, wears a trench coat and a beret."

"Not that I'm aware, but as I said, I don't mix work and my private life. I don't engage in any personal conversations either. I'm here to help run ChatSesh, to do the best job I can, not to make friends."

They talked for a while longer, drinking coffee, and as Carol felt they weren't getting anywhere, she stood.

"Where can I find Julia Grisham?" she asked on her way to the door.

Travis came over to open it for her. "She's down the hall, two rooms along. Maybe I can help with what you need to know."

"It's fine, we've taken up enough of your time, and I'm aware you have a meeting and may need to prepare. What's happening with regards to Kevin?"

"I've already issued a press statement. It'll be all over social media by now."

"Do you know who Kevin planned to leave his money and the business to?"

"I have no idea."

"Okay, thanks."

She strode out, leading the way down the foyer, stopping at Julia's door. She knocked once Dave stood beside her. A black-haired woman answered, a large bun on top of her head, her make-up flawless, no smudged mascara. Maybe she wasn't sad about Kevin. Not everyone liked their boss.

Carol showed her ID and introduced them.

"Oh, are you speaking to everyone?" Julia asked.

"Officers will be arriving shortly, yes, but we're here for a specific reason. It's better that we talk inside your office."

Julia stepped back and walked to sit behind her desk, no offer of coffee with this one. Numerous spreadsheets covered her workspace, as well as a ledger, a laptop and a computer monitor and keyboard. She gestured for them to take the two remaining seats.

"Eliza Morris said we need to speak to you about Preston Brown's details." Carol tugged the hem of her jacket up at the back where it was pulling from her sitting on it. "I need his National Insurance number, home address and a landline number."

"I'll access that information for you." Julia tapped the keyboard. A few mouse clicks, and she swivelled the monitor around. "That's all we've got on him."

Dave wrote it down. Carol read what was on the screen. Preston was supposedly born on 23 February 1991. His NI number was listed, his home address 16 Falcorpe Road on the housing estate by Sainsbury's, and he had a bank account with Barclays.

Carol folded her hands in her lap. In her peripheral vision, Dave was sending a message on his phone. "Do you know Preston well?"

Julia blinked. "Not really. Not like his private stuff or anything. He's basically Kevin's bodyguard these days, so I don't see him unless Kevin's here. Um, *was* here. God, I can't believe he's gone . . ."

"It must have been a shock."

"It was."

"Back to Preston. I know you said you don't know his private stuff, but on the off chance that you overheard a conversation, are you aware of whether he has a girlfriend?" She gave her the description of the mystery woman at the hotel.

"I don't know anything like that about him."

"When did you start working here?"

"Eight months ago. I moved up from Bicester."

"Where's that?"

"A few miles from Banbury."

"Oh right." Was there some kind of policy here where no one made friends with their colleagues? This conversation wasn't as enlightening as Carol had anticipated. Maybe the uniforms would gather more information. She stood. "Thank you for passing that information on."

"Is Preston okay?" Julia bit her lip. "I mean, you're asking about his address and everything . . ."

"He was supposed to be with Kevin and Eliza last night but has gone missing."

"Oh God, do you think he was killed as well?"

Carol didn't want to say what she was really thinking. "It's something we're looking into."

They left the office and went back to reception. Carol checked her phone. Joy had sent four officers, and one of them stood speaking to Karen, Happy to Help You.

Carol beckoned him over. "I want to know if anyone here got close to Preston Brown. I want details about his life."

"Okay, I'll let the others know."

She walked out into the autumn sunlight, Dave striding alongside her. "What did you think?"

"That no one makes friends in that place."

* * *

Incident Room

Carol fumed and paced. "What a bastard."

The address that Julia had given them was where the real Preston Brown had lived at the time of his death. The landline number belonged to that address, registered in the name of who she assumed was his mother. The NI number was also the young man's. The bank account had been opened six months ago, just prior to the fake Preston working for ChatSesh. There were no mobile contracts in that name.

He's infiltrated ChatSesh. Established himself. Got cosy, earned Kevin's trust.

"It's looking like he adopted a personality in order to get close to Kevin," she said. "What I want to know is if he killed him because of a falling-out they'd had or if he was employed to murder him."

"Like a plant-slash-assassin?" Dave asked.

"Yes. All this cloak-and-dagger stuff using the Mr Spectre name, Preston living at the hotel and not in Falcorpe Road. Can you imagine if anyone had phoned that number and asked for Preston? The parents would have been devastated, having to explain he'd died."

"Should we check that?" Katherine asked.

Carol didn't know what to do. If she spoke to the parents and asked such a question, they'd want to know why. Did she want to add to their pain by telling them their son's identity had been stolen? "No, leave it for now. Put in a request so we can see his Barclays account details, please. I'm interested to know if he's wiped it now he's fucked off." She stopped pacing and held her head in her hands.

Think! Why would he want to kill Kevin?

Will he come back to murder Eliza?

Why didn't he kill her at the same time as Kevin? Did he think the bullet had gone through into her?

It was doing her head in.

"The gun, though," Dave said. "It's premeditated if he got his hands on one of those. Normal people don't carry."

"Unless Kevin allowed it as a security measure," Lloyd said.

Carol shook her head. "Apart from his affairs, he sounds like a by-the-book kind of bloke. I can't see him condoning that, can you? It's clear he uses his money to help people. Has anyone looked into his charity ventures?"

"I'll do it," Michael said. "Katherine's got a massive job ahead with Kevin's social media."

Carol checked the clock. It was coming up to half past three already. Where had the day gone?

"Right, I'm conscious that with each new murder, the ones that came before are taking a back seat. It's not sitting well. I feel guilty."

"No," Michael said. "We've stalled and we have no leads. We're not ignoring them, it's just this case has grown long bloody legs, and there's only so much we can do at one time. All those deaths, that's a lot for us to manage on our own."

Carol felt better now. "Right, so we need to work out which scenario this is. Clem, Frank, Gail, Violet and Rebecca are one case and Kevin is another? Or are they all linked and Fake Preston is our man? Did he use a gun on Kevin to throw us off?"

"Other than Gail, what do the others have in common with Kevin?" Katherine asked.

"I don't know." Carol slumped onto a chair. "Lloyd, can you get busy with ANPR for the SUV Preston was driving? I'm going out to get food."

"Where?" Dave asked.

"It'll be a surprise when I get back."

"A Buns 'n' Bread sausage doorstep with brown sauce would be nice." He smiled.

"Wait and see."

She needed half an hour to herself, to think. Hopefully, she'd get a lightbulb moment while she was out.

CHAPTER FIFTY-THREE

Shore Drive

In her temporary bedroom, Eliza had just had a phone call from James Abbott, Kevin's solicitor. He'd asked her to go to his office to discuss Kevin's estate, but she'd told him she couldn't, she was at a safe house and didn't know when she could return to Seaview — assuming she even could, now her boyfriend was dead. Instead, he'd explained over the phone: she could most definitely live at Seaview for the rest of her life if she wanted to.

Kevin had left almost everything to her, plus some to his mother, but that was now Eliza's because of Gail's murder. It had shocked the shit out of her, she hadn't expected that at all. She acknowledged that in the six months they'd been together, Kevin had declared his love and claimed she was the one for him, but to put her in his will like that?

She'd ended the call understanding that she had to wait for probate but that Kevin had stated he wanted her to run ChatSesh alongside Travis in the meantime. Eliza didn't want that responsibility, but Travis might.

She phoned him. "It's me again. I've had some shocking news about Kevin. He's left everything to me. I can't . . . I can't run the place, you know that. I was wondering . . ."

"I'll do it."

"Are you sure?"

"Yes."

She breathed a sigh of relief. "I'm going to sell it once I'm allowed. And the house, his caravans, the lot. I don't want any reminders."

"I get that. It's fine, I'll hold the fort here. Will you be coming back in at all?"

"No."

"Okay. I'll nab one of the other secretaries to fill in for you."

"Thanks. Bye for now."

She pressed the ChatSesh icon, and her account opened. Her feed was full of condolences, users expressing their shock and speculating on who'd murdered Kevin.

She clicked the three lines at the top of her screen and selected the option to close her account. She couldn't stand to be on ChatSesh anymore. Couldn't even stomach staying in Scudderton. There were too many memories. She'd come back if she needed to with regards to the will and having everything signed over to her, but it would be a fleeting visit.

Needing some fresh air, she collected her handbag, went downstairs and tiptoed past the living room, where the woman copper looking after her sat on the sofa talking to someone on her phone with her back to the door. Some guard dog she was. Eliza went into the kitchen and left via the back, walking to the bottom of the garden and climbing over a stubby fence onto the moors beyond.

She headed towards Mollengate, the closest village, thinking about her life and what it would be like now. Still stunned by Kevin's generosity, the depth of his love for her, she smiled. He really was a kind man and hadn't deserved to be killed.

Eliza plodded on.

CHAPTER FIFTY-FOUR

Ridgebrook Close

Madeline wasn't sure what to do. Should she tell Poppy Kevin wasn't her father? Would that be too much on top of informing her he was dead? Like Carol Wren had said, Poppy would ask questions at some point as to why she hadn't inherited everything. Would anyone need to know her daughter wasn't his? It wasn't like she'd have to prove it other than by presenting a birth certificate, was it? They could claim it all, sell the business, his house, then move away, go abroad so Carol couldn't do her for fraud and Ian wouldn't know what had gone on.

She clutched Poppy's coat to her chest. Perhaps they should go to the pier, have some fun, then Madeline could explain about Kevin's murder when they got back. It would give her time to think about how to phrase it.

She climbed the stairs and opened Poppy's bedroom door.

Poppy glared at her from the bed. "I know everything."

CHAPTER FIFTY-FIVE

Ridgebrook Close

Twenty-six-year-old Sofia reached across and turned the hourglass over. In bed, she clutched a knife and stared at her mother.

Mam's mouth gaped. "W . . . H-how did you get that knife, Poppy?"

"Stop calling me that. I *hate* it."

"But you're my Poppy Poppet."

"I'm Sofia, and by the look of it, I'm not a fucking Cotter."

"Language!" Mam appeared shocked.

Good, she had reason to be, because she was one of the redheads on Sofia's list.

"Darling, put the knife down." Mam came closer, her hand out.

Sofia flung the quilt back and got out of bed. She smiled at her mother's expression.

"How . . . how are you standing?" Mam whispered.

"You thought it was such a good idea to let me inject myself, didn't you, so you could blame me if you got caught for everything you've done to me."

"I don't know what you're talking about."

"Yes, you do. I've been living as disabled for over twenty bloody years, and enough is enough. I knew what you were doing after I stopped going into hospital about the shit in my cuts. It wasn't me, I knew that, and the only other person who had access to me like that was *you*."

"You're delusional. You don't know what you're saying. Of course I'd never do that to you. I wouldn't hurt you for the world."

Anger at Mam's blatant lying exploded into flames inside Sofia. "The injections, they weren't to fix my legs, they were to stop me being able to walk. How could you *do* that to me, cage me up in this house, playing teacher, mother, father, when all along you used me to get attention. And as for this . . ." She threw her sippy cup across the room. "I'm not *two*! I can drink out of a normal cup."

Mam scoffed. "That's just silly talk."

"I saw your diaries. Loads of them. From the beginning. They explained *everything*. You're fucking insane."

"I'm sorry, I . . ."

"Don't come near me. Stay the hell away."

Sofia thought about all the times she'd left this room inside her head. The trip on the *Merry Belle*, the beaches, the amusement parks, the train trip to London, the tour bus in York. Whitby, with a man who existed only in her imagination. Nigel, the person who she wished was real so he could sweep her away to London when she'd killed Mam and claimed her life insurance.

But the pier and other places, she'd gone there. And she'd danced. So much.

Just over a year ago, when she'd stopped injecting herself, instead squeezing the fluid into the mattress, she'd found it hard to walk after so long in bed. Her muscles were so wasted she'd had to sit and do exercises that way until she'd been able to stand. Twelve whole months of teaching herself to walk again, and on the day she'd managed it, she'd had to tiptoe so Mam didn't hear her from downstairs.

And the nappies, how soul-destroying it had been to shit and piss in them, to have sores, Mam cleaning her in the shower and applying cream, and all because she wanted Kevin to take notice? How thick *was* she? If he hadn't come round here for two decades, he wasn't likely to, was he? And now he was *dead*.

Mam had wanted him to go to prison, so *she* had killed poor Clem, Frank, Gail and Violet. It had felt surreal, reading the words, the plans, Mam's viewpoint, which was a pathetic reason to kill people. There must have been others who'd encouraged her to marry Kevin. And now Sofia knew he wasn't her father, she imagined he'd found out and walked away because of the deception, yet no one had bothered to let her know.

She'd hated Mam telling her about every single girlfriend he'd had, and for what? He was nothing to Sofia, she'd only had him in her life until she was four, then she'd been abused by Mam and everything had turned into days in hospital, in bed, in that wheelchair. A prisoner in her own head.

And as for the psychotherapist being her father . . . That was in the final entry she'd read. He'd come round once, Sofia remembered it well. She'd been colouring in a peacock, and Mam and him had talked. As a five-year-old, she hadn't understood their words, but she'd stored them, made sense of them later on, and that was when she'd decided to stop injecting herself. She'd been lied to, and she'd needed to get out of the bed to find out why. She'd wanted to get out from these oppressive walls, to be free to go wherever she chose, and her first walk on the pier alone had been excruciating. She hadn't anticipated the energy it would take to walk there from Coldwater, but she'd sat for a while on one of the benches and rested. Bought herself a hot chocolate with the money she'd stolen from Mam's housekeeping jar in the kitchen cupboard.

Mam had said something about cash going missing, when Sofia had stolen enough to buy the clip-in hair extensions, the cheap mobile. Before that, Sofia had made trips out with her real hair hanging in her face, hoping no one caught a glimpse of her features, one of Kevin's old baseball caps on, his baggy clothes, the trousers held up with his belt, and the bitter pill she'd swallowed when she'd realised people would be looking for her in a wheelchair, her hair in a ponytail. No, her walking wouldn't have computed.

"The hourglass is almost empty." Sofia smiled.

"What do you mean?" Mam backed away to the door.

"Stay where you are."

"Poppet . . . Sofia, please, don't do owt silly."

"You killed those people. Did you kill Kevin, too? I heard that copper earlier."

"No! I didn't hurt Kevin. Put the knife down, love. Did you get it from the drawer? I saw two were missing."

"One's at Kevin's house."

"W . . . What?"

"While you've been murdering, I've been going out. I knew where you'd be, you put it in your latest diary, so I had time."

"What were you doing at *his* house?"

"I wanted to kill Eliza, and all the others, because you said it was them who'd taken him away from us, when it was *you*. You made me hate him when I shouldn't. The last entry, where you said he wasn't my dad, that Ian was . . . I could have killed *Eliza*, Mam."

"It's Mammy."

"No, I'm not five anymore, and I won't play your games. No more Mammy, no more stupid toys off the pier, no more talking to me as if I'm still a child. I'm an *adult*, I've missed out on so much, and what you've done is wrong." She stared at Karlos, her stuffed penguin. She'd called it that because the name meant "free man".

She glanced at the hourglass. The sand had completely filled the bottom.

It was time to kill her.

No. Don't do it. Remember what she wanted to do to Kevin. Do the same to her.

That would mean forfeiting the life insurance.

Sofia reached beneath the mattress, keeping an eye on her mother, and pulled out the pay-as-you-go phone she'd used to message Eliza. She wasn't going to admit she'd sent that text, Mam could take the blame. Sofia had already burned the hair extensions in the fire pit during the night. Mam had burned stuff too over the past few days, and Sofia could only guess it was things to do with killing.

Sofia dialled 999.

Mam's face darkened. "What are you doing? Where did you get that?"

She went to make a move forward, but Sofia jabbed the knife in the air towards her.

"*What's your emergency?*" the lady on the end of the line said.

"I know who killed those people in Scudderton." Sofia smiled.

Mam ran.

Sofia threw the phone on the bed and chased after her. The fucking cow wasn't going to get away with this. Running wouldn't do any good. At the top of the stairs, Mam paused, her hand on the newel, and she stared over at Sofia advancing.

"Look, let's talk this through, Poppy . . . S-Sofia."

"No."

Sofia darted behind her and pushed.

CHAPTER FIFTY-SIX

Undisclosed Location

Glad to have the fake beard off at last, Desmond embraced his girlfriend, Sally, so pleased to see her. She was the love of his life, a miraculous woman, and not being able to be with her properly lately had been killing him. All that work for Boss, plus Kevin, left little time for them to be alone. Still, he'd done what he needed to, and now it was time to move on before the police caught up with him.

They sat in a hire car behind a pub, him hoping she'd stick to her word and go away with him. People changed their minds, though, and ever since he'd killed Kevin, he'd tormented himself with whether she'd do the same. Yet here she was. Only . . . she could be here to tell him she wasn't prepared to leave the country.

"Are you all right?" he asked.

"Yes."

"Do you still . . . ?"

"Yes."

Desmond relaxed. It was going to be okay.

CHAPTER FIFTY-SEVEN

Ridgebrook Close

Carol and Dave sat with Poppy in Madeline's house. Alan Pitson had responded to her 999 call, but once it became clear which address he was dealing with, he'd phoned Carol to go there and see what the hell was going on. They'd gathered in the kitchen, and to say Carol had been shocked to find Poppy walking around was an understatement, given what they'd been told, that she was confined to a wheelchair. Dave made them all cups of tea, and they sat at the table.

Carol sipped some of her drink. "Let me get this straight. You're saying your mother killed all those people?"

Poppy nodded. "But she says she didn't touch Kevin. And before we go on, my name is Sofia. Poppy is a stupid name Mam's called me since I was little, and everyone else thinks that's who I am. Kevin just went along with it, I assume, and as for Ian, well, maybe he did the same, although he'd have known what my proper name is when Mam took me to therapy. It would have been on my medical records."

"Okay. Sofia, right." Carol would have to get used to this quickly. It would be weird, because she'd thought of this young woman as Poppy ever since Madeline had come up in the investigation.

Officers were out looking for Madeline. In her rush to leave, she'd fallen down the stairs then had left the house. Sofia had no idea where she'd go, not now Gail was dead. Sofia had explained that her mother had visited Gail often since the divorce, although Kevin didn't know about it. "It's all in her diaries," she'd said. Carol had yet to read them, but Dave had browsed.

"So you confronted her after we'd been here last," Carol confirmed.

"Yes. She denied it all, but once she realised she'd been caught, when I phoned the police on her silly pay-as-you-go mobile, she ran."

"Where's the phone now?"

"I threw it on the bed after I rang the police."

Carol glanced at Alan, who stood by the doorway. "Can you go and get that for me? I want to check it." She fished some gloves out of her pocket and handed them to him.

He pulled them on and went upstairs.

"What do you need to check?" Sofia asked.

"The text messages."

Sofia shrugged. "I don't know what's on there. I snatched it off her when she came into my room. She had gloves on for some reason, which is odd, considering it's not even cold out yet."

Did she have gloves on because she's the one who messaged Eliza? Didn't she want her prints on it? "Yes, that is a bit strange."

Alan returned. "There's only one sent message."

"That's what I was hoping."

He showed Carol the screen. It was the text sent to Eliza. So was it *Madeline* in the garden at Seaview? Had she worn a blonde wig?

It prompted her to ask, "Do you have any knives missing by any chance?"

Sofia nodded. "Mam told me she'd been at Kevin's and stabbed his picture with one."

"That solves that dilemma for us, then. What about when Frank was killed? Did you go to a friend's, the empty house along the road?"

"No. That's a lie on Mam's part."

It occurred to Carol that they should leave this house to SOCO. There could be evidence here. More tools. The wig. She turned to Sofia. "Did your mother ever have anyone else in the house?"

"No, it was just me and her, although Ian came years ago, when I was about five, and before that, Kevin lived here. As you can see, the place is dated. Mam left it exactly as it'd been when she was married. So much *brown* everywhere, apart from my god-awful pink bedroom."

Carol felt better now about trampling a possible crime scene. SOCO would only have to rule out a few people. If there hadn't been any visitors in years, any other prints or DNA would belong to an accomplice. *If* Madeline even had one.

Carol sent a message to Todd, requesting a couple of SOCOs, and Sofia launched into her tale. Madeline had treated her appallingly — the bit about putting faeces in her wounds was particularly disturbing, and as for injections into her legs and sending her to sleep, well . . . And Madeline used a baby monitor to watch Sofia in her room. It struck Carol as creepy.

Carol suggested therapy. "You might need help to get over all of this. You've lost out on so much already. Books and telly aren't substitutes for real life. You need to experience things for yourself."

Sofia wiped tears away. "I'm going to leave. Start again elsewhere. I'll use the money in the trust fund. She can't keep it from me anymore. It's in my name, and there's a valid bank card still stuck to the letter it was sent on. There's also a letter with a PIN. I took them just before that policeman arrived." She nodded at Alan.

"Where will you go? You'll have to go to court, so we'll need to be able to get hold of you."

"I'll let you know where I end up."

Carol couldn't fathom what it would feel like to discover you weren't actually ill, that you didn't need a wheelchair yet had spent a long time being ferried around in one.

"How did you figure it out?" she asked.

"When Mam had forgotten to leave me a syringe one day, I started to feel my legs, they weren't numb anymore." Sofia shrugged, maybe to make light of things because it was too painful to acknowledge the enormity of it. "I don't know, I just had this horrible sense of dread that things weren't right, that if I could feel my legs moving, then something was wrong. Couple that with how Mam always seemed so *glad* I couldn't walk, that I was dependent on her . . ."

"I see. What was in the syringe?"

"There's a box of stuff under her bed, almost empty now. I had time on my hands when she left the house, so I went looking. In one of the diaries, it says she stole it the day before she left the hospital as a nurse. Someone else left at the same time, and she let them take the blame. There was an inquiry, and she was spoken to, but she's such a good liar . . . She gave me just enough to numb my legs, which must be why it's lasted so long."

That sounded off to Carol, unbelievable. Twenty-something *years* using it every day? Depending on the size of the vials or whatever, surely it would have run out by now, expired, unless only a tiny amount was needed, but still. She'd let Todd know about the box. Forensics would determine what it was.

Dave raised his eyebrows. It didn't add up for him either.

"There's a boiler suit," Sofia said. "She's been putting it on to go out."

"Where is it?"

"Folded on a chair in her bedroom."

Carol would bet it had traces of the victims' blood on it.

They continued talking until Todd arrived with two forensic officers. Carol arranged for Sofia to stay at one of the B&Bs. With everything sorted, Todd aware of what he needed to look for under the bed, Carol and Dave saw Sofia off with Alan, who'd offered to take her to her new accommodation, then they sat in the car and pondered the turn of events.

"That shit about the syringes doesn't ring true," she said.

"Nope."

Carol drove away, towards the station. There was nothing much they could do until someone sighted Madeline or Preston.

If they ever did.

* * *

Good Rest Bed and Breakfast

It was wonderful to not be at home in her prison bedroom, a room that was stuck in time with pink wallpaper, pink bedding, pink bloody everything. Child's playthings in a toybox, fairy tales on the bookshelf. Mam had kept it the same throughout Sofia's life, and it was clear she'd wanted time to stand still at the point she'd been with Kevin and they'd appeared as a happy family.

Sofia smiled. The police believed Mam had sent that message to Eliza. The story about Mam wearing gloves had been a big fat lie, one Sofia had needed to tell in order to take the light of suspicion off herself. The only fingerprints on that phone were Sofia's, and it would make sense why that was the case now.

She stared out of the window and thought about Nigel. Maybe she could find a man like him, set up home and have a family of her own. She laughed to herself. Once, she'd wanted Kevin back, but now . . . No, he wasn't her dad. She'd wasted so many years pining for him, thinking he'd abandoned her.

Maybe she'd go to the hospital and find Ian. Remind him who she was. Why hadn't he wanted anything to do with her? The diaries had said Mam didn't want Kevin to find out what she'd done, but now he was dead, so . . .

For now, she had places to go, people to see. She fetched the hourglass from her bag and set it on the windowsill, the sand spilling into the bottom. She pulled a chair across to the window and sat on it, staring outside. Her eyes glazed, and she got on the tour bus in York, listening to the story of Dick Turpin and how he'd hanged himself. She dipped her head so the overhanging trees didn't grab at her hair, then she relaxed, feeling better, all the anxiety of today peeling away.

It was safer inside her mind.

No one could hurt her there.

* * *

Safe House

PC Helen May glared at Eliza, who blushed at being caught going back indoors.

"Where have you been?" Helen asked. "I had to phone in that you'd gone missing. The police are out looking for you. What if Preston or whatever-his-name-is had seen you?"

"I went for a walk. I felt caged in." That was the truth.

"Please don't do that again. You have to remain here. We can't keep you safe if you're off gallivanting."

"I'm sorry."

"I'll phone in now and tell them you're back."

Eliza walked upstairs to her room. She wasn't staying here, no matter what Helen said. She'd leave tonight, when Helen was asleep. Eliza couldn't stand it in Scudderton any longer. Yes, the police believed she might be in danger, that Preston would come after her, but she didn't believe that. If he wanted her dead, he'd have killed her at the same time as Kevin.

This was all getting too much.

CHAPTER FIFTY-EIGHT

Town Centre

Madeline had been hiding out, crouching behind a large wheelie bin at the back of a row of shops. The stench was disgusting, and she gagged for the umpteenth time. Her legs and back ached where she'd fallen down the stairs — the arm of the bloody stairlift had dug into her ribs as she's smacked into it — and her wrist was sore where it had clipped the newel post. She couldn't believe her precious Poppy Poppet had done that to her, given her a push and laughed as Madeline had tumbled down.

Tears burned her eyes. How had this all gone so wrong?

She took her mobile out of her handbag — thank goodness she'd grabbed it as she'd scrambled from the house, not to mention she'd already had her coat and shoes on because she'd thought she was taking Poppy to the pier. She opened up her contact list and selected the name she needed. This person was going to help her out one last time.

It was answered almost immediately. "What do you want? You're not supposed to contact me, I contact you."

"Poppy knows."

"Fuck. Everything?"

"Yes. She read my diaries."

"Thanks a lot, you fucking bitch. How utterly *stupid* of you to write it all down. How the hell did she find them?"

"She stopped injecting herself. She's been snooping around, even leaving the house!"

"What do you mean, snooping around? This had better not come back on me. I got you the drugs, remember. I can't have my name linked to this."

"You won't be linked to that. No one but me, you and the supplier know about our arrangement. You need to get me out of Scudderton."

"I warned you about something like this happening."

"I have to leave. I have money—"

"I know you do. Kevin paid you enough."

"There's more."

"What, money?"

"No, more news. She phoned the bloody police."

"Jesus Christ! How are you meant to spend the cash, then? They're going to be all over your bank account like a rash."

"I don't *know*! I just need to get out of here."

"No. This is the end of the line for me, and if they find out I'm involved, I'll deny everything."

"Of course you will."

The conversation had shit her up, and she swiped to end the call, switching the phone off. What if they were already onto her? They'd check her phone records, see she'd made a call. Would they be able to locate her?

She pushed up off the ground, dumped the mobile in the bin and limped along the street. Where could she go? The police might be out there looking for her, and she'd be recognised. She lifted her hood, tugging it low to hide her face. She came out near the Backstreet and walked down it. At the end, she gazed across at the marina. The *Poisson Mort* was docked far along the jetty. She thought about her time aboard with Kevin and the nosy Violet. She could hide out there overnight, couldn't she? Decide what to do. She'd have to get off in the early hours, as Callum Roberts and the crew would still likely be going out to sea, even though Violet was dead.

She scurried across the road and down the jetty, her head bent, her heart pulsing too hard. People were on moored boats, but none of them appeared to pay her any mind. She climbed up the ladder of the *Poisson Mort* and darted down some steps into the trawler's belly and sat on the bottom stair, thinking about what to do. Ahead was a room with a steel table and a long-bladed knife on top.

Poppy had really messed things up. Why couldn't she have just done as she was told and injected herself?

Why was I so stupid to have trusted her do it?

* * *

Poisson Mort

Callum hauled himself up the ladder. He wanted to give the boat a proper scrub this afternoon as someone would be coming to inspect the trawler soon — at least he assumed they would. With Violet's death, he supposed it would be sold. Yes, she'd asked him to run the business after Skipper had died, but that didn't cover what would happen when *she* died. She had family in Ireland, so . . .

He couldn't afford his own boat, and fishing was his life, so he'd have to find another job, as would the crew, but for now, he'd carry on and pay the wages out of the cash sales. Other payments went into Violet's bank. Maybe the new owner would keep him on.

He stood on deck and cocked his head. What was that noise? Was someone aboard?

"Who's there? I suggest you get off this fucking boat now or I'll phone the police. You're trespassing."

A ginger-haired woman came up from downstairs. She brandished one of the knives from the preparation room below deck and appeared insane, her eyes wide, mania seeping off her.

He held a hand out. "Now hang on a minute. No need to point that thing at me, is there?"

"Get off the boat," she said.

"Err, I think you'll find I'm allowed on here, whereas you—"

"I *said*, get off." She lunged at him and swiped the knife across his bare forearm.

He stared down at the opening cut, at the blood dripping. "What the fucking hell's *wrong* with you?" Pain flared, hot and cold at the same time, and he slapped a hand over the wound to try to stem the bleeding.

"Leave me alone," she said quietly. "If you just let me stay here for a while, everything will be all right."

Callum shook his head and backed away. "Okay, but I want you off by the time we set sail. We come on board about half four in the morning, so best you be gone by then."

"I will be."

Jesus, she was a menacing-looking cow and then some. He walked backwards to the ladder and bumped into the railings beside it. Quickly, he scooted down the ladder, trailing blood as he descended, and jumped onto the jetty. He glanced up, and she bent over the railing, staring down at him. A gust of breeze wafted her orange hair.

"Don't you *dare* tell anyone I'm here," she shouted.

"Right, whatever." *Nutter.*

He walked calmly towards the street end of the jetty, but inside he was a bag of nerves. He pressed his palm to the wound again, holding his forearm up. Blood trickled down to his elbow. He glanced back, but she wasn't there. Thinking she might be watching him out of sight, he strode across the street and down the alley beside the Devil. There, he took his phone out and rang the police. That crazy bitch needed to be arrested. He was buggered if he'd let her stay on the trawler. She was a danger to society.

* * *

Carol had been going through a to-do list. She checked up on whether anyone had located Preston or his SUV. His mobile, a pay-as-you-go bought months ago, was turned off and the vehicle nowhere to be found.

She'd phoned Heidi Welding and risked her wrath by asking whether she knew Madeline and what she thought of her. Heidi had said she didn't know her to talk to, and anyway, why should she help Carol out when Asher was being accused of all sorts?

Carol had also caught up on whether a handyman had come to fix the blind at Rebecca Larkin's and killed her, just in case the woman *had* phoned for one, despite Sam saying she wouldn't want anyone but him doing it. Nobody in the area had gone to her home.

Rebecca's name hadn't cropped up so far in the diaries — a few officers were reading them — so had Madeline murdered her without planning to do so? Or had the lad who'd collected the dog done it? There were no other sightings of him, and to be honest, he could be one of many who wore the same type of clothing.

Asher would be coming to the station soon. If he was the one killing cats, then she was glad they'd found blood on the tracksuit because at least now, he couldn't go off and kill more. If he did, they'd be on his doorstep pretty sharpish. As for the card, the bank had informed Mr Jackson it had been found. He'd put a stop on it as soon as he'd spotted it missing, and no money had been taken from the account, nor were any purchases made.

They were waiting for Madeline's phone records. She had a contract mobile, so any messages and calls she'd made might add further proof that she was a killer. Not to mention someone with obvious factitious disorder. She'd put her child through hell, and for what?

Katherine turned from her desk, swivelling her chair around. "Joy's just phoned. It looks like Madeline is on the *Poisson Mort.* She's not long sliced Callum Roberts with a fish-gutting knife."

"What the hell?" Carol glanced at Dave. "She's off her rocker. Is Callum alive?"

Katherine stood and stretched. "Yes, he was the one who called it in. Uniforms are there now, trying to get her to come down the ladder."

"Should we go?" Carol asked Dave, itching to get down there.

He nodded. "Maybe she'll come down for us two, seeing as we've spoken to her already."

It was worth a try.

* * *

Poisson Mort

Madeline stood on the jetty. Carol approached, studying her. The woman appeared unhinged, and Carol supposed she would, considering what had happened with Sofia. Madeline's world had come crashing down around her, and the game was up. Two PCs flanked her, and she was handcuffed.

"Ah, so you're off the boat, then." Carol glared at her. "Why did you have to hurt Mr Roberts with a knife?"

"He scared me."

"How so?"

"By coming onto the *boat.*"

"Right, well, he had every right to be there. You know why else we've come for you, don't you, Madeline?"

"The diaries are lies. I didn't *really* do any of it."

"Didn't you? So it's all a coincidence . . . ? No, that won't wash." She smiled at Mulholland. "Okay, take her to the station. We'll follow you in."

Carol watched them walking a struggling Madeline up the jetty. The woman cursed and spat at them, and Carol's anger burned. She didn't like officers being treated in this way, they didn't deserve it.

So much for her plan of treating Madeline with kid gloves. She'd go in hard now. No one spat at her colleagues and got away with it.

CHAPTER FIFTY-NINE

Interview Room One

Carol had read the pertinent information from the diaries, compiled by the uniforms. There had been no mention of killing Kevin or Rebecca, but that didn't mean she hadn't done it on the spur of the moment. She was clearly twisted, and Carol bore it in mind that Madeline may well need a medical assessment partway through the interview if she exhibited signs of mental distress. She would get one afterwards anyway — factitious disorder was apparent, and Carol wouldn't let that go untreated.

Carol and Dave sat opposite Madeline and a duty solicitor, Gareth Domino, who'd let Carol know in private — unprofessionally, she thought — that Madeline swung from admitting she'd done it to denying it. It seemed like there'd be a trial then if she pleaded not guilty, yet another trauma to put Sofia through. Did this woman even *care* about her daughter? That was doubtful, given the abuse since Sofia was four, but then again, despite that, she could still love her child, just not in the ordinary way.

"Madeline, I'd like to begin with the people we believe you've killed. There *will* be something of you at every scene

— a tiny fibre, a spot of DNA — and there may also be something on a boiler suit and shoes found in your home. In the coming days, we will have evidence of you being present. Couple that with your diaries, and it isn't looking good for you."

"Diaries? I don't know what you're talking about."

"Yes, you do. As I recall —" Carol read her notes — "you said to me on the jetty: 'The diaries are lies. I didn't *really* do any of it.' *You* mentioned the diaries, not me. Why did you do what you did? Why kill all of those poor people?"

"It's Kevin's fault."

"Right. How did you figure that one out?"

"If he hadn't left, I wouldn't have had to do it because I wouldn't have thought about what a waste of time being with him had been. Those people, they *encouraged* us to be together, and look what happened. They should have kept their mouths shut, then I wouldn't have married him."

Carol frowned. "So you didn't have free will? A mind of your own? You couldn't have said you didn't want to marry him? Come on!"

"We got swept away."

"So you killed several people because . . . ?"

"They said we made a good couple."

"And that's *it*? That's your reason?" *Bloody hell!*

"They ruined my life by doing that. I gave myself over to Kevin, then he cheated, he left me."

"Yet you cheated first, so we've been told. With Ian Johann." She glanced up at Madeline.

"That was a mistake."

"Is Sofia also a mistake?"

"It's Poppy."

"*No*, it's Sofia." Carol leaned back. "You systematically picked victims off one by one using tools, we presume, from Kevin's toolbox — one, I might add, he said he didn't take to his mother's when he left the family home. Do you still maintain he took it with him? I mean, it doesn't matter, not really. It's easy to see how you'd get your hands on it. Sofia said you visited Gail after your divorce. That you had a *key*. This explains no forced entry to her home, and maybe we'll discover the shears and trowel used in one of the murders belonged to Gail . . ."

"How did she know I went there?"

"She read your diaries, as have we. Did you forget that?"

Madeline's cheeks reddened. "Again, I don't know what you're talking about."

"What, regarding the diaries or the murders?"

"All of it. I don't have any diaries. I don't know owt about a toolbox, and I certainly don't know how to murder."

"Okay . . ." Carol flicked her attention to Gareth Domino to check if he felt it was all right to proceed.

He nodded and mouthed, "For now."

Carol returned to Madeline. "Are the holes left in the victims significant?"

"The only hole I know about is the great big one inside me that Kevin created when he left."

Maybe that's a subconscious thing she did. "Let's move to Sofia. Why did you poison her?"

"What? That's insane!"

Err, d'you think? "Nevertheless, you stated in your diaries — and we're in the process of getting your handwriting analysed to confirm it's yours — that you put faecal matter in her cuts and also injected her legs so they went numb. You poisoned her with raw chicken. You also used something to put her to sleep for hours. There were several hospital stays — you were a nurse, so you knew when to take her to a doctor before the blood poisoning went too far. That's a dicey game you played. She could have contracted sepsis and died."

"I was lonely."

"Pardon?"

"I wanted people to notice me, to *care*. Unlike Kevin."

"So you harmed your child for *attention*?"

Madeline bent her head and picked at a hangnail. "No one gave a shit about me after Kevin left. They didn't even come round and ask if I was okay. It was like they agreed with what he'd done, that they blamed me for him having sex with other people."

"We noted you had postnatal depression. How did you treat people during that time?"

Madeline's head shot up. "How do you think? I was angry every day. I shouted at anyone who came round."

"Yet you wonder why they abandoned you after Kevin walked out." Carol returned to one of her earlier points. "Sofia. You took her to see Ian Johann for a mental health assessment. You wanted him to say Sofia had harmed herself. Don't you feel guilty about that?"

"She *did* harm herself. She took all the poo from the front garden — there was a dog that kept shitting on our grass. I watched her put it in her cuts."

"Sofia gave us permission to access her medical files. It states the first time it was animal faeces, but all the others, it was human. It also states you had no idea how this could have happened." She checked her notes. "It said: *Mother is confused as to how this has occurred.* But you just told us you saw Sofia doing it, so why didn't you say so at the time?"

No response.

"Let's talk about the injections. A box was found beneath your bed with vials in it. They're in date, so it's not the box you stole from the hospital. Where did it come from?"

Madeline let the tears fall. "Someone got it for Sofia."

"For Sofia? Or *you*?"

"For me. For her." Madeline shook her head.

"Your bank account. Will it show cash withdrawals in order for you to pay this person? We'll be examining those closely once they come in."

"No, I didn't have to pay for it."

"So someone gave you anaesthetics for free? One of them knocks people out, and the other is local and used for epidurals."

"Yes."

"Where did they get it from?"

"I don't know. I don't care."

"Who was it?"

Madeline gave her a name.

Carol digested that, then moved on. "Rebecca Larkin. She's not in your diaries, yet she was killed with a screwdriver and is of a similar age to the other deceased people apart from Kevin, which leads us to believe you also killed her."

"No, I didn't kill Kevin and I didn't kill any Rebecca."

Madeline rocked, humming, her eyes going blank. Carol checked with Gareth who nodded.

"We're going to ask for a medical assessment," Carol told Madeline. "I'm concerned. You need help."

The woman didn't answer.

"Interview suspended . . ."

* * *

Incident Room

Carol went into a quiet corner and phoned Sofia on the B&B number. The timeframe when Alan had visited Madeline was too ropey — she could have killed Rebecca after he'd left her home. Madeline hadn't protested vehemently enough about not murdering Kevin and Rebecca. Wouldn't she have ranted and railed, claiming her innocence? Carol would. If she hadn't done something, she'd be damned if she'd take the blame for it.

Regardless of what Madeline had said, the appropriate paperwork had been sent to CPS, including the charges of murdering Rebecca. If it went to trial, it was up to the defence to prove Mrs Larkin hadn't been killed by her hand.

She checked Michael's notes on Madeline's phone records. One number had been dialled once she'd left her house after the altercation with Sofia. The name matched the one Madeline had given them as the person who'd supplied her with the drugs. They'd pay them a visit later as they were currently busy — Carol had checked with their employer.

"Owt on Preston?" Carol joined the others.

"He's just disappeared," Michael said.

"Okay, then I'm going to watch the recording of Asher's interview."

* * *

Viewing Suite

Carol sat in front of the monitor and clicked *PLAY*. Asher sat with his mother on one side of the table, and an officer sat on the other, one of the detectives from another team, Eddie Worth. The lad appeared sullen, his bottom lip poking out, arms folded.

"As you know from the officer who spoke to you prior to this interview, you're here because of feline blood found on your tracksuit bottoms and a debit card belonging to a Mr Jackson in the pocket," Eddie said. "First, I'd like to address the blood. Have you been near any injured cats?"

"It wasn't me."

"That doesn't answer my question. Have you been near any injured cats?"

Heidi nudged Asher. "Tell the truth, son."

"Yeah, but I didn't hurt them."

"Who did?" Eddie tapped the table with a pen.

"Can't say."

"Can't or won't?" Eddie stopped tapping.

"Can't. Like, he'd kill me. He said so. If I ever tell, I'm dead."

"What did he do to the animals?"

"Shot them with his BB gun. Kicked them and stuff."

Heidi gawped at her child. "And you were *there*? You watched him do it?"

Asher shrugged. "I had no choice."

"Is he a friend of yours?" Eddie asked. "Or has someone forced you to do this?"

Asher stared straight at Eddie. "It was a bloke. And yeah, he forced me."

Is he lying? Carol leaned forward to study Asher's face. She couldn't tell if he was talking bollocks or not.

"Who is this bloke?" Heidi poked him on the arm. "For God's *sake*, he needs to be stopped. What if he's getting some other innocent kid to help him? And what about those poor cats?"

"I'm saying nowt." Asher stared at the tabletop.

Eddie sighed. "We'll leave that for the moment. What about the card? Where did you get that?"

"I nicked it out of some man's wallet, but *he* made me do *that* an' all."

"When did you steal it?" Eddie wrote something down.

"The night the Ferris fella copped it."

"We've viewed the pier CCTV, and at no time were you with a man, talking to one, being forced to do owt. You were, however, with other lads. Is it one of them?"

"No, it was a bloke, I said that."

Eddie shook his head in consternation. "Look, if there's an adult making you do things, you must tell us so we can find him. When did he tell you to steal the wallet? To watch him hurt the cats? How did you even meet him in the first place?"

"I can't say owt. Trust me, fam."

Heidi tutted. "Don't talk like that. You know I hate it."

Carol watched for a while longer, but Asher remained resolute.

She phoned Richard. "Those lads you interviewed, the ones on the pier. Asher Welding and whatever. I need you to have a chat with them all again. Asher's saying a man's been forcing him to watch cats being killed, plus he made him nick a wallet. I need to know if any of the others have been used in the same way."

"Okay, I'll get that done now. There's been a shift change, but I've been swamped with paperwork so stayed on. Another hour on the job won't hurt."

"Thank you, but you could ask Oliver to do it."

"No, I've already built up a rapport with the kids, so best it's me."

"Again, thank you."

Carol switched off the recording and stood. Whoever this was had frightened Asher enough that the boy wasn't prepared to grass on him. What concerned her was that the man was still out there, waiting to use children in his sick games.

Who the hell encouraged kids to *do* things like that?

* * *

Carol's Office

Carol should be in the Lord by rights, her working day done, yet here she was, sitting at her desk, mulling things over until they could go and see the person who'd supplied drugs to Madeline. Dave had nipped into town to get them an Indian.

Richard had phoned to say none of the lads seemed to have a clue what he was talking about, and he believed them. One, however, wasn't around to speak to. His mother said he'd gone to stay with his father for a while and she'd contact Richard with his phone number when she found out what it was. Why didn't the mother already have it? Richard said he'd find the father and get hold of him that way.

Carol had rung Eddie, who was investigating the cat case. She'd told him Asher was a good lad, according to his mother, but Eddie had laughed.

"He's got belligerent brat written all over him. It stops now — because it's him and he got caught. There's sod all we can do, we've got no proof other than that speck of blood. No footage, nowt. He's a free kid until we can prove it was him. As for the stolen card, he's had a warning."

"Someone to watch out for in the future, then," she'd said. "You know as well as I do what harming animals can turn into."

"Yep."

She tidied her desk and scrubbed off a couple of things on her paperwork to-do list. Got up. Paced. Preston — or whoever he really was — had vanished, and the fact that she couldn't question him *or* the kid who'd gone to collect Rebecca's dog — which was still missing — was doing her head in. She liked things tied off neatly, but those two were loose ends.

Dave poked his head around the door. "Are we eating in here?"

"Yeah." She cleared her desk and sat, taking the orange Fanta he held out. "Thanks."

Food in front of her — she'd eat it straight from the silver tray — she tried to clear her mind. Just half an hour to be with Dave as his mate, that's all she wanted. No case cluttering her mind. No incessant voice that told her something was wrong, that all the puzzle pieces didn't quite fit.

"Stop thinking about it," Dave said. "Preston's fucked off — he killed Kevin, he left the gun behind; whether he did it for Madeline or not, I don't know. Rebecca — either Madeline offed her or it was that lad we can't find. Sometimes, we have to admit we can't bring everyone to justice."

"You know how much I hate that."

"I do, but I also know how your mind works, and you'll drive yourself nutty until you get a result. You're a dog with a bone, and you'll find out what happened eventually. It took you years to recall your dad burying your mother, but in the end, you got her justice, and you'll do the same for Kevin and Rebecca an' all. In the meantime, there's a curry to get down your neck, so chop-chop."

Carol smiled. He was right. She'd find those two loose ends one day.

Just not today.

Except . . .

"We need to go and visit someone, don't forget," she said.

"Oh yeah. We'll do it after we've finished our dinner, shall we?"

Carol nodded. *This* particular loose end might very well get tied up if she played her cards right.

* * *

He opened the door and stared at them, his mouth dropping open a little.

Carol held her ID up. "I suspect you can guess why we're here. I know you've not long got home from work. Late shift, was it? Are your wife and children in?"

"No."

"Lucky you."

He stepped back, and they entered his house, a bloody nice one by anyone's standards. Modern furniture, all sleek lines and gloss. The living room he led them to didn't show signs of any children living in the property. Maybe his wife tidied everything away.

He sat, as did Carol, but Dave remained by the door.

"So you know, then," the man said.

"We know a fair amount, yes, but the main thing we're here about is you allegedly acquiring anaesthetic and epidural drugs for Madeline Cotter."

"*What?*"

"Please don't play games. I'm tired. Just admit it, will you?"

"Shit."

"Hmm. So she wasn't lying to us, then?"

"Unfortunately not."

"Why did you do it?"

"Why do you think? To keep her mouth shut. If I didn't, my wife would have found out. I haven't told her about *you know who*. Obviously."

"Why not?"

"I've told you why. I could never be sure if . . ."

"I see. How did you get hold of the drugs?"

"A friend of mine's a delivery man. He happens to drop a box on the ground every so often, and some of the contents smash. He removes a few of the intact vials and breaks the rest that didn't get damaged. It works."

"And no one is suspicious it's the same drugs every time? Or that he's clumsy?"

"He does it with different drugs as well. As for clumsy . . . he's never been called out on it, so I suppose that sort of thing happens a lot."

"Or maybe he's in on this with a few other drivers."

"Probably."

"Who is he? The supplier?"

"I can't . . ."

"You may as well tell us. Why take the rap for all of it?"

"Christ." He swiped his forehead. "My wife's going to find out everything, isn't she?"

"Probably. If you plead guilty, there doesn't have to be a trial. Your dirty laundry won't have to be aired in public, you'll just get sentenced."

"But what am I supposed to tell her about the reason why I was doing it?"

"Use your brain. You'll think of something. Please stand."

He did so, and Dave stepped forward to walk behind him and apply the cuffs.

"Ian Johann, I am arresting you on suspicion of supplying drugs illegally. You do not have to say anything. But it may harm your defence if you do not mention when questioned something which you later rely on in court. Anything you do say may be given in evidence. Do you understand?"

Ian nodded.

Carol sighed. "It would have been so much easier if you'd insisted on a DNA test and helped to bring Sofia up, don't you think? Madeline had you over a barrel."

She led the way out of the house, holding the front door open for Dave to usher Ian through. She'd interview him in the morning, but in the meantime, he could spend the night in a holding cell. It was nothing less than he deserved. He'd knowingly provided drugs to cripple his own child.

He was no better than Madeline.

CHAPTER SIXTY

The Beachfront Hotel

Eliza stirred and lifted her head. "I thought you were never going to get around to it. And great, I've got his blood on me. You could at least have gone for the forehead."

A bedside lamp flickered to life. Eliza had scarlet spray mist on one side of her face and the rounded hump of her bare shoulder. "You've got half an hour, then I'll 'wake' and find him dead." Naked, she reached for her phone.

Desmond smiled. "I'll wait for you at the agreed place tomorrow. The police should be finished with you by then."

"They could put me in a safe house with a police guard."

"Then you'll need to get creative and find a way to leave, won't you? Fuck, you look beautiful."

"Not with this red hair. I can't wait to dye it back."

"You did well. Even I believed you loved Kevin. I got jealous, though."

"I only love you. And don't forget to let Boss know you're done."

Desmond shrugged. "Why bother? This will be all over the news come tomorrow."

"Fair enough. Now get out of here. Some of us still have work to do."

"Wait. Did the money come through?"

"Yes, I just couldn't risk telling you — that's what I was doing at the window in your room, sending the message. I managed to check the bank when Kevin went to sleep. Five million was rerouted in the end. Boss won't even notice it until he employs a new accountant."

Desmond relaxed. He blew her a kiss and left the suite, going to his room. He stashed the gun beneath the mattress, annoyed Boss had handed it over with gloves on. It would have been sweet justice if the prick's fingerprints had been on it. Boss owned one of the other big social media sites and had taken exception to Kevin telling the world about users being listened to via their phones. It had cast a shadow on Boss's integrity, and he hadn't liked it.

Now he'd be after Desmond — and Eliza. Or, as she was known in real life, Sally — but they'd be in the wind, sunning it up and living it large.

Boss had no chance of finding them.

CHAPTER SIXTY-ONE

Marbella — One Month Later

They'd agreed to meet here and relax for a bit. Julia Grisham, who'd booked the suite at the Beachfront in disguise, Lee from accounts at Boss's company, Sally and Desmond. Their other ally was missing. Travis Underhill would remain at ChatSesh until Sally sold it. He was good at lying, was Travis, and so far, no police had gone back to question anyone. All employees had been cleared of any involvement in Kevin's murder.

Sally had told Carol Wren she'd moved to Hampshire. To all intents and purposes, Eliza Morris *did* live there. They'd shared the five million that Lee had stolen from Boss, and she'd rented a cheap flat and let one of her old school friends live in it — on paper, they were roommates. Sally would go back when probate had gone through, to claim Kevin's estate and use his solicitor to help sell everything, then her stolen existence would disappear. The real Eliza Morris had once been a young woman who'd died of cancer. Sally was going to reroute the cash from Kevin's assets with the help of Lee, whose brother knew a thing or two about disguising money trails.

It had been a long two weeks in Marbella while Sally had remained in Scudderton so it didn't look suspicious. Plus it gave her time to complete the ruse that she was packing up and moving to Hampshire. As for Boss . . . Desmond laughed. He'd be steaming by now. All along, he'd thought he'd employed trustworthy people, when from the start, they'd begun working for him on staggered dates, weeks or months apart so it wasn't obvious they knew each other. Desmond had planned this, the theft of the five million, and they'd pulled it off, even if it did mean he'd been roped in to kill Kevin as well.

Shame. Like Sally had said this morning, he didn't deserve to be killed, but Desmond had to maintain his cover with Boss, so he'd had to commit the murder.

One thing Desmond had struggled with was Sally shagging Kevin. It had been necessary, though, and he had to shove it to the back of his mind every time it popped into his head.

Today, everyone would be parting ways. This little layover had come to an end, a celebration of what they'd achieved, a pause so they could purchase properties in other locations, their forever homes. Desmond and Sally had chosen a little island, population five thousand. They'd settle, have a few kids, but first, they'd live like the king and queen they were.

Desmond smiled.

CHAPTER SIXTY-TWO

The Oak Tree

Nathan had gone back to see Mam. It was weird how he'd been called home by some force or other, and there was nothing he could do to stop it. He wanted to kill her, but it would be too obvious it was him. He wasn't stupid. There'd be CCTV at the train stations, and the coppers would work it out. When he was old enough to drive, though, he'd steal a car, and there'd be no stopping him.

The smell of the sea air . . . He hadn't realised how much he'd missed it until now. While he'd thought Scudderton was a shithole, a place he couldn't wait to leave, it had taken him a while to settle in Leeds. Dad was an all right bloke, and they got along well, which was weird when you thought about them not really knowing each other until the day Nathan had turned up at his office.

Now he was back, if only for the day, Nathan's old persona returned. He was the Cat Killer, the pickpocket, the kid who'd murdered some old dear and nicked her dog. Herbie loved it at Dad's, and Nathan brushed him every day. That mutt was one of the best things that had ever happened to him.

Mam had been the same sarky bitch as she'd always been, pummelling him with questions about Dad and what life was like there. He'd answered in the most spiteful way he could, saying it was a better life than she'd ever given him and that Dad's parenting skills far outweighed hers. He had two half-brothers as well, aged six and eight, and Dad treated them all the same, unlike Mam, who'd always favoured Chantal.

Mam had said something that had bothered him, though, and it meant he had to go and see Bestie. Asher had been hauled into the police station, something about having cat blood on his tracksuit, plus that debit card from the old fucker on the pier. Asher couldn't have told them anything because Nathan hadn't been pulled in by the coppers in Leeds. A good kid, was Asher.

Nathan tapped his foot on the grass in front of the oak tree. Dad had replaced the trainers and the tracksuit, and he'd bought a shedload of other clothes, too. Nathan bet Asher wouldn't be able to afford the gear he had on today. His outfit had cost five hundred quid.

Unless Asher was still robbing purses and wallets.

Nathan peered across at his old friend walking towards him. Asher grinned and ran, hurling himself into Nathan for a chest bump and a bit of back slapping.

"Fuck me, what have you been up to?" Asher asked, pulling away. "It's well boring now you're not here."

"I had to get out of here. Mam was doing my nut in."

"So's mine. She goes on and on, and since I was in the cop shop, shit, she watches me all the time. Like, she says she believes me, that I didn't do owt, but I can tell she's not sure, know what I mean?"

"Yeah. Mam told me about it. What happened? What did you even say?"

Asher smiled. "I said some bloke forced me to watch him killing cats and that if I told on him, he'd kill me."

Nathan cracked up laughing. "Fam, thanks for that. What about the card?"

"I said the bloke made me nick it."

Nathan smirked. "And they bought it?"

"What else could they do?"

"Are you still nicking?"

"Nah. That Prince copper came by last week, asking if the man had bothered me again, and I said no. Has he not spoken to you?"

"Yeah. He found Dad and phoned him. I said I didn't know owt about any bloke getting you to do shit."

Asher sat beneath the tree. "Want a spliff?"

"Yeah, then I have to catch the train."

They smoked until blackness scoffed the daylight, joking, talking about old times.

One day, Nathan would come back here for Mam. He'd bash her fucking head in and be rid of her for ever. Until then, he'd play the good son for Dad, although Christ, he could just do with shooting a cat. He'd missed that little game.

Maybe he'd strangle his little brothers' hamsters instead.

CHAPTER SIXTY-THREE

Scarborough

Carol stood on the promontory in the spot she'd scattered the majority of Mam's ashes. She leaned on the black mesh fence and looked down at the sea. White-capped waves crashed against the rocks, spume rising, and she pulled back, a sudden bout of vertigo hitting her. She'd come here alone, needing space, time to think. It still bugged her that they hadn't found Preston or the dog-walking kid, but her working life had gone quiet since the murders, and she was grateful.

A colleague who used to work at her station had phoned her for a chat last week. Someone had been killing dogs in Leeds, smearing their entrails inside the homes where the animals had been slain. He was worried this was a precursor to something more — to humans being killed. It had brought that lad to mind, the one Richard had finally spoken to. Nathan Pottersby. He now lived in Leeds. She'd hoped the kid was the one who'd walked Rebecca's dog, but no, it wasn't. Nathan had a solid alibi for that day, he'd been shopping in Leeds, and his dad had vouched for him afterwards because he'd driven him back to Scudderton so Nathan could collect some belongings before moving in with him. As for the dogs, again, he'd had alibis, but it seemed a coincidence that the cat killings had stopped when Nathan had moved away, then the dog killings had started in Leeds.

She'd passed his name on to her colleague.

It was looking like Madeline would go down for killing Rebecca, although there was a sticking point. None of Rebecca's blood had been on the boiler suit, but Madeline's height had matched the blood spatter analysis, so the prosecution were trying to pin that on her.

Gail's palm print had been on the chisel, so Carol had surmised she'd yanked it out of her neck, then Madeline had used it between the woman's eyes. The smear of blood on the hammer in the shed had belonged to Gail. Madeline, in one of her rare "I did it" moments, had said she'd put it there to frame Kevin.

As expected, all the guests who'd stayed at the Beachfront were cleared of being involved in Kevin's murder. Fake Preston's vehicle still hadn't turned up.

The clothes Kevin had handed over had come back clean, of course, and the people who'd sent hate mail to Eliza had been caught, except for whoever was using the Tor account. She'd since relocated to Hampshire to live with a friend, and Carol was hopeful she'd be able to move on from this.

Carol pondered why Madeline had remained in the house in Ridgebrook Close when she had so much money. Why hadn't she started again? Or even redecorated? Not that it mattered. She often thought about small things like that.

Sofia had gone to London. She rented a studio flat in a blue house and attended therapy sessions. Hopefully, she'd come out on the other side of this a different woman. She deserved happiness.

Carol sighed.

"I wish I'd known you for longer, Mam," she muttered to the breeze. "I wish *he* hadn't . . . hadn't killed you." A lump formed in her throat, and she walked down the steps from the landing. She moved over to those random stones on the grass and sat on one, lifting her face to the overcast sky.

Autumn was properly in residence, winter just around the corner, and soon, coming up here would mean she'd either freeze her tits off or get blown over by the wind. She closed her eyes and cleared her mind, concentrating on the rush and *whoosh* of the sea. She was at peace here.

She opened her eyes to find a wren perched on one of the other stones. A stocky thing with a pot belly, it cocked its head at her, and she took comfort in its presence. After all, birds of a feather stuck together.

THE END

THE JOFFE BOOKS STORY

We began in 2014 when Jasper agreed to publish his mum's much-rejected romance novel and it became a bestseller.

Since then we've grown into the largest independent publisher in the UK. We're extremely proud to publish some of the very best writers in the world, including Joy Ellis, Faith Martin, Caro Ramsay, Helen Forrester, Simon Brett and Robert Goddard. Everyone at Joffe Books loves reading and we never forget that it all begins with the magic of an author telling a story.

We are proud to publish talented first-time authors, as well as established writers whose books we love introducing to a new generation of readers.

We have been shortlisted for Independent Publisher of the Year at the British Book Awards three times, in 2020, 2021 and 2022, and for the Diversity and Inclusivity Award at the Independent Publishing Awards in 2022.

We built this company with your help, and we love to hear from you, so please email us about absolutely anything bookish at feedback@joffebooks.com

If you want to receive free books every Friday and hear about all our new releases, join our mailing list: www.joffebooks.com/contact

And when you tell your friends about us, just remember: it's pronounced Joffe as in coffee or toffee!

ALSO BY EMMY ELLIS

DETECTIVE CAROL WREN MYSTERIES

Book 1: SPITE YOUR FACE
Book 2: HOLD YOUR BREATH
Book 3: GUILT BURNS HOLES
Book 4: BEST SERVED COLD

Printed in Great Britain
by Amazon

26439666R00179